The Fallen

Book 1 · Dark Genesis

Sean M. Bazaar

iUniverse, Inc.
Bloomington

The Fallen
Book 1 - Dark Genesis

Copyright © 2012 by Sean M. Bazaar

All rights reserved. No part of this book may be used or reproduced by any means, graphic, electronic, or mechanical, including photocopying, recording, taping or by any information storage retrieval system without the written permission of the publisher except in the case of brief quotations embodied in critical articles and reviews.

This is a work of fiction. All of the characters, names, incidents, organizations, and dialogue in this novel are either the products of the author's imagination or are used fictitiously.

iUniverse books may be ordered through booksellers or by contacting:

iUniverse
1663 Liberty Drive
Bloomington, IN 47403
www.iuniverse.com
1-800-Authors (1-800-288-4677)

Because of the dynamic nature of the Internet, any web addresses or links contained in this book may have changed since publication and may no longer be valid. The views expressed in this work are solely those of the author and do not necessarily reflect the views of the publisher, and the publisher hereby disclaims any responsibility for them.

Any people depicted in stock imagery provided by Thinkstock are models, and such images are being used for illustrative purposes only.

Certain stock imagery © Thinkstock.

ISBN: 978-1-4759-5899-7 (sc)
ISBN: 978-1-4759-5898-0 (hc)
ISBN: 978-1-4759-5897-3 (e)

Library of Congress Control Number: 2012920379

Printed in the United States of America

iUniverse rev. date: 11/02/2012

Journal of Alisha Grace

TIME, PEOPLE SAY, IS NEVER-ENDING. No matter what happens to people, plants, animals, or the planet itself, time is the one thing that never changes.

None of us could have fathomed that one day our time would be up. That day is now.

Everyone knows of the story of Armageddon, the battle between the forces of Heaven and the demonic legions of Hell. And we all just figured it was a no-brainer, which side would come out on top. But we were wrong.

Every time I go to the window, I smell only blood, fire, and brimstone.

It happened so quickly that no one had time to react: portals forged from demonic magic opened all over the world, and pouring through them were agents of macabre death, tidal waves of destruction the likes of which we had never seen. The sky filled with beautiful, white-winged creatures full of deadly grace and determined precision, intent upon stopping the demon armies. The final war had been brought to our very doorstep.

Across the planet battles raged. Blood and death spread across the Earth, with both sides suffering heavy losses.

It didn't take long for us to realize that the tide of war was shifting to darkness. And if the light fell, what hope would humans have?

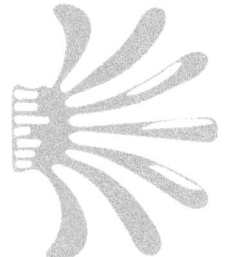 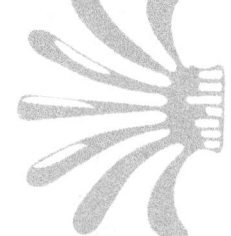

Chapter 1
Earth

THAME WAS MAKING HIS WAY through the throng of Seraphim warriors, looking for his commander, Krillion.

Krillion was a captain in the Fury Legion, a force dispatched from the Crystal Palace by Gabriel himself to ensure that Armageddon was halted and mankind would prosper through peace and free will. Thame finally saw Krillion standing on a small rock outcropping, studying the landscape upon which the upcoming battle would be fought. At six feet four and 275 pounds, he had a massive physical presence, standing head and shoulders above the rest of the warriors gathered around him.

Standing a few meters behind Krillion, Thames felt admiration and love swell in his chest as he looked upon one of the most respected commanders in the All-Father's army. He thought back to his first battle millennia ago, when Krillion had saved his life as two goat demons under Azazel's banner were about to impale him upon their horns.

Krillion had appeared out of nowhere.

With his massive frame of raw brute force, he wielded his mighty war hammer like a man possessed. In a single swing, Krillion collapsed the rib cage of one demon, sending it spiraling through the air, while he grabbed the other demon bare-handed and snapped its neck.

As Krillion stood over Thame, his broad chest heaving, a smile spread across his face and he extended his hand to the young archer, saying, "On your feet archer, no Seraphim will die this day!"

Such a long time ago, thought Thame. Ever since that day, Krillion had taken a liking to the young archer warrior and had been a surrogate father to him. The two of them had grown to respect and love one another and had shared many battles together.

Now Krillion stood on a hillside, looking across the valley that would be the place of the upcoming battle, and he saw the enemy army. The denizens of the underworld were flooding the surrounding landscape like ants.

"Too many," Krillion said to no one in particular.

"What are you thinking about, old man?"

Krillion turned his head to slightly to see his oldest friend, Thame, standing behind him. With a crooked smile and just a trace of arrogance, he replied, "I think we're in for a long day."

Thame laughed and put a hand on Krillion's shoulder. "Good times… good times," he said.

"Let's do what we came here to do, then," Krillion said, reaching for the mighty hammer strapped to his back. Then the two friends turned and headed back to where the legion was awaiting orders to begin the attack.

They had been named Fury Legion, and rightly so: they were one of the fiercest units ever assembled in Heaven. Standing five thousand strong, these were veteran angels hand-picked by Gabriel himself to combat the most savage of demons.

"Archers, ready!" thundered Thame.

The command echoed down the lines. In one fluid movement, hundreds of angelic warriors took flight to hover fifty feet over their own lines. Arrows forged in heaven, each imbued with a small amount of light, were nocked to bows, awaiting the command that would start the battle.

From across the green valley came the response: the snarls and grunts, the clacking of teeth and scraping of claws from more than eight thousand demons ready to crush the force standing before them and feast upon their flesh.

The demon commander, Rai, stood there, a dark shadow. Rai had been an angel a long time ago. When Lucifer revolted from heaven, Rai was one of the first to join his cause. Afterward, when he was cast down to Hell, his mind was wiped clean of any memory of his former life. The only evidence that he'd once lived in the heavens was the pair of black wings protruding from his back. Even with no recollection of his former existence, Rai had regretted his fateful choice ever since.

"Rai, the dark mage's are in position." It was the gritty voice of Valafor, Rai's right-hand man.

"Excellent, Valafor," Rai replied. "Soon this... army will be nothing more than a memory for us. Tell me, are your legions ready?"

"Yes, ten legions strong—and all eager to spill blood."

Thinking for a moment, Rai said, "Valafor, you have served me well through all these years. Remember that Hell doesn't tolerate failure, and I would hate to lose you at my side."

"Ha! You're worried about me?" Valafor laughed and held up his massive right forearm, which looked as if it had been horribly charred by fire. Then he flexed his muscles and the charred flesh crazed as radiant blue light exploded through the cracks.

"Every time I see that, I'm still impressed," said Rai. "The power of a thousand demons harnessed in one weapon."

"Yeah, well, when you lose half an arm, you tend to get very creative," Valafor grinned, showing a mouthful of razor-sharp, yellow teeth.

"Look up, Val," Rai said. "Their archers have risen. Give the command and let's end this."

"Yes, sir," Val said, his voice suddenly serious.

"Fire!"

At that command, hundreds of arrows were loosed upon the demon horde, now starting their deadly advance across the valley. But just before the arrows could find their marks, a dark cloud of smoke rose up out of the ground to engulf them, reducing them to ash.

"Thame!" Krillion shouted to the captain of his archers. "They've got dark mages out there somewhere. Search and destroy!"

"Got it!" Thame shouted back. He gave the command, and then he and his archers sped through the air across the battlefield to find the masters of magic. Meanwhile Krillion and his ground forces rushed headlong into the fertile valley to meet their accursed enemies.

Throughout the valley, angels screamed and demons howled, the lust of battle coursing through their veins. All across the battlefield was violence and death, with Krillion leading the charge in the center, crushing heads and shattering bones with every swing of his mighty hammer. Out of the corner of his eye, he saw something rushing at him. It looked like a massive gray rock golem with a red visor for an eye.

"I see you, ugly!" Krillion yelled, turning to face this new opponent.

Krillion raised his hammer high, ready to strike the killing blow, when the rock demon smashed straight into him with its shoulder, sending him sailing into the air. Krillion grunted as the wind was knocked from his body, but fortunately he was just as deft in the air as he was on the ground. His wings expanded to their full width, catching the wind, and he shot back to where the demon was standing triumphantly.

"*Fury!*" came the battle cry, followed by a deafening crack as Krillion's hammer found its mark this time, shattering the grey rock demon into thousands of pieces.

Breathing heavily, Krillion took in the whole battle raging around him. His legion was holding the lines, maybe even pushing the demons back. They were going to win this fight. Pride and satisfaction spread across his face at the notion.

Just then something scraped the back of his arm. He looked back and saw a little demon latched onto him by its teeth. Reaching around with his opposite arm, Krillion grabbed the demon by the neck and crushed it, feeling its body go limp in his huge hand. Then he tossed the lifeless corpse to the ground. "Little bastard," he said, wiping away the blood.

Off to Krillion's left, dozens of his warriors were being thrown back through the air by an unseen force. He knew at once that the dark mages were still out there and, if left un-checked, could easily turn this fight. "*Thame, you'd better hurry up,*" he thought. Then, raising his hammer and giving another mighty war cry, Krillion rushed back into the fray.

Flying as fast as their wings would carry them, Thame and his archers flew across the battlefield in search of the dark mages. Time was of the essence: the longer the mages stayed active, the more casualties would befall Fury Legion.

Looking at the ground stretched out before him, Thame saw his targets. Hidden in a small cluster of trees that had turned black and ugly from their presence, they stood—seven short, hooded figures, surrounded by a host of demons, minor foot soldiers. Nothing Thame and his legion couldn't handle.

"To the left!" Thame shouted to his archers, and with a twitch of their muscular wings, they turned and sped toward their targets. Swords drawn, they landed right in the middle of the demons, striking them down from all angles.

"We have to get the mages," Thame shouted as he gutted a vile-looking creature missing the top of its head. Then he heard the distorted sounds of magic as the mages started working their dark arts. It was too late. In the span of a heartbeat, Thame and his legion were frozen in place.

It was as if someone had tied weights on them to hold them in place. Thame stared in hatred and fear as hundreds of demons emerged from the trees to form a semicircle around his trapped archers. He shouted and cursed the demons, struggling to free himself from his invisible prison.

One of the hooded mages stepped forward from the semicircle. "Who is in charge here?"

No one answered.

"If you don't tell me who is in charge, you will all be brought back to Hell and tortured for eternity."

"I'm in charge," Thame said, still struggling to move under the spell. "I'm in charge."

"Good," the mage said as a red beam of light shot from his hand, striking Thame in the chest.

A second later, Thame was on the other side of his legion, tied to a tree at the edge of the forest. The dark mage glared at him with a look of unrivaled evil in his eye.

"Kill them," he said.

Behind the dark mage, the demons fell upon the archers—clawing and biting, spraying blood and bits of flesh everywhere.

"*Noooo!*" Thame cried. All he could do was watch as his legion of archers, frozen in place like statues, were torn to pieces right in front of him.

This is it, thought Thame. *I have failed. Failed my men, failed myself... and worst of all, failed Krillion.* His neck went limp, and a single tear fell from his eye to land on the blackened grass at his feet.

"Forgive me, Krillion," Thame said under his breath. "I'm sorry."

"Now then," said the mage, pulling a bloody knife from the sleeve of his robe. "Let's talk."

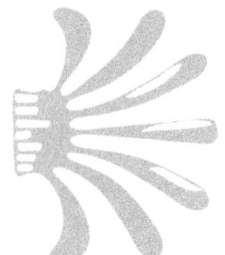 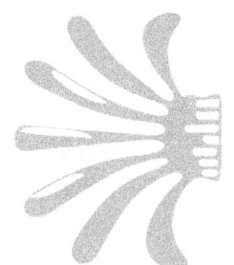

Chapter 2
Earth

"LET'S GO, MEN—SEND THESE SOULLESS bitches back to their fiery pit in Hell!" Captain Zara screamed, encouraging her legion to victory over the immense onslaught of the demons around them. Her long, curly, black hair hung over her face, matted by sweat and blood. Her armor hugged a very curvaceous body with muscles toned from years of training with sword and dagger.

Most of her legion didn't hear Zara; her words were lost in the noise of battle all around. Everywhere she looked, angels and demons were fighting, each battle a small part of Armageddon to determine who would dominate Earth and lock in mankind's fate.

Zara was a captain in the Twelfth Legion of Light. She had spent her short life preparing for this one moment, this one battle, but as she looked around Earth's landscape, her instinct told her that something was not right.

Off to her left, cutting a swath of devastation through the demon ranks, was General Wranti, the commanding officer for the Twelfth. "Zara, watch your right side. They're starting to flank you," he said, pulling his sword from the gut of a demon in the thrall of death.

By now Zara was trading blows with a demon that barely resembled anything humanoid. "It's not that I don't see them, sir," Zara said through bloody, clenched teeth. "It's just that I can't keep up with the sheer numbers of them! For every one I kill, three more take its place." Ducking under the demon's massive claws, which were dripping with blood from her fallen comrades, Zara, swift and deadly, sank both her short swords into the creature's spine, killing it instantly.

For a moment she stood, bloody and triumphant, over her foe, and then she looked out across the battlefield. All hope faded from her heart. Her mouth went dry as a sliver of fear crept its way into her thoughts.

They had lost.

The demons were too many and too powerful to be stopped by the Twelfth.

Gripped by the terrible reality of the situation, she barely had time to react when a demon standing close to seven feet tall almost cleaved her in two with a claymore as big as she was. She rolled out of the way just in time; the sword came down on the precise spot where her head had been not a moment before. Now Zara knelt before this unholy, malicious creature, her guard up.

"What's the matter little birdie?" the demon said with a guttural snarl. "Not as high and mighty as you thought you were? Don't worry—when this is over, I will feed your head to my children so they will know never to fear you and your kind!"

Feeling the bile rise up in her mouth, the rage churning in her stomach, Zara lunged with every ounce of strength she had left. One of her twin blades bit deep into the creature's neck, severing its head from its shoulders.

Zara was trapped in the grip of madness. She knew that losing this battle meant surrendering Earth and mankind, and quite possibly Heaven itself, to the demons.

Her thoughts were a twisted mess; adrenaline pumped through her veins. If they didn't stop Hell's armies and halt Armageddon, women, children, and every facet of life on Earth would become corrupted and warped. It would all blacken and die.

By the All-Father and everything she was taught to believe in, she would not let this fate befall the planet. Not while her lungs held breath and her hand a sword. Panting, wiping the blood from her face, she turned to find her next opponent.

Instead she found the sharp tip of a rusty, bloody spear that plunged through her breastplate and into her back left wing before it was quickly pulled back out.

Eyes wide, lost in panic, Zara fell to her knees, and time itself seemed to slow to a crawl. The ground was wet with the blood of fallen angels and vile demons. She saw most of her legion on the ground, where demons had stopped fighting to feast upon them. When an angel fell, the demons didn't stop hacking and tearing at the bodies; instead they tore flesh and rendered limbs until there were nothing left but gore.

Off in the distance, through vision blurry from blood loss, Zara made out the form of General Wranti surrounded by demons of all sizes and colors. She watched in hopeless horror as he sank to one knee in the dirt.

Looking up to the heavens that were once clear and blue, all she could see were the black shapes of demons silhouetted against the dark skies. While the angelic Seraphim once ruled the skies, filthy demons were now its masters, infesting it with their presence. There was no sun anymore. Ever since the first portal opened up, unleashing demons upon Earth, the sun just blinked out, as if it had never been there.

As dark-red venous blood oozed from Zara's chest, her anger raged.

"Not like this," she said through bloodstained teeth. "Not... like this ..." Darkness consumed her and she slumped over. The last thing she saw was a massive sword being driven through the chest of the demon that had stabbed her ... and then nothing.

† † †

"Ungh."

Zara moaned and opened her eyes, a painful process. All she could see was darkness. Smoke and the metallic smell of blood still hung in the air. When she tried to sit up, she gasped and winced at the sharp pain in her back. Then she remembered that she had been stabbed. She could feel the dried blood sealing the hole in her chest from the spear's entry point.

Rolling onto her side with great effort, she was able to get to her knees. There was anger in her voice. "I swear by the All-Father, if I get my hands..." Her words trailed off as she saw the remains of the battlefield. The countryside, once lush with its meadows and rolling hills, was now a barren wasteland. Dead bodies from both sides littered the blood-soaked ground.

She had been right, then. The battle was lost. The demons had left nothing intact. Wincing again, Zara got painfully to her feet and took a staggering step. "So many," she whispered, raising a hand to her mouth.

Everywhere she looked she saw dead demons and the remains of her legion. *How could this have happened?* she thought.

She spotted her twin swords a few feet away, one lying on the ground, the other embedded in the torso of a goat demon. Her knees shaking, every nerve in her body yelling at her to stop, she walked toward them and knelt to pick them up. She placed them in their scabbards, the dried blood sticking to her hands. Then, stepping carefully over the bodies strewn across the field, she found General Wranti, or what was left of him. Kneeling down beside him she felt her eyes well up. "No," she said softly. "There will be no tears—only vengeance. This will not go unpunished, I promise you, General."

Anger and vengeance rising in her heart, Zara stood, facing no one. "*Noooo!*" she yelled, arms raised to the sky. "Vengeance will be mine! I swear by everything I hold sacred, every filthy servant of Lucifer will pay for this! Do you hear me, Lucifer, you piece of shit? Your fucking head is mine!"

Her last bit of energy faded, Zara fell to her knees beside the broken body of the general, her rage dissolving into sorrow at the state of her leader and her legion.

Looking down at the mutilated corpse of her once-proud commander, she removed the medallion around his neck that signified he was commander of the Twelfth and placed it inside her left gauntlet.

I need to get back and tell Gabriel what has happened here, she thought. Perhaps the other legions had fared better?

"Hell, no. We're the frickin' Twelfth," she answered herself aloud, her voice again filling with anger. "We've never been beaten before. We led the charge when Lucifer rebelled against the All-Father. These demons should have fallen before us like pawns on a chessboard." She stood up to leave, taking one last look around her. The carnage from both sides was massive. She took in the smells of fire, blood, and brimstone, took in everything, and burned it into her mind.

Unfurling her wings, Zara tested them for damage, gently flapping them and wincing from the sudden pain that shot through her back. It would be rough going, she knew, but she had to make it back.

She had to. Someone had to warn Gabriel and the Seraphim of the atrocities that had been committed this day. With that final thought, Zara jumped into the air and began the slow, painful journey back to Heaven.

Chapter 3
Journal of Alisha Grace

ITS DARK OUTSIDE ... IT'S ALWAYS dark now. The only light visible comes from the fires.

Fires were burning parks, buildings ... people. We were so incredibly arrogant. We thought that we were the top of the food chain, that nothing could stop us. We had created weapons capable of destroying entire countries overnight.

It's ironic, in a way—it took less time than that for us to fall.

The portal appeared on the street outside my mom's apartment shortly after the sun went down. Mom wasn't home at the time. She had left earlier to get milk and cigarettes, saying she would only be gone a few minutes.

It was the first time she had let me stay home alone.

Every time I close my eyes, my blood runs cold in my veins and my body is gripped in fear from the high-pitched screams of the people on the street, all echoing their death song.

Men, women, children—all the people unfortunate enough to be out there were dead before they knew it. It happened so fast no one had a chance to react, much less survive. Tears streamed down my face and my throat went dry as I watched these monsters tear people limb from limb, spraying blood and guts everywhere.

Then I ran to the closet and slammed the door shut. Slammed it shut from the grotesque sights, the horrific sounds. From the nightmare that had become my new reality. Sitting in the dark with my knees pulled into my chest, sobbing uncontrollably and shivering with fear, I prayed to God to make sure Mom was safe and to send these creatures away, I didn't care where. Anywhere but out there.

Hundreds perished within the first few minutes, their mutilated bodies strung up like hunting trophies.

There was no mercy from the monsters, no pity. No one was spared.

Men and women, old and young ... it didn't matter. Within an hour the streets were red; it seemed blood covered everything.

Now, rocking back in forth in my dark closet, I can close my eyes and visualize that day. It will stay with me forever ...

A creature that looked half-goat, half-human had grabbed two full-grown men by their necks and, lifting them off the ground, smashed their heads together, splattering brains and bits of bone along my window, painting it red not a foot in front of me. It ripped their spines right out of the bodies. And that's not even the worst part.

That was two days ago, and the sun hasn't risen since.

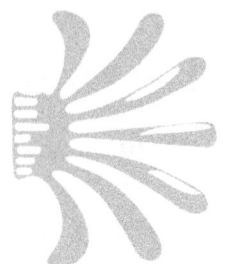 

Chapter 4

THE CRYSTAL PALACE STOOD AS testament to the might and will of the angels. Built in the time of Lucifer's revolt from heaven, Gabriel had the palace erected as a first and last line of defense should Heaven ever go to war again.

This was the second time the angels had gathered in its mighty halls. Once again, their intent was to stop evil in any form that threatened the prosperity of love, hope, and mercy.

Afriel, the angel of youth, was walking about the stone courtyard, admiring the tall towers, which had a slightly blue tint when the sunlight touched them. Gabriel and the rest of the council had met here to prepare for Armageddon, the final battle.

Afriel had never cared much for battle plans or wars; he was, after all, the angel of youth, not an angel of death or judgment. He possessed the ability to feel the life force of the young, human or angel, discern when they were in trouble, and help guide them through trying times.

Looking up at the window of the war room, he could hear voices arguing.

Afriel knew that Gabriel and the others were handling the war down below, and if Afriel could hear them from his position on the palace grounds, he knew it wasn't going well. Gabriel was known for having a short temper, and it was his voice that rose above all others, bringing a vision of Gabriel into Afriel's mind. Standing roughly six feet tall, with well-proportioned muscles and a shaved head, Gabriel was the All-Father's champion among the Seraphim. Here was an angel that Afriel would not want on his bad side.

After listening for a few minutes and deciding that it was all just too much for him, Afriel unfurled his wings and flew up to the battlements on the palace walls to talk with the guards. The number of guards there had been doubled due to the war, and so it was difficult finding an open space to land on. Finally Afriel descended gracefully on the crystal walkways.

Then, with no warning, his legs buckled and he fell to the ground as if he had been hit in the chest with a hammer. "Oh no," Afriel said, gasping for air. His pulse raced and his palms went sweaty.

One of the guards dashed over. "Afriel, are you all right?" the guard said, grabbing him and helping him to his feet. When Afriel's face turned and met his, the guard could see that he was not all right; his face was flushed and tears raced down his cheeks.

"I have to see Gabriel right away," Afriel gasped, wide-eyed with dread, trying to refill his depleted lungs.

Meanwhile, in the main war room of the palace, the conversation was reaching a boiling point. In the center of the room stood a massive table that, when viewed from above, resembled a flaming sword.

Seated around this table, engaged in a heated discussion, were Gabriel, angelic messenger; Metatron, angel of the divine plan and the voice of God; Azreal, angel of death; Israfil, angel of Judgment Day; and Abdiel, angel of faith.

"This is the last stand of the angels—is that what you're saying?" demanded Gabriel, staring at Israfil.

"As I told you, something has happened in Hell, something that has changed the outcome of the war ... something we could not have foreseen." Israfil was clearly taken aback by Gabriel's wrath.

Gabriel then turned his icy glare to Metatron. "And what of the All-Father—have you spoken with him on this?"

"No, not in as many days," Metatron replied in his normal monotone, looking down at the table. "What he is thinking he has not told me, and that is what worries me the most."

"Gabriel, I think you are underestimating the force of our army," Abdiel said with a calming air of confidence. "We have never been defeated, and just because Israfil is saying that his vision of Armageddon has changed does not mean we shall lose."

In a fit of rage, Gabriel threw his goblet of water across the room. "Really, Abdiel? Tell me, then, one time Israfil has been wrong. One time!"

A pounding on the door caused Gabriel to shift his gaze from those gathered around him. "Enter!" he yelled.

The doors opened and Afriel walked in, supported by the guard.

"Afriel, what happened to you?" Gabriel's voice softened, although it still held residual anger.

Still reeling from shock and struggling to lift his head, Afriel spoke, his voice coming in shallow breaths. "We're in trouble. The warriors we sent to Earth to stop the advance—"

Gabriel sighed; he knew what Afriel was going to say. "How many?" he asked.

"Over two-thirds, Gabriel," Afriel said as he began coughing, his whole body racked with pain.

Gabriel shot an icy look at Azreal and yelled, "You knew about this, didn't you? You knew we would lose, and you didn't say anything." As Gabriel spoke he began to draw his sword out of the intricately carved gold scabbard that hung at his side.

Azreal shot up from the table, dagger in hand. "You know that's not the way my power works," he shot back, "so I'd suggest you put the sword away or you'll soon find out why I'm the angel of death!" Azreal was never one to back down from a fight, no matter the odds or with whom. He'd never lost a fight.

Gabriel thought better of it and returned his sword to its rightful place. Then, never taking his eyes off of Azreal, he said in a calmer voice, "Guard, take Afriel to rest, and fetch Raphael. Metatron, see if you can contact the All-Father. Israfil, look to your vision and tell me what transpires on Earth with our forces. And Azreal ..." He let the name hang in the air for a moment. "Nothing," he finally said.

As everyone left to carry out his orders, Azreal glared at Gabriel with hate in his eyes. "One day, Chosen One, you and I are going to have a serious disagreement," he said. And with that, Azreal turned and walked away.

Abdiel came to stand next to Gabriel. "We have faced dark times before," Abdiel remarked. "It is the faith and fortitude of angels that allows us to overcome any and all obstacles."

Gabriel shook his head. "We have lost over two-thirds of our forces, the Earth is practically lost, the humans have been decimated, and Israfil's vision has almost become a reality. Tell me, old friend, how much faith do you have right now?"

"Enough to know that we will make it through this and that the All-Father will not abandon us, nor shall we abandon our sacred oath to protect mankind," Abdiel said softly. Then he turned and went, leaving Gabriel to ponder the severity of the situation.

Outside the war room, from the palace walls, the alarm rang out:

"Intruder coming from the north!"

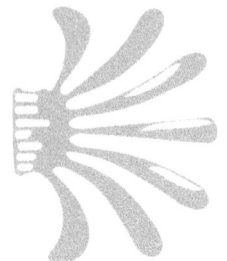 

Chapter 5

BLUE LIGHT EXPLODED THROUGH THE air as Valafor's blackened weapon arm connected with angelic swords. Grinning to show a set of teeth perfectly sharpened for rendering flesh, Valafor pushed back the two soldiers who were attempting to cut him down. He was relishing the adrenaline of the fight.

Through the darkness all around him, more and more angels were speeding toward Valafor, intent on making this demon suffer as he made so many of their brothers and sisters in arms suffer.

With one deft movement, Valafor side stepped left, backhanding one of the soldiers so hard that the soldier landed ten feet away, unconscious. The demon used using his free hand to pick up the other soldier by the neck. "Die, worm," he said, punching a hole through the angelic soldier's abdomen and spraying blood all over the new wave of attackers.

"Worthless, all of you!" Valafor shouted at them. "Fucking worthless. How did Lucifer ever lose to the likes of you? Before this day is out, I will strip the meat from your bodies and use your bones as toothpicks, meat!" Then, with a sadistic laugh that would have given pause to even the bravest of warriors, Valafor drew back his arm and punched the ground with such force that it created an explosion of blue hellfire, engulfing everything within arm's length, burning wings and melting flesh. His laughter was drowned out by the screams of the dying.

As Valafor stood there amid the chaos of burning warriors, his hairy body covered in sweat, he threw his head back, closed his eyes, and breathed in the aroma of searing flesh. All around him, the warriors of the Fury Legion fell to the unholy fire that engulfed them. The smells of hot metal and burned tissue permeated the air.

Feeling a new rush of adrenaline, Valafor looked up to see another angel right in front of him—wings fully expanded, hellfire gleaming off a bloodstained breastplate, sword ready to plunge—rushing through the air to stop the monster that had brutally butchered so many.

Hmmm, missed one, Valafor thought, jumping up at the last second to land on the back of the angelic warrior, who flew under his intended target. Now sitting between the angel's wings, Valafor leaned down close to his ear and whispered in a gravelly voice, "You're not having any fun, birdie."

Before the warrior could react, Valafor sank his claws into his neck. Reeling in the ecstasy of feeling hot, fresh blood course down his hand, Valafor ripped out the angel's throat and rode him straight into the ground, laughing as together they struck the dead of both armies.

† † †

The battlefield was a nightmare. Everywhere there were dead demons with heavenly spears sticking out of them. Among them were the heads of angels, mounted on rustic poles that had been jammed into the ground. Demons were busily feasting on the remains of the fallen Fury warriors.

Krillion, covered in blood and gore, his armor dented, continued to swing his hammer with unstoppable, rage-fueled force.

The look on his face said two things: one, his legion could not, would not lose this battle; and two, Krillion was a warrior who loved a good fight.

In the midst of the fight, lost in the thrill of the kill, Krillion threw his hammer to the ground and ran after a demon with greenish skin and an extended jaw like an alligator's. Wrapping his arm around its neck and wrenching its back, he began choking it. With his free hand he grabbed the wrist of a sword-wielding demon who was about to stab him. Securing his grip on its wrist, he jerked its hand up, feeling bone and cartilage snap under the pressure. As the sword fell from the now-deformed appendage, Krillion smashed the demon in the face with his gauntlet. Blood shot everywhere, adding yet another layer of gore to Krillion's armor. The demon collapsed.

Having seen what happened to his comrade, the other demon struggled beneath Krillion, trying to get free. "Where you goin', bitch?" Krillion asked through clenched teeth. Flexing his massive arm around the demon's neck, Krillion felt a crunch and then dropped the limp body to the ground.

Retrieving his hammer a few feet away, Krillion continued surveying the battleground. Both armies had been at it for over an hour, with neither side seeming to have the advantage.

The dark mages hadn't acted for a while, thought Krillion. That meant Thame had done his job and taken them out. But where were he and the rest of the archers? Their arrows could easily bend this war to the light.

Doubt and worry seeped into Krillion's mind as he pondered the potential fate of his friend. This was war, and war had casualties. Krillion just prayed that he hadn't sent Thame to his death when he saw the potential of the young archer many years ago, taking him under his wing and teaching him how to command and be a leader.

Come on, Thame, where are you? he thought.

Just then, a massive, eight-foot-tall demon with grayish skin and three sharp horns protruding from the top if its head ran up behind the Fury Legion commander and let out a mighty snarl, covering him with droplets of putrid demon spit.

Placing all thoughts of Thame in the back of his mind, Krillion turned around to face this gigantic monster, smiling as if to say, "Who runs up to somebody and growls at him?" In a flash, Krillion sent his hammer sailing into the kneecap of the monstrosity standing before him, completely laying him out in the dirt. Then Krillion walked over and placed his boot on the demon's neck, pinning it to the ground as it howled in pain. A little ways away, Krillion saw some of his spearmen, hard-pressed and outnumbered.

Time to get back to work, old man, he said to himself between deep breaths. Glancing once more at the sky in the hope of seeing his old friend, he sighed and crushed the demon's neck with his boot, then stepped off to aid his spearmen.

Rai stood atop a hill at the edge of the battlefield, his long, jet-black hair pulled into a tight ponytail at the back of his head. Rai was six feet four with a slender build, and strapped to his back was a slender sword roughly the same length as him.

As Rai watched the battle unfold all around him and saw the angels soar through the grayish skies, he pondered his own origin. Rai knew that at one time he had been somewhere other than Hell, that he hadn't always been a commander of demented demons and cruel monsters.

He didn't look like other demons; he had a more humanoid form. And then there were the massive black wings protruding from his back. His body and face were covered with scars he couldn't remember getting.

His thoughts snapped back to reality and the battle as a small, hideous creature ran up to him.

"My liege," the creature snarled, saliva dripping from two overly long fangs protruding from the front of its mouth. "We cannot break their lines. No matter what we do, they hold."

"Summon the dregs!" Rai shot back, anger in his eyes.

"Yes, sir," he heard, as the creature ran away to do its master's bidding.

This was to be Hell's crowning moment, Rai thought, the time when they finally inherited Earth from the accursed Seraphim and their weak god. Rai was determined that he would not be the one to fail and lose it all.

Dregs were savage flying creatures from a remote part of Hell that had been added to their ranks as a means of fighting an aerial battle against the resilient angels. They stood five feet tall and weighed around 150 pounds. They were small, but their quickness, ferocity, and numbers more than made up for the lack of size.

Rai's thoughts drifted again, this time back to when he and Valafor had led a legion into the dregs' domain to make them commit to the upcoming battle for Earth.

They didn't need much convincing after Rai cut the eyes from the dreg chief's face and handed them to Valafor, who ate them.

Focus on the task at hand, Rai thought, scolding himself. Snapping back to the fight, he drew his long blade, fastened the red-and-black mask that covered his nose and mouth, and ran down the hill to join the fight. *Time to finish this.*

† † †

After an hour on the battlefield, every swing of Krillion's hammer was starting to take its toll on the huge angel's muscles. The fighting seemed to have gone on for days, and he was beginning to fatigue.

Suddenly a flash of light shattered the black sky. All the combatants set their eyes upward as a massive portal opened up, and out of it flew hundreds of reasons why Krillion's legion had just lost this fight.

"Fuck," was all Krillion could say, looking up with wide eyes, wondering how and what they were going to do now.

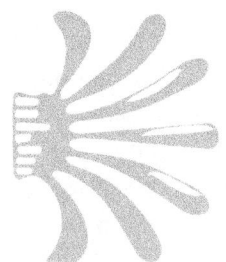 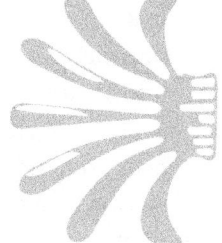

Chapter 6
Hell

"You there, halt!" boomed Geryon as a hooded stranger approached the massive creature who guarded the flaming gates of Hell. "You must have a death wish to be here so far from home, fool," Geryon said.

Geryon was a centaur: his lower half was that of a horse, while his upper body was that of a man. He had been assigned as the guardian of the gates by Lucifer himself. Geryon took an enormous amount of pride and pleasure in the job.

Brandishing the massive claymore that was always strapped to his back, he approached the stranger, ready to end his life. "I know who you are, and I'm not impressed," Geryon said.

"Your master has requested me, you filthy beast," the stranger said in a matter-of-fact tone.

Geryon returned his sword to its leather sheath on his wide, muscular back. Even a creature of his immense power and position in Hell wouldn't defy the orders of Kobal. "So the demon master of hilarity wants to see you?" Geryon asked, rubbing his chin and stepping out of the way. "You are free to pass."

As the stranger resumed walking, he turned back to stare straight into Geryon's eyes. It was the death stare of one who could back up everything his reputation entailed, and it sent shivers up and down the centaur's spine. "If you ever raise a blade against me again," the stranger said, "I will gut you where you stand and nail your sorry fucking ass to your own gate." With that, he turned and headed toward the castle.

Hell was a barren wasteland of fiery geysers and jagged rocks. From all directions could be heard the screams of souls unfortunate to be trapped in that dismal realm.

Walking was not the stranger's preference, but he was not about to draw any more unnecessary attention upon himself in the land of the damned. So he walked through Hell on the only thing remotely resembling a road, noticing demons of all kinds lingering around.

They noticed him, too. They knew that he didn't belong here—that he wasn't one of them, that he didn't look right and didn't smell right.

As long as Kobal kept his minions in line, there would be no problem.

The trick with Hell was that though it was a physical realm, you could get to where you wanted to go there merely by thinking of the location. So bringing his gaze back to his front and closing his eyes, the hooded stranger focused his thoughts upon Kobal's castle.

When he opened his eyes moments later, he was standing before towering double doors guarded by two humanoid demons that looked like they had been dumped in acid, their skin randomly falling off their bodies as if they were decomposing right in front of him.

One of the guards pushed opened a door, saying, "The master is expecting you." Its skeletal jaws clacked together as it talked, and both guards looked ready to jump on him and tear him to pieces, their desire held in check only by the threat of what their demented master would do to them.

Once again, the hooded stranger noted that Kobal seemed to rule his guards and minions with an iron fist. Very surprising that there would be such order and discipline in such a realm.

Upon entering the main chambers, he saw the master, and as he came to stand before him, their eyes locked on each other's for a long moment. The stranger would not kneel; Kobal had not expected that he would.

Kobal sat upon a throne comprised of the skulls of angels who had been killed in past battles. What made the scene truly grisly was the fact that all the skulls were smiling. That was one of many sick reasons Kobal had earned the title "demon master of hilarity."

Kobal was not a particularly large demon. He was however, exceptionally ruthless. The more things he killed, the more fun he had. His ability to manipulate people and creatures always worked itself into a game for his amusement.

There were two other creatures in the chambers, but the stranger didn't recognize them. Kobal noticed his eyes darting to the other figures and decided that introductions were in order if they were to work toward the common goal of mankind's destruction.

"Allow me to introduce Leonard, master of black magic and sorcery, and, to his left, Azazel, lord of the hairy demons—or 'goat demons,' as you refer to them," Kobal said, gesturing toward them with a wave of his hand.

The stranger said nothing as he glanced from demon to demon, sizing them up.

"Have you completed your task?" Kobal asked with a slight chuckle in his voice.

"No, the moment has not presented itself yet," replied the hooded figure.

At this disappointment, Kobal stood up from his throne and approached him. "I will decide when the time is right, scum! You will do as I command or you—"

The stranger cut him off. "You'll do what?" he asked, his hand moving quickly to the hilt of his sword. "Please let me know what you'll do to me. I'm dying to hear this one."

Kobal shot a sharp warning look at Azazel, whose hand was moving over his head to grasp his battle-ax. Then Kobal turned back to the stranger with a grin. "If you wish to attain that which you believe is rightfully yours, then I advise you to complete your task," he said. "At this point I don't think even you would be stupid enough to oppose us."

"You double-cross me in any way, demon, and you'll find out exactly how stupid I really am. And while you're at it, you'd better tell your lackeys here to remember their place and sure as hell remember who the fuck I am." The hooded stranger spoke with an arrogance that let all present know he was more than capable of backing up his words. "I'll let you know when it's completed. And you'd better have your end done by then, Kobal, or I swear I'll carve your fucking face from your skull."

Giving the gathered demon lords one last look, the hooded stranger strode out of the chamber and headed back toward the gates of Hell.

"Why must we suffer his threats, Kobal?" Azazel demanded. "Were it up to me, I'd have gutted him on my horns right now and been done with him. We don't need him, not at this point." Azazel was half snarling as he spoke, his hooves scraping on the stone floor.

"I have to agree with Azazel," Leonard said with his distinctive hiss. "Kobal, the war isss pretty much over. The Earth is oursss. The humans fell to us within hours across the Earth, and the angels are scattered."

Kobal walked back to his throne of skulls and sat down, deep in thought. Finally he spoke. "We tolerate him because he has one use, and only one use. Plus I seriously doubt either of you two could kill him. You know his reputation is well-earned." Kobal gave a little laugh. "You two just need to sit back and enjoy the game."

"That's the problem with you, Kobal," Azazel roared. "You think everything is a damn joke. We have waited too long for this time to come, and I will not see it ruined by of your stupid fucking games, just so you can have a laugh!"

Kobal continued to grin and, with a dismissive wave, said, "Trust me, Az, soon we will all have what we desire. Until then, go back to your legions, hunt down the scattered angels left on Earth, and slaughter the remaining humans."

Azazel stared at Kobal as though he wanted to strike him. Orders were orders, though, and Lucifer had left Kobal in charge of the war over Earth. Azazel turned and began walking toward the exit.

Kobal and Leonard watched him leave the main chamber, his hooves clacking on the stone floor.

"You play a dangerous game, master of tricksss," Leonard hissed. "I wonder if one day your games won't get the better of you. How funny would that be to you then?"

"Leonard, you're right," Kobal answered. "Perhaps one day I will fall to my own designs. But how funny would that be? That would be the greatest punch line of all time!" And Kobal broke into hysterical laughter at the thought.

Shaking his head in disgust, Leonard began reciting an incantation that would transport him back to his own castle—away from this demon who found everything so damn funny, back to his books, spells, and mages.

When Kobal stopped laughing, he looked around the chambers and realized he was alone.

He straightened himself in his throne. "No one has a sense of humor anymore," he said.

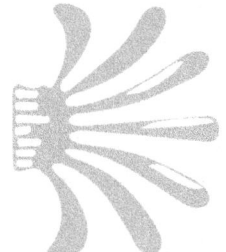 

Chapter 7

GABRIEL STOOD ON THE BALCONY of the war room, watching the sunlight glint off the sharpened spearheads and polished breastplates of the Crystal Palace's angelic guard, who were racing through the sky toward the possible oncoming threat flying towards the crystal palace.

This was a dire time for the Seraphim—a time of war and death.

Gabriel had just received news from Afriel confirming what Israfil had spoken of earlier: almost all the forces Gabriel had sent to Earth had been destroyed in the war against the agents of Hell. Legion upon glorious legion had fallen to the demonic onslaught.

Here at the Crystal Palace, Gabriel wasn't about to take the off chance that this intruder was anything more than an enemy. The palace was the first and last line of defense should Hell ever try to attack Heaven.

His hand on the hilt of his sword, his wing muscles twitching, ready to take flight should the palace guards need him, Gabriel watched them work like a well-oiled machine.

"Talon formation," commanded Sandalphon, captain of the guards, over the onrushing winds.

Upon his command, the handful of angels with him formed a spearhead pattern in the air. There was only one aerial target, but this was not the time to take chances.

† † †

"Come on, just a little further." Zara urged herself forward, gasping for air as her strength faded from blood loss and a severely damaged wing.

Her world was quickly fading into oblivion again. Try as she might to clear the cobwebs from her vision, all she could make out before her were blurry silhouettes racing toward her, for all intents and purposes to finish what the demons had started.

She needed a way to let them know she was an ally.

With the little bit of strength she had left, she pulled up to hover in midair so her pursuers could see she that was one of them—that she possessed the celestial gift of wings. But the strain was too much on her wracked body; her damaged wing completely failed her, and she began a free fall.

Recognizing that the intruder was, in fact, one of them, a young guard said to Captain Sandalphon, "Sir, she's one of us!"

"Catch her! Now!" ordered Sandalphon.

Without a word the young guard tucked his wings to his side and sped his way toward her. "Let your body go limp!" he yelled, as if she had any choice in the matter. If she tried to fight him, both of them likely would plummet to Earth, far below.

Zara's world was a twisting mess of colors, sights, and sounds. Her stomach clenched as she began to dry heave from the spiraling fall.

The little air she was able to breathe in exploded from her lungs as she landed hard in the guard's arms.

Upon impact, the young guard spread his wings, catching the air to slow their decent. The force at which Zara suddenly stopped falling was too much for her already abused body. Once again, blissful darkness consumed her.

Flying back to the Crystal Palace, the young guard couldn't help but notice how bad Zara looked. Her curly, black hair was stuck to her head in various spots with dried blood and sweat. The gaping hole in her chest was oozing fresh blood over her armor, which was dented beyond repair.

Meeting up with the rest of his party, the guard briefed Captain Sandalphon of his initial observation of the female angel he carried in his arms.

"She's a survivor of the war. Bring her straight to Raphael; I'm going to get Gabriel. The rest of you, back to your posts and stay vigilant!" Sandalphon barked.

"Yes, sir!" the guards said at once, and the formation broke off.

Noticing Gabriel standing on the balcony, watching the episode unfold, Sandalphon banked right and headed toward him. Gabriel took a few steps backward to give him room to land. "What news, Captain Sandalphon?" he asked.

"The intruder turned out to be one of our own, Gabriel. She's near death from wounds suffered in the battle below. My man is taking her to Raphael as we speak." Captain Sandalphon spoke with the calm, steady voice of a veteran soldier who had seen more than his share of blood.

"Excellent work, Captain. See to the guards and meet me in the infirmary. We have much to discuss."

"At once, Gabriel," Sandalphon replied. He then arched his wings and took to the air to make his rounds.

As Sandalphon jumped from the balcony ledge, extending his wings and soaring toward his guards positioned around the battlements, Gabriel took solid note of the captain's work of late. *If any of them survived this new evolution,* he thought, *I'll promote him to legion commander.* Then, turning to leave, he was struck by his own word: *if.*

† † †

"Raphael" the young guardsman shouted in a panic. "Raphael, you are needed quickly!"

"I'm always needed, young warrior," laughed Raphael, stepping out from another room in the infirmary. His chuckle faded as he glanced at the female warrior so close to death and bleeding in the guard's arms. "Lay her here and fetch me water and bandages," he said, clearing a nearby table.

As the guardsman hurried about this task, Raphael's hands and mind took over, and he started removing the breastplate which had taken too many hits to be of any use anymore. Once it was off he began watching the barely perceptible rise and fall of the angel's chest to determine the strength and frequency of her breathing. While looking over her still form, Raphael noticed a small piece of metal protruding from her left gauntlet. He wiped the blood from it and examined it closely, his eyes widening as he realized he held the medallion of a general in his shaking hands. "No," he whispered.

Worry and concern now fueled his actions as he began to shake the warrior's body in hopes of waking her. "How many are left?" Raphael asked desperately, still shaking her. A brief flutter of eyelids was all he received for his efforts. Wherever she was, it wasn't in this room with him.

"Here Raphael. This is all I could find. Is it enough?" The guardsman asked handing over several clean, white bandages and a pitcher of warm water.

"Yes, yes," Raphael said, distractedly. "You may go back to your duties now, guardsman. And thank you." As he spoke Raphael never lifted his gaze from the bloodied body lying prone on the table. The questions raised by her possession of her general's medallion brought thoughts of dread and fear for the warriors left on Earth.

With one more worried look at the battered warrior's limp body, the guard bowed his head to Raphael and turned toward the door. But just as he reached it, it shot open again, and in walked Gabriel. Upon seeing the guard and the female warrior, Gabriel realized this was the angel who had saved her from free-fall and certain death. "Well done, spearman," Gabriel said, clapping the young guard on the shoulder.

Standing in the presence of the mighty Gabriel, the guard lost his nerve. "Y-y-yes, sir," was all he could stammer out.

"Back to your post. And make your captain proud," Gabriel said, smiling at the guard, who was clearly in awe of the All-Father's champion.

"At once, sir," the guard said, and holding his head high, he left to report back to his post. As he exited, he was smiling ear to ear. *Wait 'til I tell the others this,* he thought, racing out the door to resume his duties.

"Gabriel, this is Commander Wranti's medallion," Raphael said. "If she's back here with it, we have to assume the worst." Raphael spoke in saddened, hushed tones, passing the bloodied medallion to Gabriel.

"Old friend, I don't see how this could get much worse," Gabriel said, taking the medallion in his hands and studying it. "Remember, though—we haven't lost yet. As long as one of us breathes, we will fight to reclaim the Earth and mankind. This is what the All-Father created us for, and we shall obey and defend to the last of us." Gabriel walked over to the table where the girl lay. "Heal her with all haste," he said gravely. "She'll have knowledge that we'll desperately need, if we are to survive."

"Of course, Gabriel, of course," Raphael said, continuing to clean and dress the wounds on her body.

The sound of armored feet on the balcony outside brought Gabriel's attention away from the medallion in his hand. Captain Sandalphon usually didn't walk through the palace hallways or use its doors, as most rooms in the palace were equipped with ledges and balconies to provide easy flight access. Due to the constant rounds he made checking up on his guards all along the palace towers and battlements, he spent most of his time traveling around the outside of the palace walls, not inside.

But here Sandalphon was, inside the palace and bowing before Gabriel and Raphael. "What is thy order, Gabriel?" he asked.

"Find me Azreal," Gabriel said. "I need to speak with him on certain matters. Also, once she wakes up"—and here he looked down at the female warrior—"I'll need everybody gathered in the war room. We'll need to find out specifically where the battles took place, what the demon numbers were. I also need you to assemble three search parties to look for our comrades who might not have been able to make it back." Then, as an afterthought, he added, "Give them light armor, short swords, and crossbows. If they come into trouble they can't handle, I want them to be mobile enough to escape and return here to report on what they have seen."

"Yes, sir. Scouts will be ready within the half hour, and I shall send Azreal to you immediately upon finding him," Sandalphon replied.

Sandalphon was a credit to the Seraphim, a soldier through and through, thought Gabriel as he watched the captain walk away to complete his tasks.

As Sandalphon strode toward the balcony, Gabriel and Raphael resumed talking about the girl on the table, wondering aloud who she was and whether or not she was the only survivor. Rolling her gently onto her side and examining the wound in her back and wing, Raphael remarked, "She's lucky to even be alive. The fact that she flew back here is a testament to her devotion to her oath and to the Seraphim."

Gabriel sat down on a stool next to Raphael, watching him work. "I wonder how large a force her legion saw." he said. "What types of demons were there? Who were the enemy generals in charge? So many questions need answering."

One thing was certain, he thought: whatever her legion had been through, if they lost, that meant there were demons running around Earth, unchecked and unopposed. Killing those who wouldn't serve them. Razing buildings to the ground. Pretty much turning Earth into Hell.

Looking down at the ground, Gabriel put words to his thoughts. "It has been rumored that some demons have the power to transform humans into twisted versions of themselves and use them for their own purposes. If that's happening, their numbers are being replenished daily."

"That's a worst-case scenario, Gabriel," Raphael said, trying to comfort his leader.

"Best case is the legions are still out there, fighting … fighting and dying," Gabriel said softly. Then he collected himself and stood up, still staring at the seemingly lifeless girl. A million questions tore through his mind. "Raph, inform me the minute she wakes and is able to talk," he said.

"Absolutely," Raphael replied, trying to dislodge a small splinter of spear still lodged in her wing. "If she wakes up at all."

As Gabriel left the room, Raphael sat on his stool, his hands working methodically to repair the damage this mysterious soldier received. His mind, however, focused on what must have been an immense amount of pressure and guilt placed on the shoulders of the All-Father's champion.

Chapter 8
Journal of Alisha Grace

It was sometime around 2:30 a.m., I think. (It's hard to keep track of time now. There is no day or night anymore, just a gray darkness broken by the fires outside.)

Screams and shouts erupted from outside, shattering the silence. It wasn't the same type of screaming I heard on that first night when the monsters came. This was rage and vengeance.

People were shouting orders, and my first thought was that the army had finally arrived to save us. I opened the door of my hiding place just a bit and peeked out. My living room was illuminated by huge bursts of light from the street outside. There were fresh flames everywhere.

I crawled to the window, expecting to see men in green uniforms, tanks, and planes. All the wonderful stuff from the movies. Instead I saw a sight that I don't know if I can put into words.

My heart leapt into my throat. For the first time since it all began, I allowed myself to feel hope. Hope that all was not lost, that we would be saved from the monsters that had threatened and massacred us. My mouth opened wide as I gazed upon the most magnificent creatures I had ever seen. From what I could tell, they were all over the city, as far as I could see. They were everywhere. In the air, on the ground—everywhere.

The men were tall and muscular, and the women were graceful and beautiful, more beautiful than the girls you see in the magazines. All of them had enormous white wings, and they all wore dazzling armor that gleamed in the burning fires of the city below. Some wielded swords and spears, and others utilized bow and arrows with deadly aim.

I knew right away what they were: angels. They were angels who had come down out of Heaven to save us ... or what was left of us.

I stayed on the floor on my hands and knees, in utter awe, silently cheering and hoping they would kill every last demon. My heart was pounding, and I kept watching out my window until the happiness and hope I had allowed into my heart began fading away.

The monsters were starting to win. I could see it. As each minute passed, there were fewer and fewer angels left. Then a horn sounded in the distance, and within seconds, the few angels that were still alive and fighting—fighting for us—leapt into the air ... and flew away.

The demons roared in victory. The sound was deafening.

My body trembled with horror and fear; I could do nothing but silently watch them leave. I felt hot tears running down my cheeks as I started crying uncontrollably, my body shaking. I wanted to call out to the angels to come back, to beg them to take me with them, but I was so afraid of the monsters finding me that I didn't say anything.

All hope was lost as I watched them fly higher and higher until I couldn't see them anymore; my face and shirt were wet with tears.

Finally I looked away, and I crawled to the kitchen.

Staying as low to the ground as I could, trying to be quiet, I opened up the cupboard and carefully took out some cookies and juice boxes. My mom and I used to play in the park down the street and have cookies and juice afterward on the bench by the swings, so we always had a lot of them in the house.

Inching over to the refrigerator, I grabbed a photo of my mom and pulled it down. I hurried back to my hiding spot in the closet and closed the door. Then I wrapped myself in my blanket and I cried.

I cried for what seemed like forever, thinking how much I missed her and wondering if I would ever see her again ... At some point I fell asleep, still holding the picture.

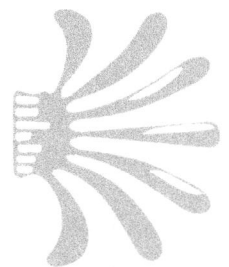 

Chapter 9

KRILLION WAS A WARRIOR WHO had seen more battles than he could count and had even more scars that he couldn't remember how he got. Since he was able to wield a sword, his whole life had been dedicated to being a soldier. Starting out decades ago as a lowly swordsman, he had quickly worked his way up the chain of command to the position he now held.

Reflecting back on his first battle, he remembered that he had barely been able to hold up his sword and he'd been likely to do as much harm to his allies as to his demon enemies. He'd come a very long way since those early days.

Now, looking up at the portal in the sky and this fresh wave of attackers, and seeing the inevitable death of his men, he was at first taken aback, wondering what the hell he was going to do. But his hesitation was brief, as his warrior instinct and years of training took control of his thoughts and actions.

Scanning the field, he saw that the majority of his legion was still holding its own against superior numbers. If he didn't act quick and decisively, however, the situation was going to change quickly. His men, bruised and battered beyond belief, already had fought well past the point of what they should have been capable of—and still they fought the oncoming demonic forces, still they clung to a hope of victory that was fading by the minute.

They all knew what was at stake here, and Krillion could not have been more proud of them than he was at that moment. As he returned his gaze to the skies, battle plans and formations started taking shape in his mind.

Suddenly Krillion heard laughter all around him: reality had just surrounded him in the form of hairy demons—half goat, half man, and full of malicious intent. This bunch, he knew, belonged to Azazel, the lord of the goat demons.

Old fool, Krillion thought, scolding himself for losing his focus.

"Well, well, well. What do we have here?" one of them said in a strange, buzzing voice.

"Looks like we got us a little playmate," said another one, staring at Krillion with glowing red eyes.

The veins bulged in Krillion's massive arms as he gripped the handle of his war hammer, preparing for the pain he knew was coming. He didn't say a word, deciding instead to let his hammer do the talking. His strategy gelled just as the first demon charged him.

Swinging his hammer around with all his strength, Krillion caught one goat demon in the chest, sending it up and away from the brawl. Spinning his body as he followed through with the full circle of his swing, he smashed his hammer into the next demon, reducing one of its arms to little more than useless skin and bone hanging from its socket.

The third demon hopped back as the hammer whisked past where its torso had been a second earlier, and the fourth, Krillion knew, was on the attack. Dropping down on all fours, the creature gouged the back of Krillion's leg with its gnarled horns. Refusing to cry out from pain and show weakness before these insignificant creatures, Krillion reversed his swing, smashing the third demon in the face, breaking bones and spraying blood. Then he reached down with a single hand, grabbed one of the horns that had just punctured his leg, and snapped off, driving it straight into the third demon's neck with full force. He felt the bone slide through flesh to hit the creature's spine.

A shrill buzz came from the dying demon, followed by a sick gurgling sound as the creature choked on its own blood.

Eyes filled with hate, Krillion slowly moved his gaze to the last of the demons, which was lying on the ground, clutching its head where its horn used to be. He saw fear in the goat creature's eyes as he brought the head of his hammer down directly on its temple, killing it.

Krillion dropped to his one good knee, allowing himself a second to rest and regain control. And once again he looked around and took the measure of the fight. When he did, fear gripped him; he was shocked to see far fewer of his troops engaged in battle. Risking a quick glance up, he noticed several of his men engaged in aerial combat with the dregs.

It was clear to Krillion that they were hopelessly outnumbered by this fresh wave. It was just a matter of time until they were overwhelmed completely.

For the first time in the Fury's glorious history, he would have to call a retreat.

† † †

On the other side of the battlefield, Rai pulled his bloody sword from the stomach of an angel who had had the audacity to challenge him. Rai had seen the whole fight between Krillion and the goat demons, and his eyes lit up with evil joy. *The legion commander,* Rai thought. *What better way to end this scrap than with his death?*

Barely sweating, as he had joined the fight so late, Rai sprinted toward the commander at full speed, determined to present Krillion's head to his master as a trophy. Without missing a step, Rai pulled a dagger from his belt and jammed it into the back of an angel as he ran past. He forced his legs to move faster until it seemed as if he were flying.

Rai's target was almost within his reach when, at the last second, Krillion turned his head and saw the demon general racing straight for him. Acting on sheer instinct, Krillion jumped into the air, his wings spread to their full, majestic width. Rai came to a stop right in front of him, staring up at him with hate in his eyes.

Hovering well out Rai's reach, Krillion could only stare in disbelief at the sight before him. "Impossible," he whispered, wide-eyed, as waves of raw emotion hit him.

"Commander!"

Krillion looked up to see one of his lieutenants flying toward him.

"General, we have to get the hell out of here," the angel yelled. "Order the retreat, sir!"

But Krillion was again staring, mouth agape, at the figure on the ground before him. He seemed frozen in place, unable to move save for the wings keeping him aloft.

"Sir!" the lieutenant yelled again, this time grabbing Krillion by his arms and shaking him back to reality.

The Fallen | 37

"What? Yes… yes! Sound the retreat! Everyone able to fly, grab any survivors unable to fly and head to the trees!" commanded Krillion.

The lieutenant turned in the air, catching a gust of wind that sent him high over the battlefield. He could see that it was littered with the dead from both sides. He produced an ivory-colored horn carved with angelic symbols, put it to his lips, and blew one deep note that resounded through the chaotic landscape.

Less than a minute later, the sky was filled with fleeing angels—some barely flying on their own strength, others helping the more seriously wounded to escape. The warriors of the Seraphim had begun their tactical retreat, with scores of dregs closing in fast.

"You men are with me now!" the lieutenant yelled to the first twenty warriors who reached him. "We have to protect the commander!"

Krillion was still fixated on the figure below him as if he were staring at a ghost from his past. And in a sense, he was.

"General, get out of here, now!" the lieutenant shouted as he fended off blows from two dregs that had caught up with them. "Go, sir! We'll cover the retreat—get out, now!" He turned to some angels hovering nearby. "You three—stay with the general. Ensure he makes it out of here!"

With a final glance at the death and destruction below him and at the figure still standing there on the ground, Krillion turned and flew with his guards to the trees at the far end of the valley.

The lieutenant and what remained of his small group now faced an impossible number of claws and fangs, all speeding toward them. "We are Fury!" the lieutenant yelled to his men. "By all you hold dear, do not let them pass until our brethren have escaped! For the oath and for the All-Father!"

"Fury!" he yelled, flying straight into the storm. His battle cry was followed by an even louder one from the men who flew by his side. They knew they had no chance of surviving. They could only hope to buy the precious time their general needed to escape, and pray that the All-Father would embrace them in his arms when all was said and done.

In a matter of minutes, the horde of dregs had completely engulfed the defenders. The lieutenant, who was being bitten and cut from too many angles at once to defend himself, began swinging his bloodstained sword wildly, trying to stall for a few more seconds. "All-Father, protect me and my men. Embrace your faithful servants …" The lieutenant's cry trailed off as the last of drops of blood fell from his deathly white hands, and his body plummeted to Earth like a dart, hitting with enough impact to reduce his every bone to dust.

Rai walked over to where the lieutenant lay and stared at him. The once-white wings were shredded and covered with blood; the body itself was horribly disfigured, twisted unnaturally from the impact. Rai looked up at the dregs.

"After them," he commanded, and the chase was on.

Rai looked down again upon the remains of the lieutenant who had so valiantly sacrificed his life so that his general could live. He wondered if any of his minions would do that for him. *Only Valafor,* he thought, seeing his loyal friend running toward him.

When Valafor reached Rai, he was panting and covered in sweat, but he had a huge smile on his face. "Damn good fight, boss," he said in his gravelly voice. "Victory is ours! See how they flee from us?" He pointed to the sky, where the angels were in full retreat. Then he noticed Rai's expression. He could tell something was wrong. "What is it, Rai?" he asked, genuine concern in his voice.

"Something about the enemy commander, something from … my past. It's as if I should know him, but I can't remember," Rai said, confusion spreading across his face.

"Let's go find him, then. He couldn't have gotten far," Valafor suggested. "This fight is over here, and I'm bored, anyway."

"He headed to the grove of trees over there," Rai said, gesturing with his sword.

"We'll have to match pace to get to him before the dregs do," Rai said, glancing up.

"Well, shit—let's go, then," replied Valafor, as he started running toward the trees, maneuvering over the bodies of the fallen from both armies. A second later Rai was at his side—still unsure what compelled his own actions, but glad that his friend Valafor was with him.

The angel lieutenant had bought moments, at best, for what remained of the Fury Legion. The dregs had broken ranks and now flew in all directions, hunting down and picking off the angels who didn't have the strength to outfly them. Four dregs were in pursuit of Krillion and his band of three.

Try as they might, Krillion and his guards didn't have the strength to escape the dregs. The hours of fighting had taken their toll on them all. The dregs' high-pitched screeches pierced the air as they forced their smaller wings to flap harder and faster to gain on the fleeing angels.

Risking a glance behind him, one of the guards nudged his fellow guard and nodded toward the immediate threat to their rear.

"The All-Father watch over you, sir," the warrior said, and just like that, before Krillion could react, the two guards banked sharply, circling around to meet the dregs head-on. Hovering there, swords brandished, ready to offer the ultimate sacrifice, their lives, for their commander, the two beaten, bloody warriors removed their helmets. The little wind there was in the gray sky cooled their heads, allowing them a moment's respite. Then they exchanged salutes with their swords and rushed to meet their end.

Their wings straining from the hours of fighting, the two guards moved as quickly as they could toward their targets in order to put as much distance as possible between them and Krillion. The guards glanced at each other, nodding in agreement at their unspoken plan.

They sped at the dregs full-force, stopping midflight just as they seemed destined to crash into them. Then one of the guards threw his sword with all his might straight at the lead dreg. The blade found its mark, sinking deep into the creature's face, ripping through flesh and skull. Clutching at its face in a frenzied panic, scrambling in the throes of death, the dreg plummeted to the ground.

The second guard, who still had his weapon, was locked in a battle with the second attacker. Meanwhile one of the remaining dregs attacked the first guard from behind, slashing and biting him savagely. Blood and feathers flew everywhere. In his last act as mankind's protector, the guard swung around to face the dreg, locking his arms around the small creature and pinning its arms and wings to its side. "For the All-Father!" the guard yelled, clutching the dreg as they both fell to their deaths.

The second guard, who had just run his sword through his current foe's neck, turned to see his partner falling to earth with his victim in tow, too far down to be saved. He swung his body around in the air to find the last of the dregs—but he was too late. The last thing the airborne warrior saw was the mouthful of razor-sharp teeth that clamped over his face.

The dreg tossed the faceless carcass away and returned to the chase.

He saw his prey a little ways ahead of them, still trying to make it to the trees. The dreg flew higher so that he had an elevated view from which to strike. Then he waited.

† † †

"Sir, what are we gonna do?" the last remaining guard asked his commander.

"Make our way back to the Crystal... *oof!*" The dreg landed on Krillion's back, slashing at him with one clawed hand while fending off the guard with the other. His strength depleted, Krillion started falling. At this the dreg lunged at the guard, determined to kill off the stronger of the two and come back for the weaker.

The guard was ready. With one swift motion, he plunged his sword deep into the dreg's chest just before the dreg ripped out his throat. Clutching the gaping hole in his neck, the guard stared, terrified, as his commander fell to Earth below. *I have failed*, he thought. *I failed to protect my commander.* And then he himself succumbed, plummeting to the valley floor.

† † †

Krillion hit the ground hard, trying to roll with the momentum of his body to cushion the impact. After lying still for a minute, catching his breath and trying to shake off the numbness he felt all over, he realized that he hadn't landed on grass. Straining every muscle in his huge frame to bring himself to a sitting position, he looked around and saw firsthand what had happened to Thame and his archers: there were body parts everywhere, most of them unrecognizable except for the few pieces of armor that remained. That's what had cushioned his fall and probably saved his life.

The commander of the now-fallen Fury Legion tasted bile as he looked around, overwhelmed by feelings of dread and failure. Getting to his feet and taking a shaky step, he headed for the nearby tree line. *Just a few more feet*, he thought, *and I'll be safe.* And then he saw his worst fear made real.

Tied to a tree at the edge of the forest was the body of his oldest friend, Thame. Never had Krillion seen a body so desecrated. Thames's wings were extended out and nailed to the tree by giant wooden stakes; his arms were bound behind him with evil cords that bit into his flesh. Walking closer, Krillion noticed the worst part: Thame had no eyes, no ears. His head had been shaved and his breastplate removed, exposing his bare chest.

The Fallen | 41

Carved on his chest was a single word: *Kobal*.

Krillion dropped his hammer on the ground and fell to his knees in front of the ruined corpse. His legion was wiped out, and now his best friend was dead because Krillion had sent him to deal with the dark mages. Krillion hung his head in silent surrender.

He knelt there for several minutes, covered in blood, his head hanging low.

Then from behind him came the sounds of someone or something running up the hill toward him. With an anger even he would have found frightening had he seen it, Krillion grabbed his hammer and forced himself to stand.

Turning, he saw the enemy general racing up the hill. With him was another demon with a massive black arm radiating a deadly-looking blue light.

One last fight, Krillion thought. *Then it will be over.*

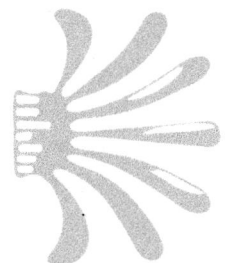 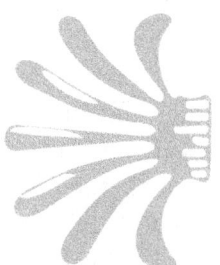

Chapter 10

IF THE SERAPHIM EVEN SURVIVED the oncoming days and weeks, then surely this morning would be remembered as the turning point in the war, Afriel thought, walking to the infirmary window to stare at the skies surrounding the Crystal Palace.

"On this morning," he whispered, "the Seraphim suffered their first and possibly last defeat at the hands of their most hated enemies."

The normal calm of the heavens was shattered by the deafening sound of death cries. The warriors of light had returned home in droves this fateful morning. Many flew alone, propelled by their own strength and determination; twice as many carried ones that could not fly.

The angel guard, dispatched by Gabriel days ago to stop the invasion of Hell's forces onto Earth, had failed miserably. They had failed to protect Earth, and they had broken their sworn oath to defend mankind.

Today would be the darkest day in the history of the Seraphim.

How did this happen? Afriel wondered, staring in awe at the sheer number of wounded flooding in from all directions. *Israfil's visions have never been wrong, and they always clearly portray Heaven's victory. Something of late has tipped the scales in favor of Hell. But what?*

Throughout time, the angels had always triumphed over the demons in any war or skirmish. But not this time. This fight was different, Afriel thought. Perhaps some would call it arrogance on the part of the light. Arrogance from never having been defeated, arrogance at the stature they held on the Earth below... Who knew?

What Afriel and the rest of the Seraphim did know for certain was that the war had been lost and Earth was now firmly secured in the hands of the demons. Would it be just a matter of time before the Crystal Palace was next?

I can't even imagine what the humans are enduring right now, Afriel thought, clutching his stomach in pain.

Ever since the first human was cut down, wave after wave of fresh pain washed over Afriel's body. Such was the price he paid for being the angel of youth. It was his burden to guide the dying and help bear their pain—and it was a position he had accepted with great honor. Now, though, the numbers of the dying were too many, the pain too great for his body to withstand.

Looking around the infirmary, Afriel couldn't even fathom what the warriors there had seen or done below. If Heaven itself was in chaos, what had happened on Earth? There were so many wounded arriving all at once it was hard to keep up with the sheer number of them. There were warriors with fatal gut wounds, missing arms and legs, eye sockets filled with dried blood instead of eyes. The stone floor of the infirmary was slick with blood. There wasn't a single spot in the room where Afriel could look without seeing horrors that would stay with him until his days ended.

"Afriel, come here quickly—I need your assistance!" Raphael's voice snapped Afriel back to reality.

Afriel ran to a table where Raphael was working hard to keep his patient alive. "Apply this bandage over his chest ... right here," Raphael said, guiding Afriel's hands over a bloody wound the size of his fist.

If the palace itself was in a chaotic state due to the war, then the infirmary was an absolute nightmare. Not having seen the warrior's share of blood and death, it was hard for Afriel to grasp the enormity of the situation. He had never seen combat or its aftereffects. Still, although he was completely consumed by the constant pain he felt every time an angel or human died on Earth below, he was handling himself pretty well.

"Is he going to live?" Afriel whispered meekly, applying pressure to the wound.

"That depends on many factors," Raphael said. "Right now if we can't get this hole closed and stop the bleeding, then no, he will not live." Raphael spoke with the cool, collected tone of one who had seen this type of bodily damage so often that it didn't panic him anymore.

Raphael was the angel of healing, and he was the best the Seraphim had to offer. Afriel closed his eyes slightly as the power of the All-Father coursed through Raphael's arms and into the wounded warrior on the table. Then, wincing at the sight of the warrior's bruised and battered body, Afriel watched as his cuts and bruises began to disappear.

Afriel gasped at the sight of wounds healing before his very eyes. He began to say something to Raphael but stopped when he saw that Raphael was lost in deep concentration, harnessing the power of the All-Father and channeling it to save the life of the warrior who lay before them.

The air around the three angels began to glow red as the power continued to surge through Raphael and into the warrior. The gaping hole in the warrior's chest started to close up, and then… nothing. The light quickly faded and the warrior's head slumped to one side.

Confusion showed on Afriel's delicate face as he continued looking up and down the fresh corpse on the table before him, searching for some sign of life.

"Raph, what happened? Your power—why didn't it work?" Afriel stammered, stunned by the loss of the angel lying in front of him.

"It wasn't enough. His wounds were too severe even for me to heal," Raphael said, closing the departed warrior's eyes.

Afriel sank to his knees near the table. Being so close to death brought him fresh waves of pain. Placing his head on the fallen warrior's body, Afriel began whispering a prayer to the All-Father to accept this brave angel with love and grant the angel a place by his side. When he finished he said nothing; he just lifted his head and looked at Raphael, his face streaked with tears.

"Come, Afriel," Raphael said, placing a comforting hand upon his friend's shoulder. "We cannot dwell on this, not while so many others need us."

Afriel looked around the room at the warriors of the Seraphim who had given everything they had and paid the ultimate sacrifice so mankind would not live under Hell's heel. He felt more tears form in the corners of his eyes. "Yes, Raph, you're right. Let's go," he said. And following Raphael's lead, he did not wipe the tears away.

☦ ☦ ☦

Standing in formation in the courtyard below the war room were 150 warrior scouts assembled by Sandalphon. They were lightly armed so they could get to Earth, do their mission, and get out quickly should the need arise.

In front of them stood Sandalphon himself, captain of the palace guard, addressing the captains of each unit.

"Captain Cassiel, Captain Raziel, Captain Tabbris: plain and simple, this is a search and rescue operation," Sandalphon said, looking each one in the eye. His expression spoke volumes about the severity of the situation each captain faced. "Find our men down below, if there are any still alive, and get them back here as soon as possible. Fight only if you can win. I'm not going to lie to you: Earth is lost for now; I don't know what you'll face down there. Keep your heads on straight, focus on the mission, and keep your men in line. Are there any questions?"

"Sir, what if there is no one left?" Tabbris asked.

"In the event that we're all that's left, make haste back here," Sandalphon replied.

"What about the humans, sir?" Cassiel asked.

"If you come across any that you can help, do so—but not at the peril of our own men."

The captains looked at each other uncertainly. Every angel, soldier or spiritual, took an oath administered by Gabriel and passed down from the All-Father to lay down his life for the salvation of man. Sensing their emotions, Sandalphon continued, "I know it sounds harsh and goes against the oath, but we can't do anything for them if we're all dead. Anything else? No? Captains, you have your orders. Good luck to you all. May the All-Father watch over you."

As Sandalphon departed for the war room, Tabbris, Cassiel, and Raziel gathered their units, double-checked their supplies, and promptly left the safety of the Crystal Palace to complete their mission.

Waiting for Sandalphon in the war room were Gabriel, Israfil, Metatron, and Abdiel. They were gathered around the majestic table that stood in the room's center. While many of the seats were empty now, the one that caused Gabriel the most distress was Azreal's.

"Anybody know where Azreal is?" Gabriel asked with a sigh. He knew that no one would. Azreal had never been what you would call a team player. Yes, he was an angel of the highest caliber, but he never quite fit in with the rest of them. Gabriel had always suspected that Azreal had his own agenda, that he was always keeping secrets or with withholding vital information.

It was Abdiel, the angel of faith, who responded. "I haven't seen Azreal, but I know that Raphael and Afriel are in the infirmary, tending to the wounded. And there are many, Gabriel."

"My apologies for being late."

Gabriel looked up to see Sandalphon walking to his appointed seat at the table.

"I have organized three scout parties to search Earth for our brothers and sisters," Sandalphon said, taking his seat among the others. "The guards manning the palace have been rotated and given their orders, and there is no sign of Azreal anywhere around the palace that I have seen."

Just as Gabriel was about to commend his captain on an outstanding job, the door to the war chamber opened and in walked Azreal. "Why is everyone so concerned with where I am these days?" Azreal said smugly, his black armor clanking as he took his seat. "It's not like any of you have cared about the angel of death before." Azreal's voice was mocking, and as he spoke his eyes darted from one angel to another, as if he dared anyone present to challenge him.

If it had been an arrow, Gabriel's icy stare would have pierced Azreal's twisted heart right then, wiping that smile off his face.

"There's a war going on, or have you all forgotten?" Azreal asked.

"That will be enough, Az," Gabriel said, cutting him off with a wave of his hand.

Everyone knew what was coming: every time these two were in the same room, a fight broke out. Gabriel was short-tempered, and Azreal was never one to take orders or back down from a challenge.

"Tell me, where have you been?" Gabriel asked. "I sent Captain Sandalphon to retrieve you for this meeting. He couldn't find you, and no one has seen you." Gabriel eyed the angel of death carefully, looking for anything out of sorts.

The blood in the room was about to reach a boiling point.

"You may be the All-Father's chosen, but that doesn't mean I answer to you, Gabriel. Also, if you doubt my sincerity, ask your captain if he checked the top of the signal tower. As to what I was doing, my business is my own and of no concern to you—or to any of you, for that matter." Azreal again stared hard at each angel seated around the table, as if daring any of them to speak out against him.

Seeing Azreal's challenging look, Gabriel felt his anger again take hold. He shot up out of his chair. "We are at war, Azreal—a war that we are losing badly. If we do not stand together in this, we will fall individually. What part of that are you having trouble understanding?"

Just as Azreal stood to respond, Metatron spoke, breaking the challenge between the two. "Gabriel, I must leave. The All-Father summons me."

"Right," Gabriel said, regaining his composure. He sat back down, never once taking his eyes off of Azreal. "Please inform me of his plans once you have finished. And Metatron … make haste."

"Of course, Gabriel," Metatron said, his voice emotionless as always. Then his head fell forward to rest upon his chest, his eyes still open and his body slumped in his chair. No matter how many times Gabriel saw this, it was still a little unnerving to know that though Metatron's body was there sitting in his chair, his mind was off somewhere with the All-Father.

Returning his attention to the matter at hand, Gabriel started again. "We know that Hell has invaded and taken control of Earth. The forces I sent down to stop them, from what we gather, have been soundly defeated. Reports coming in from the survivors say that they have taken heavy casualties across Earth, but all is not lost. Captain Sandalphon, if you would?" Gabriel said, bringing the attention of those assembled to the captain of the palace guard.

"Yes," Sandalphon said, standing up. He waited a few seconds, clearing his throat and collecting his thoughts, before laying down his defense plan.

"We need to regroup as many of our warriors as we can here to prepare for a secondary attack upon the Crystal Palace. It's unlikely that we will be attacked here soon; the most probable course of action for the demons is to set up and fully secure Earth first. I have dispatched three scout groups with specific orders to search and rescue any Seraphim left behind. The palace guards also have their orders concerning the situation and anyone heading toward the palace. This is all I have right now," Sandalphon said, and he sat back down, looking at Gabriel.

"Israfil?" Gabriel said. Those assembled turned their attention to the angel of Judgment Day, who stood to speak.

"There have been extreme changes in my visions as of late. Yes, the world was lost to us, but somewhere in the world there is a girl. I do not know what she represents or what part she will play in the end game, but regardless, the sight of her in my visions must mean something. Along with her, others have shown themselves to me. Some we know, some we don't. And others…" Israfil's voice trailed off, and he seemed lost in thought.

"Speak plainly, Israfil," Gabriel said. "If we are to have any hope of surviving, we must have solid facts with which to work."

Israfil nodded and resumed. "First, the female warrior who came to us the other day, the one who lies unconscious in the infirmary under Raphael's care… Krillion, commander of the Fury Legion … There is a demon with a blackened arm that harnesses awesome power and …"Israfil's voice again trailed off, and he stared down at the table.

"What is it?" asked Gabriel.

"Gabriel," Israfil said, lifting his face to look him straight in the eye. "It's Rai."

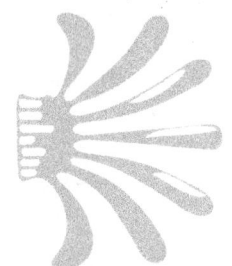 

Chapter 11

As Tabbris and his men flew in between buildings, gazing at the ground below, it began to dawn on him how dire their situation had become. Buildings were in shambles, and random fires lit up the dead city, their flickering light dancing upon the piles of decaying corpses. In many areas, large sections of the street were ripped up. Everywhere Tabbris looked he saw human remains, and the sight made his stomach churn and his heart pound with sadness and rage.

He noticed immediately that no angels or demons were among the bodies below. That meant only one thing: the Seraphim never made it to this city.

He couldn't even imagine, didn't want to imagine, the events of that night. It was obvious by the carnage alone that the humans had never had a chance. Even if they could have mounted some kind of feeble defense, what good would that have done? Forget any attempt at retaliation—the strongest and bravest of them would have been brought to their knees by fear at the mere sight of a demon.

No, Tabbris thought, this was massacre on a scale he had never borne witness to.

Tabbris gave the hand signal for his unit to spread out among the rooftops. They would operate as security while he and three others went down to street level to get a better look. Even though the city appeared dead and quiet, he wasn't going to take any chances on a random encounter with an unknown force. Tabbris was a young captain, but his youth didn't counteract his good training and sound judgment.

Within seconds of their landing, one of Tabbris's men fell to his knees, spraying vomit on the pavement. The smell of rotten flesh was everywhere in this city of the dead. Holding an arm over his own nose and mouth to try and filter out the putrid odor, Tabbris began walking, taking in the magnitude of the destruction around him. Tabbris didn't fault his soldier for getting sick or even consider it weakness. Most of the people they saw were torn apart or partly eaten. Exposed organs and partially intact faces of horror were everywhere. It was a wonder that he didn't throw up himself.

He'd been in battle before, seen the worst it had to offer and its aftermath, but this... this was something entirely different. The sight before them made all his battles look like Sunday picnics by comparison. Tabbris didn't know what to feel or think as his senses took in the carnage laid bare before him.

Some of the bodies in the area had been left intact, strung upon upside-down crosses as a gruesome reminder of who was in charge now.

Walking farther down the road, Tabbris stumbled over something that appeared to be a body. Yes, it was a woman, horribly burned. Tabbris gently lowered himself to one knee to close the eyes that were still open. Fighting back tears that seemed determined to escape, he offered prayer and apologies to the woman for their failings of protection. Then something caught his eye.

The woman was clutching something to her chest.

As gently as he could, he pulled back the brittle, black arms. He looked and immediately closed his eyes, got to his feet, and turned his back to the burned corpse. One of his men saw his sudden movement and, careful not to step on the dead, made his way to his captain, asking softly, "What is it, sir? Did you find something?"

"N-no..." Tabbris stammered and walked away from the body.

The scout looked at the body and shuddered. Melted to the woman's chest were the charred remains of a baby.

Suddenly an arrow struck the pavement next to the scout, bringing his attention upward. "Captain Tabbris, look!" he yelled, pointing to the rooftops. They were under attack; the dreg had found them.

"To arms!" Tabbris yelled, drawing his sword and flying up to join the fight, all thoughts of the woman and her child replaced by hate and anger. His men followed suit, flapping their white wings to gain height and leaving the dead to their peace on the streets below.

Soaring in between buildings, Tabbris gripped his sword like someone possessed. Now he had something of flesh and blood he could

The Fallen | 51

strike down. Now he had dreg demons from which he could physically carve his revenge.

The Seraphim might not have been here in the beginning, but they sure as hell were here now. He couldn't help the humans on the ground below, but he could pay them some small amount of respect by shedding the blood of their enemies.

Flying as fast as his wings would carry him, Tabbris saw the first of the dregs. Flying directly under it, his sword at the ready, Tabbris let out a fearsome scream. By the time his victim saw him it was too late: one clean cut of the sword sent a line of red from the demon's groin to its face as Tabbris swept past. Shrieking in rage and pain, the demon fell to the street below to join its victims.

He is but the first this night, thought Tabbris, looking for his next target.

Throughout the skies, Seraphim scouts and howling dregs were engaged in brutal aerial combat. Taking a quick count, Tabbris realized that this fight wouldn't last long. There were only about twenty of the flying creatures against his fifty angels. It would be a quick fight, but one that would let him and his command vent their anger for the atrocities he was sure the dregs helped commit below.

Flying up behind a creature already locked in battle with one of his men, Tabbris threw his arm around its neck, pulled its head and chest away from his warrior, and plunged his sword directly into its chest. At the same time one of his scouts crashed into something mere feet behind him; apparently one of the dregs was about to perform the same tactic as Tabbris.

That's the trick when fighting in the air, Tabbris thought. *You have to have eyes in all directions—up, down, left, and right—and you have to trust your comrades with your life.*

Within minutes of its beginning, the fight was over, the last of the dregs retreating through the dark sky, clearly recognizing that they were outnumbered and outmatched. A triumphant cheer erupted as angels raised their bows and short swords high in victory.

Tabbris had all the warriors land on the same rooftop right below him so he could take count. Just as he had figured, they hadn't lost any, and only four of his men had sustained minor injuries. Finally, spirits were high. After so many losses, one victory, no matter how small, was what was needed to boost morale.

But the celebration was short-lived.

"Quiet—keep it down, all of you!" Tabbris ordered.

In the distance could be heard the shrieks and wails of a whole host of dregs, which apparently were just learning of what had happened to their own kind and were en route to the scout's position.

"It's time we got back," Tabbris said. "This mission is over."

Within seconds the whole unit was airborne, making their way back to the Crystal Palace and leaving behind the dead city and its eternal inhabitants.

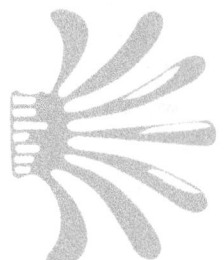 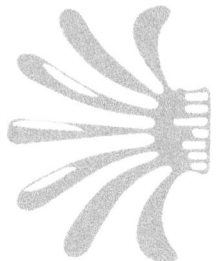

Chapter 12

THE UNHOLY BLACK TOWER STOOD in a remote part of Hell, away from the general population of demons and tortured souls. Surrounded by a mote of bubbling lava, the tower was guarded by massive stone golems created from the very ground around it and filled with life by the tower's master.

This was the tower of Leonard and his dark mages. Here, the master of the dark arts was able to teach his apprentices the ways of demonic magic and enhance his own powers through enchantment and experimentation. Like Leonard, the mages were feared throughout the realm; they could weave spells that wrought horrible destruction and devastation unto their enemies.

It was here in his tower, with his prized apprentice, Mullin, that Leonard sensed a deep, soft power residing on Earth. Now, extending his senses further and deeper across the planet, he had found what it was that disturbed him. Standing in the center of his pentagram, harnessing all his power, hands outstretched, Leonard dropped his spell, breathing heavily and pondering what he had uncovered.

"Master, what is it? What do you see?" Mullin asked.

"There is a presssence on Earth that we have overlooked or failed to sssee in our haste to secure a foothold," Leonard hissed. Wondering how a power of this magnitude could have escaped him earlier, he walked across the inlaid pattern on the floor to his desk, where he began to shuffle through random scrolls scattered on its metal surface. "The angel you interrogated—did he mention anything of thisss to you?"

"No, Master. If the archer commander knew anything, he would have talked," Mullin said, following Leonard with his eyes. "If there is such power on Earth, it's possible that the accursed angels don't know of it either. I will dispatch the—"

"No!" Leonard cut him off. "No, you will go yourssself. We don't want to arouse anyone's sussspicions, especially that imbecile, Kobal. That damn fool thinksss everything isss a damn game, and this situation has the potential of being our undoing, even at this late stage. I will send word to Azazel to meet me at the slave penssss." As Leonard spoke, his serpent-like tongue flickered out from within his hood. "Now go. Find this power and bring it to me immediately. I will be awaiting you at the pens. I must concoct a containment spell."

"Yes, Master," Mullin said, and then he recited a teleportation spell that would carry him to the realm of man.

His apprentice gone, Leonard was left alone with his thoughts. He walked over to stand on a symbol carved into the floor. It was a sigil, a five-pointed star surrounded by a circle. It had been a gift from his master, Lucifer, as a way to enhance his already extraordinary powers. Stretching his arms toward the ceiling so that his scaly fingers extended slightly past the cuffs of his robe, Leonard shut his eyes and began murmuring the language of magic. He was careful to pronounce every sound and pitch perfectly, as even the smallest mistake could have disastrous effects.

Red and yellow beams of light coursed through his body, illuminating the room as the spell grew in strength and neared completion. A shape began to take form in front of him, a few feet off the ground. As the spell continued to gain power, the shape became clearer.

In seconds, the fur-covered face of Azazel was floating before him. "Leonard, what is it?" Azazel asked. "I have strategies to plan and battles to win. Why have you called me?"

"Meet me at the pens with all hassste," Leonard said to the ghostly face. "An unexpected turn of events has occurred. It could be our undoing."

Azazel sensed the urgency in his ally's words. "I'll be there in ten earth hours," he said. "We'll talk then." The horned head of Azazel blinked and disappeared.

Leonard stood alone in the empty room for a moment, gathering his thoughts. Then he, too, blinked out.

† † †

Mullin blinked himself into a small space at the entrance of the pens. *The pens*, thought Mullin. *Where captured angels and humans are kept.* The pens served many purposes. The main one was that they were where mages turned human captives into "biters"—mindless demon-slaves who would do the mages' bidding.

All around Mullin, locked in hastily built cages, were hundreds of humans and dozens of angels stripped of their weapons and armor. The angels' morale had been crushed. It was bad enough that the Seraphim had lost the war and mankind was on the brink of annihilation. But then to be brought here and subjected to even more torture was too much for some to bear.

Some of the captured angels were used in sadistic, gruesome ways for the entertainment of demon soldiers, but most were taken to the mages in the only building, at the far end of camp. There the mages methodically and with great pleasure ripped the wings from their backs and threw their mutilated bodies into cages for all to see. The severed wings were then piled up in the center of the camp and set aflame in front of all the cages housing the prisoners. The result was a massive bonfire that illuminated the entire camp and the dark gray skies above. The symbol of the angels' heavenly power being burned before the humans and captive angels created an atmosphere of fear, dread, and hopelessness throughout the camp.

Mullin took all this in as he walked past the goat-demon guards to stand in front of the raging inferno at the center, admiring the sight of charred and withered wings crackling in Hell's awesome flames. He looked around, studying every cage in the half circle around the fire, and he allowed himself a brief smile. It appeared that the burning wings were having the desired effect on the inmates.

Now he had work to do.

Returning his gaze to the flames, feeling their magnificent heat, Mullin let the magic spread outward from his body to find this power source his master spoke of.

Within minutes, he had found what he was looking for. It was in a city the demons had already destroyed, a short ways away.

Looking around at the prisoners one last time, Mullin again smiled. "Our time—finally," he whispered. He was still smiling as another teleportation spell whisked him away to his destination and this mysterious power.

Chapter 13

Journal of Alisha Grace

EVERYTHING WAS QUIET OUTSIDE AGAIN. I don't know how long I'd been hiding in the closet. It's hard to tell how much time has passed when you're huddled in the dark, fearing that at any moment the door will burst open and death will come for you.

The only sound now was the crackling of the fires that consumed everything outside. The fires seemed to burn forever, illuminating for any survivors the carnage that had been wreaked upon mankind.

Even the pitiful moans of the dying and suffering had ceased.

I was in the kitchen, rummaging through the last of the food and staying as low to the ground as possible, when the realization hit me: if I wanted to survive, I would have to leave the safety of the apartment soon. Just the idea went against my every instinct.

My heart jumped as screams ripped through the street, the shrill sounds penetrating my window and sending me into instant panic mode. I crawled to the window and peeked out onto the street. I didn't see anything, just the flickering firelight.

Suddenly something flew past the window. I think it was a human body. I screamed and ducked down, praying that the monsters weren't back again.

My mind realized the truth in seconds, and then seconds felt like minutes as I sat there shivering with dread and uncertainty on the carpeted floor. I heard people running down the street, yelling and screaming in panic. I peeked out the window again to see what was happening.

There were three of them, all running with no apparent destination—just running to get away from whatever was chasing them. Behind them came the grating sound of claws scraping on pavement. The putrid smell of fresh death hung in the air. My blood ran cold at what I saw next.

Coming around the corner were people—at least they looked something like people—who appeared to have been horribly burned. Their arms were much longer then a normal person's, with fingernails resembled a hawk's talons and abnormally large, muscular legs that looked like they had been made for jumping.

The closer they came to my house, the better I was able to see them. The creatures' jaws were extended, with multiple rows of razor-sharp teeth protruding from their dark, gaping mouths. Some of them had bits of flesh and cloth stuck to their teeth.

The creatures howled their bloodlust in anticipation of catching the prey still running from them.

One of their trio of intended victims—a woman with a long, blonde ponytail, sporting a black miniskirt and a bright-blue halter top—saw me inside as she ran by my window. She stopped and stared into my pale, tear-stained face. Then she started yelling at me to climb through the window, saying that she could help me, she could get me to safety.

Help me? She couldn't even help herself. They were already dead. They just didn't know it.

I began crying again, for I knew the monsters would find me for sure this time, and I began shouting at the woman through the window, begging her to go away. Instead she ran down the sidewalk to the front door of my apartment building.

Her two companions had run down the street out of sight, to whatever new terror awaited them. With tears streaming down my face, I watched some of the monsters veer off course to follow the blonde woman into my building.

Fear gripped my soul, and my heart felt as if it were going to burst in my chest. I ran to my hiding spot in the closet, grabbed the picture of my mom and held it close, praying that they would not find me. That I would remain safe and unseen.

I didn't.

There was a loud crash on the front door, and then another one. On the third, the door caved in.

This is it, I thought, my heart pounding. Because of her the creatures had found me, and now I was going to die like everyone else in the city.

But then I realized I wasn't hearing monsters swarming in to kill me. It was the woman from outside. She was running from room to room, looking for me and calling out. I opened the door and poked my head out.

"Come on, sweetie," she said, relieved, as she grabbed my hand, and into the hallway we went. Behind us I heard the scraping sounds—the creatures were hot on the mysterious woman's trail. Death echoed in the empty hallways as the nightmarish creatures had entered the building and were looking for our blood.

The woman took off in a sprint away from the noise, dragging me along behind her. Burned out hall lights and closed apartment doors smeared with blood passed in a blur as we ran straight to the emergency exit at the far end of the hall. The woman sucked in her breath and hit the door hard with her shoulder. The force of the impact caused the door to shoot open, colliding with the wall behind it and shattering glass everywhere in the back alley.

Once we were outside, behind the building, the woman squatted down next to me. "Honey, you run that way," she said, pointing down a stretch of dark back road. "I'm going' to lure them away from you. Find help. There are people still left alive in the city. Now go. Find them—they'll take care of you."

"What about you? Please don't leave me!" I cried, my lungs still burning from our sprint down the hallway moments before.

"Don't worry about me, sweetie," the lady said, half-smiling as she pulled out the largest handgun I had ever seen. There was a gleam in her eyes that radiated pure confidence.

She turned me around and told me to run, and, still crying, I obeyed. After running a few feet down the road, I risked a final glance over my shoulder at her. Her back was to me, and I saw two long streaks of blood soaking through the top of her blue shirt. Aiming her handgun into the hall we had just exited, she fired off three shots, the noise echoing through the alley.

Then, with a final, sympathetic look at me, she turned and ran back to the main street.

I turned and I ran. The last thing I heard was more gunshots, and I turned again to see demons pouring through the doorway after her. Now I took off running, and I didn't look back.

I ran blindly, not knowing exactly where go. I ran and ran until my veins pumped acid and my lungs felt like I was breathing in shards of glass. When I stopped running sometime later, I found myself in a park. Even here, in this once beautiful place, were signs of the massacre. People, demons, and angels, all mingled together. Blood and body parts were everywhere.

Walking through the park, picking my way across the bodies, I came across a grotesque statue. It had been formed from the bodies of people who had been broken into pieces, a mass of contorted limbs and horror-filled faces like some gruesome kind of Play-Dough. They had been compressed into one solid shape: an upside-down cross. Heads, arms, and feet protruded from this monstrosity of a structure.

I gaped wide-eyed at this visage of death, unable to speak or move. Then my legs gave out and I fell to my knees, unable to breathe. And then I threw up.

On the far side of the cross, the head of a woman was sticking out: eyes frozen wide, mouth opened in an eternal scream, face stained dark red from dried blood.

I had found my mom.

All was quiet now except for the screams emanating from the deep haze of my mind.

My screams, I realized. Echoing through the park, shattering the silence, were the sounds of my own screams.

And I didn't care. I didn't care if the demons found me. Nothing mattered anymore. Scream after scream ripped through my raw throat as I gripped the sides of my head in disbelief. I wanted to die. I wanted the demons to find me and end this nightmare reality.

Then a hand fell upon my shoulder, and darkness consumed me…

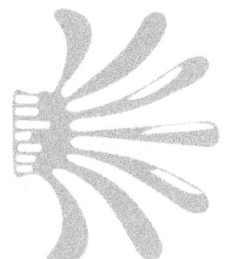 

Chapter 14

SUMMONING EVERY LAST OUNCE OF strength in his weary, bruised body, Krillion got to his feet. His head held high, his war hammer poised and ready for bloody action once more, he refused to show weakness to the two enemy combatants rushing up the hill to his position.

The enemy general closed the distance between them, stopping short a few feet away. "Lower your weapon, Commander," Rai said, calmly eyeing the huge angel on the verge of collapsing at his feet. "I have some questions for you, and the way you're looking at me right now tells me that you have the answers I seek."

As his adrenaline rush faded, Krillion's facial expression softened at the sight of one he had not seen in a very long time. Trying to find his voice through the flood of unexpected emotions, Krillion's throat went dry. "Have your man lower his weapon first," he said, choking the words out.

For all his arrogance and bravado, Valafor had never challenged Rai's authority. At Rai's quick glance, Valafor relaxed the muscles in his right arm. The cracks that appeared all over his charred arm began to close, sealing in the deadly power that resided within it. A little disappointed that there wasn't going to be a fight with the mighty warrior before him, Valafor walk away, toward the angelic corpse nailed to the tree. "I'll be over here if you need me, Rai," he said without looking back.

"Now then," Rai continued, "I want to make something perfectly clear to you, Commander. Your legion is scattered. You yourself can hardly bear your own weapon. Answer my questions truthfully and you have my word you are free to go. None of my minions will hinder you."

Sorrow filled the eyes of the Fury Legion commander as he looked upon Rai. "Why would you let me escape?" he asked.

"Look around you," Rai said. "You have lost all. Mankind is on the verge of extinction, and the Seraphim have been thoroughly defeated." Waving his arm around him to prove his point, Rai continued. "Even the Earth has begun merging with Hell. Believe me, Commander, letting one angel go will not tip the scales in Heaven's favor."

Ready to drop from exhaustion and injury, Krillion allowed his hammer to fall to the ground. "One angel," he whispered softly, repeating Rai's words. "You don't recognize me, do you?"

The question caused Rai's eyes to widen. It was as if this commander of the light could read his mind. "Should I recognize you?" Rai asked. "I don't recall ever meeting you in battle before."

"You and I have been in many battles together before this one," answered Krillion. "As enemies … and allies."

Looking down at the grass, which was blood-spattered from the archer massacre hours earlier, Rai tried to sort out his twisted thoughts and emotions. He knew this angel had something to do with the pieces of his past, of his life before Hell, but the more he tried to remember, the emptier his mind seemed to be. He paced back and forth over the mutilated corpses of Thames's archers, and then he stopped and looked Krillion directly in the eye. "Tell me," he said. "Where and when have we met in battle before today?"

Krillion lowered his head slightly, recalling the shame of that fateful day. In the space of a heartbeat, the events of that day replayed in his mind's eye.

The sun was just rising over the horizon, filling the countryside with unending light. Sharpened swords and freshly polished armor reflected the light, sending it to dance upon the ground as the angelic warriors overhead flew to combat. On that day Gabriel led the final charge against Lucifer's rebellion to conquer Heaven.

Seraphim fighting Seraphim, brother versus sister, father against child.

Krillion vividly recalled how tears stung his eyes as he locked weapons with his final opponent that day, and how his emotions nearly drove him to the edge of madness in the weeks afterward.

Before the battle Gabriel had approached him, telling him to stay behind, away from the fighting. Gabriel realized what was at stake for the big warrior should he enter the fray. Ever the faithful servant of

Heaven, Krillion declined with a heavy heart, saying it was his sacred duty to uphold his oath in the upcoming battle.

With a heart full of bitter rage and guilt, he flew into battle that day, defeating any traitor to Heaven that got in his way, including his last foe—one with long, black hair pulled tightly into a ponytail, wielding a sword the length of a man and slender enough to pierce armor like a hot knife through butter.

"Rai!" Valafor's voice brought Krillion back to the present. "Something's going' on back at the battlefield. Look!" Valafor was pointing into the air with his blackened arm.

Turning to stare at the place where he had just attained glorious victory over Heaven's mightiest legion, Rai saw the flight of angels. They were fresh warriors, not the weary, beaten Fury Legion that had retreated just minutes before. His mind raced. Where had these new foes come from? Were they fresh legions come to reinforce the depleted Fury?

Turning on Krillion, all patience from his voice gone, Rai shouted, "I ask again, Commander. Where have we met?"

Killion took a deep breath and looked Rai directly in the eye. "Lucifer's last stand," he said. "You're my twin brother."

The Fallen | 63

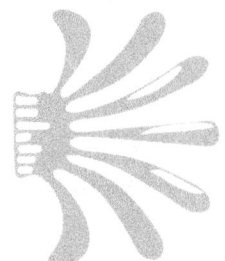 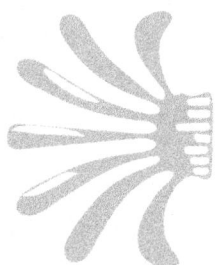

Chapter 15

RAZIEL'S GROUP HAD BEEN SEARCHING Earth for the past couple of hours, occasionally running into small groups of demons wandering around the desolate landscape. At every encounter her unit had cut them down without a shred of mercy or dignity. Her wings tired from the arduous search, she spotted a clearing a short ways off, in the middle of a grove of pine trees.

The only trees left alive, she thought.

She'd noticed that the longer the demons remained in control, the more the two realms—Earth and Hell—merged into one. Even though the sun had been gone for days, the skies were not yet completely black. It wasn't much light, but it allowed for limited visibility to the ground below. Alighting on a floor of dust and sharp rocks, Raziel wiped sweat from her brow with the back of her hand.

Calling a halt to their mission so her group could rest, she quietly signaled her scouts to move in close so they wouldn't give away their position to any unwanted company that might be in the area. "Okay, here's the plan," she said, her voice hushed and a serious look in her eyes. "Two men, two teams, low recon. I want a perimeter search of a twenty-mile radius. Meet back here in fifteen minutes. Any trouble, blow your signal horns—even if you can handle it—and we'll head right to you. Fly fast and safe. The All-Father be with you all." With a silent nod of understanding, her scouts paired up and flew off in opposite directions around the grove of trees.

Pulling out the water skin that was hanging by her side, Raziel popped the top and took a healthy pull from it. As the lukewarm fluid passed her lips, quenching her thirst, she felt renewed energy flow back through her muscles. Her unit was out in the middle of nowhere, so she didn't fully lower her guard; she walked a few yards away from her scouts so she could peek out of the trees into the dark, barren landscape spread before her.

Earth was turning into a no-man's-land, a constant, painful reminder of the Seraphim's failure in the last few days of war. In fact, it felt to Raziel as if the war had started and ended in just a matter of days. The number of demons across the globe was overwhelmingly high. She hadn't been part of the initial defense wave, so she could only guess what those warriors had gone through trying to fight them.

Taking in her surroundings and thinking back to all she learned as a warrior in training, she wondered how this could have happened.

As far as she looked in any direction, the Earth and Hell appeared to be merging into one. Bare mountains of sharp rock were erupting from the ground, killing all the vegetation and animals that had survived any demons they might have encountered. The warm, golden sunlight had been blotted out within moments of the demons entering Earth's realm; now, the sun's feeble light was barely noticeable. She could smell the smoke and brimstone that spewed forth from geysers of fire that had appeared across the land.

It was a sight she thought she would never live to see: the sight of their defeat and failure.

Seeing the silhouettes of her returning scouts high above her, she crept back into the clearing to await their report. She prayed it was good news of some kind.

As the scouts alighted in a semicircle around their captain, Raziel handed the lead scout her water skin. "Report," she ordered impatiently.

"Captain," the lead scout said after swallowing a mouthful of water and passing the skin to his comrade, "there is a small encampment posted about eighteen miles east of here. It's filled with human prisoners and captive angels."

Raziel's eyes grew wide and her heart raced. Was it possible that through all this devastation, some of her brothers and sisters, as well as the humans in their charge, could still be alive and perhaps even saved? She was buoyed by the hope that after all this time their search would not be in vain, that they had finally found survivors. A million questions zipped through her mind.

"How many demons and what type?" she asked.

"An entire legion of goat demons, plus the captain and at least one mage, probably more," the scout replied solemnly.

"Damn," Raziel said, looking around. Her fifty lightly armored warriors were no match for a legion. "Fifty against a thousand… impossible odds," she murmured. "Sergeant," she said to the lead scout, "I'm going to inspect this prisoner camp. These three will accompany me. Post guards and wait for our return. If we're not back within a half hour, fly back to the Crystal Palace with all haste and tell Captain Sandalphon what you heard here. He'll know what to do."

With a nod of her head, the sergeant left to carry out Raziel's orders.

"Okay, men. Show me this camp," Raziel said to the three scouts standing before her. As one, all four angels spread their wings and took to the air, heading east. Fully aware that somewhere before them was a legion's worth of goat demons, possibly with scouting parties out and about, Raziel ordered her men to fly low to the ground. After several miles they finally spotted firelight off in the distance.

The makeshift compound was in a small valley that was surrounded on three sides by massive cliffs overlooking the entire camp. It was a great defense for ground troops, and all but useless for aerial attacks.

Raziel and her scouts landed on the hard ground atop one of the cliffs, out of sight of the camp's occupants, and she gave the signal for silence. The last thing she wanted was to bring an entire legion down upon their heads because they'd made some noise that could have been avoided. The trio of guards returned her signal, signifying that they understood her.

Crawling on their stomachs they began the slow, painstaking trek toward the open edge of the cliff. They moved inch by inch; it was a slow process, but absolutely silent.

After a few minutes Raziel was lying on her stomach, peering over the edge of the cliff at the camp. Even from a distance it was a horrible sight; tears formed in the corners of her eyes.

The camp itself looked like it had been hastily assembled. Cages were arranged in the center of the camp, forming a semicircle around a huge bonfire. Inside the cages were captured humans and angels. Guards—members of Azazel's clan of hairy goat demons—stood erect at the only gate.

Half goat, half man, Raziel thought. *If they're here, their lord probably isn't too far off.* She also took note of the black-robed figures walking around. "Not good," she muttered to herself. The magic the dark ones wielded was to be respected and feared as a tide-turner of wars.

The bonfire illuminated the entire camp in its red glow. At the far end of the grounds Raziel saw a few of the fallen warriors of the Seraphim nailed to a wall, enduring horrendous torture—and who knows what else—by their captors' hands.

Another group of angels was being herded by goat demons toward a building in another corner, the only solid structure in the whole camp. As her senses focused on the unholy structure, Raziel could hear bloodcurdling screams from within its rock walls.

Raziel's mind raced to piece together all the elements of the scene before her and then the answer came to her, along with a flare of emotions. She looked back at the bonfire and saw a group of demons tossing something into it—and then she covered her mouth and choked back the bile that rose in her throat. She could see charred bones and brittle, blackened feathers as flames leapt around the celestial gift of the All-Father.

The demons were severing the wings of the captive angels and using them to fuel the evil fire below.

Her eyes widened in horror as realization dawned, her gaze darting back and forth between the fire and the building from which cries of pain were continuously erupting. She had to hold back the urge to fly down and kill every evil minion of Lucifer, even if it meant her death.

She couldn't waste another second while this camp of unimaginable horror remained. She had to get her men and report this to the Crystal Palace. "Sandalphon must hear of this atrocity," she whispered to them. Reluctantly, with a heart full of sorrow and despair for those below, she began to creep back from the edge.

When they had retreated far enough, Raziel and her scouts stood up. "Let's go," she said, the hate and pain evident in her voice. "We have to get back to the palace immediately and tell them of this."

As the three of them flew through the dark-gray skies back to the clearing where her command waited, Raziel heard in her mind the voices of her brethren enduring torturous acts the likes of which no Seraphim had witnessed before. And she heard the laughter of the demons, and the awful snapping, popping sound of the fire as it desecrated the eternal gift from the All-Father to his children.

After a minute she couldn't take it anymore. Followed by her scouts, she flew as quickly as she could, trying to distance herself from the horrors behind her.

As her winged form flew into view of the warriors below her, Raziel didn't even land; instead she signaled for them to follow her back to the Crystal Palace. Within seconds she was speeding upward, her unit behind her. But all she could think about was the screaming and the building it came from.

She propelled herself faster through the sky, a single thought burning in her mind: *Vengeance!*

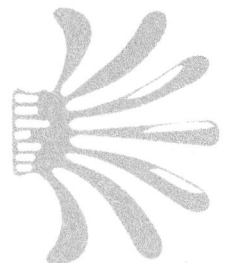 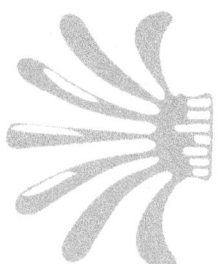

Chapter 16

"Fire!" Cassiel's command echoed through the desolate ruins of what had been a battlefield. In their search of Earth, her units had stumbled upon a valley where the demons and Seraphim had met, force on force. From the seconds she'd had to evaluate the carnage, it appeared that the angels had lost yet another battle in the great war. Bodies were strewn everywhere across the trampled valley floor—the forces of light and darkness forever entwined in an eternal grave.

The dregs that now hounded her and her scouts had caught them unawares as they searched the vicinity for survivors, and more blood was spilled in the span of a few heartbeats. At Cassiel's command, her remaining scouts hovering above the horrific valley floor loosed a volley of arrows infused with light, aiming at the dregs that were closing in quickly to finish the job. Without waiting to see if they hit their marks, the front row of angelic archers turned and sped about fifty meters back, away from their attackers. As they retreated, they passed through a second row of archers who waited, arrows set, kills in sight, covering their comrades' escape.

"Leaping and bounding," the strategy was called: as soon as the first line of archers passed, the second took aim and loosed a volley; then they would, in turn, move back behind the first line. This is how the angels under Cassiel's command were making their slow retreat.

The only flaw to this strategy was that they were running out of arrows. Soon they would have to stop and make a break for it, in a dead flight to outrun their aerial pursuers. To stay and fight meant to die, and there were enough slain holy warriors on the ground already.

"Fire... Bound!" The commands kept coming through the gray skies

One of Cassiel's sergeants came rushing up to her side. "Captain, we need to flee now," he said, panting.

"Give the sign—full retreat. Go!" Cassiel retorted, studying the increasingly dire situation. Now she regretted having disobeyed the order not to fight. But it wasn't as if she had looked for this battle; she had wandered into the wrong place at the wrong time. She was losing her warriors to endless waves of flying, screeching death that never seemed to stop or slow down, regardless of how many they killed.

The retreat horn sounded, blowing loud and clear across the sky. The remaining airborne angels threw down their bows, turned from the fray, and sped away from the dregs.

The chase was on. Wings flapped frantically as the angels gained speed, trying to outdistance the dregs.

As Cassiel neared the end of the valley, something below caught her eye. It was three small figures standing on a hill near a grove of trees: a lone angel and two demons.

Whistling to get the attention of the two scouts nearest her, Cassiel pointed down to the hilltop, hope and desperation showing on her face. She had mere seconds to react before the demons attacked and overpowered what she believed was the sole survivor of the terrible battle.

Her scouts glanced down to find their target and then dove without hesitation.

From his vantage point on the hilltop, where he stood at the edge of a tree line, Valafor had seen the influx of fresh angels enter the valley and engage the dregs. Krillion watched out of the corner of his eye as Valafor came rushing from the tree line, the cracks in his right charred arm opening again as the blue energy that was his to command illuminated the area.

"Deal with them!" Rai shouted to Valafor. Then he glared back at Krillion, who had just told him they were brothers from Heaven, and drew his sword. "You are free to go, Commander," Rai said. "Fallen though I be, I still have honor."

Valafor ran to the edge of the hill to await this new threat, muscles tensed and ready for the oncoming conflict. He stood, feeling the cooling wind whip past his hairy body. He clenched the muscles in his charred right arm, expelling even more energy for the attackers to see and fear.

"Lambs to the slaughter," he said, laughing, as the two angel scouts sped toward him, swords shining in the blue light released from his weapon arm. Valafor's mind and body tensed as the angelic scouts closed the distance between them. Violent blue power radiated from his arm as Valafor flexed it in anticipation of the oncoming fight.

Just as Valafor was about to strike them, the angels changed course and flew right over his head, straight toward Krillion, and sheathed their weapons. Each grabbing one of Krillion's huge arms, the scouts never missed a beat of their mighty wings. They hauled Krillion off the ground, gaining height with every passing second.

"Hold on, commander! We'll get you out of here!" shouted one of the scouts.

Fighting with the little energy he had, Krillion tried to struggle against them. "No, let me go! I have to go back!"

Cassiel flew up beside them.

"Commander, get a grip," she shouted in her most commanding voice. "Your legion is defeated and my own unit is dwindled. We are breaking right now. If you don't like it, deal with me when we get back. You two, fly!" The scouts let go of Krillion, who took reluctant flight on his own.

Behind them the dregs were screeching in anger and frustration as their prey slowly widened the gap between them.

† † †

On the hill below, Rai stood watching the warriors of light make a hasty retreat into the dark air. "Call back the dregs, Val" he said.

Giving his friend a puzzled look, Valafor pointed his weapon arm toward the sky. A blue beam of demonic energy burst forth, filling the space between the pursuing dregs and the fleeing angels. The dregs stopped midflight as the massive beam appeared directly in their path. Screeching in fury, they looked down to see Valafor looking up at them, wagging a finger back and forth. He could only assume they were cussing him out in their strange language, but he didn't care; none of them was stupid enough to fly down and attack him.

Valafor turned to Rai, eyeing him curiously while powering down his own arm. "So," he said in his rocky voice. "You want to tell me what's up?"

Rai returned his own weapon to its strap and sat on the ground. "You wouldn't believe me if I told you," he said. "The enemy commander said we were brothers."

"Yeah I would," Valafor replied. "You weren't always a general in Hell, you know."

Rai stood up at this statement. "What do you know, Val? If you know something of this, now is the time to tell me."

"Sometimes it's better not knowing the truth," Valafor said.

"Tell me now," Rai said, his eyes glowing red.

"Fine… He is your brother. And once you two did look alike, until the day Lucifer lost and you were cast from the light."

Red light streamed from the corners of Rai's eyes. "You knew about this and didn't tell me!"

Valafor shrugged. "What did you want me to do, Rai? After you fell from Heaven in the final battle, your memory was wiped clean of any knowledge except for the fact that you remember Heaven—the place you turned your back on. I was placed as a guardian to make sure you stayed in line and did your job. Only problem was that I started to like you—and as much as I wanted to, I couldn't tell you the truth." By now Valafor was staring his friend straight in the eye.

"Couldn't tell me … or *wouldn't* tell me?" Rai asked.

"Kobal gave strict orders that you were not to be told anything of your former life so you would be better prepared to serve Hell."

Rai walked to the edge of the hill, staring off into the valley, the scene of a victory that now felt hollow. Valafor walked up and stood beside him, putting a hand on his shoulder. "What now, Rai?" he asked.

"Now," Rai said, red beams shooting from the sides of his eyes, "now we go have a talk with Kobal." He turned to Valafor. "Understand, Val, I won't be serving Hell any longer. Kobal has lied to me, made me fight my own brother while he sits back getting his laughs. I promise you, the last laugh will be on him when tonight's over." Rai hesitated, then spoke again, quietly. "As my friend, don't feel obligated to come with me. I'll understand if you don't."

To Rai's surprise, Valafor started laughing hysterically in his odd, gravelly voice. "You're going' to take down the demon of hilarity and you expect me to sit this one out? No, Rai, I got your back," he said.

Rai looked at his friend, a slight smile on his face. "You sure?"

"Hell yeah," Valafor replied, smiling back. "I got nowhere else to be."

The two began walking into the woods, away from the valley, past the slain archers and their captain still nailed to the tree. "Rai?" Valafor asked

"Yeah, Val."

"You know we're walking into a shit storm here, right?"

"Not for us, Val… not for us," Rai said, a malicious grin on his face.

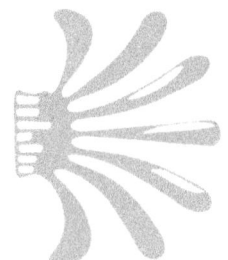 

Chapter 17

THE PENS WERE ALIVE WITH terror and pain-filled screams. Humans and angels alike were kept as animals in makeshift cages, both races serving a specific purpose to the demon horde.

Upon entering the pens, the humans were turned over to a group of dark mages to be experimented upon and transformed into biters, hideous creatures designed to serve the sadistic demands of their demon masters.

As the incantations rippled through the air and the transformations began, jaws lengthened and extended from once-human faces. Row after row of sharpened teeth erupted from bloody gums. Arms grew longer until claw-like fingernails almost scraped the ground. Soft pink skin turned black and brittle as bodies began to burn and warp under the power of the dark mages.

They had been aptly named by their demon handlers: biters tore and ate their victims' flesh by means of tooth and nail. While they still had a semihumanoid form, their minds focused only on their masters' bidding. Only their basest instincts were left.

The captured warriors of the Seraphim had it much worse.

Off in the corner of the camp was a single, dreary building, a stone structure extending high in the air. It was a lone tower void of any windows, and inside it, the unimaginable took place. The horrific screams from within could be heard throughout the compound.

It was here where the last vestiges of glory and dignity of the once-proud celestial warriors faded into oblivion. In the center of the single-roomed tower, Leonard's dark mages and Azazel's goat demons ripped the celestial white wings from their backs; the precious gift that

All-Father bestowed upon every angel was torn from their bodies in a horrendous and merciless fashion. The goat demons would then take the bloody wings to the center of the camp, in front of all its inhabitants, and throw them into a raging inferno of hellfire for all to see.

The effect was everything that Leonard had hoped for and more.

Seeing the salvation of mankind defeated and forever shamed was enough to bring even the hardiest of angelic warriors to his knees. All traces of fight had left the solemn prisoners.

† † †

Inside the tower, the dark mages were in the process of destroying another life when a flash of blue light exploded in the room, stopping all work and turning all eyes upon the source. As the light faded and eyes readjusted, Leonard, demon master of the black arts, stood before the current occupant of this tower of horrors.

A young female warrior's legs were anchored to the ground, her arms suspended from chains that hung from the ceiling, her body exposed.

"Welcome, Master," one of the mages said with a respectful bow.

Staring, taking the measure of the holy warrior stretched out before him, Leonard could see she had the look of one who still had fire in her soul—but how much? He drew back his scaly hand and slapped her across the mouth with all the force he could muster, snapping her head back.

"Ssstill some fight in this one," Leonard hissed, glaring at her. "We shall soon sssee about that."

The angel, cut and bruised, looked directly at the reptilian face under the black hood and spat a mouthful of blood straight at him. "We shall see who still has fight left in them when this day is over, monster!" she retorted, grinding her teeth with anger and pain. Do what you will to me, bastard, but as soon as Gabriel discovers this camp, he will—"

Leonard's hand shot from the hem of his robes, and he wrapped his scaly hand around the angel's throat, cutting off her air flow before she could finish her threat. "Don't worry about your pressscious Gabriel; plans are already in the works for him. You should be more worried about your own fate, holy scum!" Leonard shrieked, his serpentine tongue flicking out to taste the blood on his captive's face.

He turned his head toward two goat demons who were standing by, smiling eagerly at the thought of sating the bloodlust that characterized their race. "Are you ready?" he asked. Pure malice spread across both their faces as they nodded in anticipation of the gory ecstasy to come.

In his snakelike voice, Leonard began chanting the garbled syllables of a spell. As he finished the quick incantation, the slack in the chains that bound the warrior's wrists went tight, pulling her arms straight up to the ceiling and fully stretching her body out. She hung in the center of the damp room, unable to move even an inch in any direction. She knew that with whatever happened next, her fate was sealed. Still she fought feebly against the chains that bound her, her gaze never leaving Leonard as she tried to kill him with a hate-filled stare.

The two goat demons moved to stand directly behind her, one on each side.

The warrior's anger gave way to a fearful reality. Breathing in the foul air of the tower, she shut her eyes, bracing for the pain she knew was coming.

As her vision dimmed, her thoughts left the demons and the unholy tower and she allowed her mind to float up to the Crystal Palace in the land of tranquil light—back to her peaceful life in the skies before Armageddon shattered everything. She thought about how it felt to soar through the blue skies on routine patrols, the wind whipping through her hair. She recalled walking the battlements of the castle, talking with Abdiel about the importance of having faith in themselves and of the oaths they took to protect mankind and free will.

Through the years, she had never regretted becoming a soldier, no matter how hard the training was or how many battles and friends she lost along the way. All her long years were spent training and preparing for this moment in time. Right here, right now.

On this day, she and her brethren would free mankind from Hell's tainted influence forever. It was her life's duty to serve the All-Father and to uphold the oath in any manner she could, even if that meant paying the ultimate sacrifice for the greater good.

Please be proud of me, Gabriel, she thought.

Come what may, the angelic warrior knew the All-Father would not abandon his faithful servant. Empowered by the strength he'd given her, she would suffer through the physical trials ahead.

She felt the demons place their hairy hands upon her pristine wings, wrapping their crusty fingers around the place where the wings connected to her back. She began a whispered prayer: "All-Father, hear my words in this, my darkest hour. Deliver me from the clutches of evil, and grant me the strength to persevere as the darkness spreads, intent on extinguishing your graceful light."

Tears began to form in the corners of her closed eyes as the demons began pulling down on her wings. Through the pain and tears she sang, "Remember your faithful servant and embrace me with open arms when—" Her words turned to screams of pain. The body of the once-proud warrior was pulled so tight she couldn't squirm away, and her memories of Heaven and the Crystal Palace gave way to the harsh reality of the tower and the pain wracking her battered body.

Gritting their foul teeth together, the goat demons pulled harder.

One of her wing bones snapped with a horrible popping sound that echoed through the vast room. Tears streamed down the angel's face, and she convulsed in the throes of unimaginable pain.

Still the demons pulled.

Another pop, as the other wing broke free from the joint, tearing through tendons and cartilage.

Still the demons pulled, as Leonard looked on with pleasure. The flesh around the base of her wing bones stretched and began to tear free. Her memories completely blotted now, the angel could only scream in horror and pain.

Finally, in one final burst of power from the goat demons, both wings were ripped from her back. Blood sprayed everywhere. Little pieces of bone and cartilage hit the walls, while bits of muscle and flesh hit the ground with a dull splatter. In shock, the warrior fainted, her head slumped forward.

As the two demons walked past Leonard, smiling—a wing in each hand, fresh fuel for the fire—Leonard turned to one of his mages. "Cut this one's eyesss out before you send her to the cages."

"Yes, Master," replied the mage, pulling a small knife from the cuff of his sleeve.

Leonard walked toward the door, hearing screams from behind him. The warrior had awakened, unable to do anything but scream her eternal suffering for the rest of the captives to hear.

Leonard smiled: this was the time of demons and evil intent.

He opened the door to the tower and stepped out into the open-air compound. Since the initial assault on Earth, days back, the sun had been blotted almost completely from view. The camp and its semicircle of pens were illuminated by the light of the glorious, grotesque fire, which now burned a little brighter.

As Leonard began walking to the cages to admire the show, he heard a horn in the distance. *Ah, perfect,* he thought. The horn meant that Azazel was en route to the camp, and not far off. Leonard abruptly turned around and headed to meet his ally at the gate.

When he arrived he saw a formation of goat demons, five hundred strong, walking toward the compound across the dusty landscape. At their head walked Azazel, a massive demon even by the standards of his own race. He stood around eight feet tall, with jet-black fur. His upper body was bare, exposing his massive chest and arms. Strapped to his back was a double-bladed battle-ax too heavy for any human to lift, much less wield.

Azazel stopped a few feet away from the makeshift front gate, where the guards snapped to attention, saluting their clan lord.

"Make way for Lord Azazel! Open the gate!" ordered the lead guard. With a high-pitched screech, the rusted metal gate swung inward to reveal Leonard, standing and waiting. Azazel and his unit entered the camp in orderly fashion; then the gates were shut to the outside world.

Once inside, Azazel commanded his unit to disperse and receive new orders from the captain of the pens. As the small army scattered, Azazel turned to his mysterious ally.

"Let us walk," Leonard said, bowing and showing Azazel the fire behind them.

"What is this about, Leonard?" Azazel asked in his harsh, buzzing goat voice. "I'm still in the middle of the search for hidden humans. Also, there have been rumors of wingless angels blending with the human cattle. What have you heard on this?" As he spoke they walked a short ways through the pens to stand before the fire.

"Of the angels, I can't say. I wouldn't be surprised. I have though, detected a random, mysterious power source that could upset our plansss and give Earth back to them," Leonard sneered, pointing a thumb at some humans huddled in the back of one of the cages. "I have tasked Mullin to find and retrieve this power. There is no doubt as to my pupil's ability to retrieve it, but we don't yet know what it is or what it is capable of doing to us."

Azazel stomped over to the fire, glaring at its fiery center, feeling the heat on his exposed skin. "Does Kobal know of this? Do the angels?"

Leonard walked up to stand beside him, "Of the angelsss, I have no idea. And Kobal wouldn't know what to do even if he were aware. He believes this war is nothing more than a game and not to be taken seriousssly. No, we must handle this in our own, my friend. How many demons have you brought with you?"

The fire popped and crackled, and Azazel watch as the feathers on a wing turned black and withered and the ashes floated away. "I have brought five hundred," he said. "Add that to the legion already here…" He thought for a moment. "We'll have around fifteen hundred, counting your mages. Why do you ask?"

"If Mullin succeedsss in his task, which he will, I have ordered him to bring the power here. If the angels have discovered this, they will track the power to this location. We must be ready for a full assault," Leonard said.

Azazel snorted in disgust. "How many warriors can they possibly have left? We have won damn near every battle in the war. The few that survived have been scattered or have fled back to their accursed palace. No, Leonard, I don't think we have anything to fear from them."

"Don't underestimate them," Leonard hissed. "That hasss been our folly and downfall every time we've lost. What we fought was just the first wave. Granted, Gabriel probably sent the majority of his army, but there are still many out there."

"Fine then, let them come!" Azazel yelled in frustration, stomping his hoof into the dirt. "They will come, and we will crush them again!" As if to prove his point, Azazel stomped over to a cage filled with wingless angels, little clouds of dust rising with his every hate-filled step. Ripping the door from the hinges, Azazel snagged one of the prisoners by the neck, lifted him off the ground with one hand, and carried him outside. Gasping for air and weakly grasping at Azazel's hand, the angel put up little resistance in the mad grip of his enemy; his spirit had been broken in the pens.

"This is what you're worried about, Leonard?" Azazel smashed the blood- and mud-stained face of the angel into the side of the cage, the force of the impact shattering bones and splattering blood and bits of flesh on the floor inside the cage. At the sight of their comrade being smashed and disfigured before their eyes, the few remaining angels were filled with a frenzied desire for vengeance. Rattling the bars of their cages, the imprisoned angels yelled curses and spat at the lord of goat demons.

Acting on instinct from an eternity of practicing his craft, Leonard murmured an incantation and the cell door shot up from the ground, sealing the prisoners inside before they could reach Azazel.

"Fuck that—let them go, Leonard," Azazel snorted, his eyes bloodshot with rage. He was scraping his hooves on the ground like a bull about to charge, the animal in him taking over. With a single word and a deep sigh from the master of mages, the cell door fell back to the ground, releasing the three prisoners for the brutal assault. Already prepared for the conflict, Azazel threw the lifeless angel at his attackers. The first two angel prisoners ducked out of the way, but the third moved too late. The corpse struck him with the force of a dump truck, killing him instantly.

By now Azazel's bestial nature had completely overtaken him. Lowering his head to show his spiraled horns, he charged straight at his foes, growling his rage. Bracing his neck for impact, he skewered the first angel, piercing flesh and bones and flinging the body away with a toss of his muscular neck.

The last angel rolled under the gnarled horns and came up behind Azazel. Years of training kicking in, and the angel jumped in the air, twisting his body, to face his foe. But he went only about two feet up before landing back on the ground, eyes wide with horror.

Azazel laughed hysterically. "What's the matter flyboy—missin' something?"

The wingless warrior, so enraged by this final humiliation, gave the Seraphim battle cry and charged Azazel head-on, ready to beat the lord of goat demons with his bare hands.

Azazel stood waiting for his prey. He had nothing to fear from this little angel with no wings, no weapon, and no hope.

Upon reaching his target, the angel began hitting Azazel on his massive chest, although he knew it had no effect on the demon. He would not cower before a minion of the dark prince. If he was going to die here and now, at least they would know the strength of the Seraphim, even in the face of hopeless odds.

Towering over the desperate warrior, Azazel reached out, wrapped both hands around his neck, and twisted in one fluid motion, ripping the angel's head from his shoulders. Standing there, holding the head and part of the spine that was still attached to it, dripping blood, Azazel watched the mutilated body pitch forward and begin to twitch, squirting blood to the fading rhythm of a dying heart.

"We will never lose again, Leonard," Azazel said. He walked back to the fire and tossed in the head, smiling as flames danced over the face whose mouth was still open in a silent scream.

Following him, Leonard said, "You need to control that temper of yoursss; it's going to get you killed one day."

Laughing his weird goat laugh, Azazel pounded his chest. "You might be right about that, but that day is a long ways off."

Taking once last glance at what remained of the head sizzling in the flames, Azazel walked off to issue defensive orders to his unit. He had to prepare for what he believed would be a ludicrous act of desperation from the angels to save their former comrades and the humans in the camp.

Gazing after him, Leonard knew had more important matters to attend to. He had to create a field in which to contain the mysterious power before Mullin returned. He was still standing in front of the fire, pondering what type of spell he would need, when a flash of light and the smell of brimstone erupted behind him. He knew it was Mullin before he even turned around.

"Isss it done?" asked Leonard.

"Yes, Master... but I don't understand how *this*"—he sneered and gestured toward the unconscious human girl lying on the dirt floor by his feet—"could be a problem for us."

Turning to look at his most promising apprentice, Leonard gasped in disbelief. "This is it?" The power source before him was not what he had expected or planned for. *No matter,* he thought, *it can still be subdued.*

"Master, look," Mullin said, pointing to the prisoners, who were all staring in their direction. "It's as if they sense something, as well."

"No matter, it is time, apprentice. Follow my lead—we've no time to lossse on this," Leonard said.

Leonard began the incantation to the most powerful containment spell he knew. As demonic magic began to take shape before his eyes, Mullin joined his master, reciting the well-memorized words. To someone untrained in the dark arts, it might have sounded as though the two mages were about to die, choking on their own vomit.

Within moments an oily, midnight-black bubble was floating in the air, grower larger the longer they kept the spell active, until it was roughly seven feet in diameter. It was a prison of sorts, infused with dark magic to sustain it and keep all energies within. It dropped upon its intended target, who was lying on the ground, and swallowed her up. Then it resumed its eerie hovering.

That done, Leonard looked at Mullin. "I have one more tasssk for you. Go to Kobal and deliver this." In an instant, an off-white scroll appeared in Leonard's hand. "What is written inssside will explain everything to him," Leonard said, handing over the message. "Make haste, apprenticcce. Time is of the essence."

"Right away, Master," replied Mullin, and once again the apprentice blinked out of sight to do his master's bidding.

Leonard looked at the black ball hovering in the air. It was an unholy device most angels had seen in battles before. *I'll leave this one hanging by the fire for them*, Leonard thought. *Another reminder of their utter defeat and shame.* Then, adjusting his robe slightly, he made his way back toward the solitary tower to inform the rest of his mages of the impending attack.

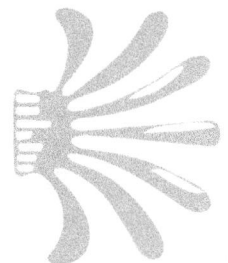 

Chapter 18

As his unit neared the massive front gates to the Crystal Palace, Captain Tabbris called a formation halt.

"Identify yourself!" sounded the voice of the senior guard at the palace gates.

"Captain Tabbris, returning from my scouting mission to report back to Captain Sandalphon," Tabbris replied, sucking air into his depleted lungs.

With respectful nod from the lead guard, the blue-tinted, arched crystal gates slowly opened.

When his men flew into the courtyard, Tabbris instructed them to rearm themselves and get some rest in the event of another mission.

Sandalphon, who was flying across the east battlements making his rounds of the palace defenses, saw the young captain and abruptly tucked his wings and banked hard to the right, descending into the courtyard to get the report from Earth. A smile played across his old face at the sight of at least one of his scouting parties returning from the nightmare below.

"Captain Sandalphon," Tabbris said as Sandalphon alighted on the ground a few feet from him. "Search and rescue reporting in, sir."

"Rest easy, son," Sandalphon said, throwing up a hand to put Tabbris at ease. "Catch your breath and give me your assessment of Earth. Did you find any survivors, angel or human?"

Fidgeting with a strap on his breastplate, which had gotten dented during his earlier fight, Tabbris replied, "Nothing and no one. Our mission was cut short due to a host of dregs. The city we searched was completely wiped out, sir. Our men never even made it there."

Pulling a small knife from his belt, Sandalphon walked over and cut the difficult strap, allowing Tabbris's breastplate to fall to the ground. "Take that to the armory when we're done," Sandalphon said, nodding at the breastplate lying on the ground before him. "Now, from the beginning, tell me what you saw and what happened down there. We need all the details we can get."

Pulling out his water skin, Tabbris drank heavily; then he poured the rest over his head, shaking out his blonde hair, which was saturated with sweat and grime.

"First sir, I must ask—have Cassiel and Raziel made it back yet?"

"Not yet. Yours is the first unit back. But don't worry: if they followed orders and the All-Father is willing, they'll be back. Now tell me of your recon."

Starting from the beginning, Tabbris described the macabre slaughter they had seen in the city, as well as the beginnings of the merging of the two realms, and his personal theory of what had happened.

Sandalphon took all this in and processed it, tapping his fingers on his the hilt of his sword, and then he dismissed Tabbris, telling him to stand down until further notice. Not wasting a second, Sandalphon made his way to where he knew Gabriel would be waiting, eager for the return of any of the scouts and the news they bore from below.

† † †

In the war room, all the chairs were empty except for two. One held the comatose body of Metatron, who was still communing with the All-Father. The other chair, at the head of the table, held Gabriel, who was leaning back, eyes closed, and rubbing his face with his hands in an attempt to bring a little life and energy back into him.

It seemed to Gabriel that since the war began a few days ago, he had hardly left this room. "Well, Metatron, old friend, this could finally be it," he remarked to the motionless body slumped in the chair a few feet from him. "After all this time and all the battles, is this to be the angels' last stand?"

Knowing that his friend wasn't likely to lift his head and answer, Gabriel concentrated on the task at hand. On the table in front of him were battle plans, maps showing where portals had opened and the demons had struck, information passed down from survivors of previous skirmishes, and notes regarding the remaining strength of the Seraphim.

Running through his mind was Israfil's new vision of a last-ditch team to save Earth. Gabriel had come to trust and respect the fact that Israfil's gift had never been wrong. But how could Rai possibly be one of the "chosen"? Rai had chosen to follow Lucifer and, as a result, had become a fallen. And as odd as that was, there was a demon in Israfil's vision as well.

Try as he might, Gabriel couldn't understand how the fate of Earth and the angels depended on these five individuals. "Don't forget the human girl," Gabriel whispered to himself.

The idea was ludicrous, and it went against his every military instinct.

"Gabriel." The voice came from the balcony. Captain Sandalphon entered the war room, shaking Gabriel from his reverie. "Captain Tabbris has returned … with dire news, I'm afraid."

Gabriel gestured Sandalphon to sit.

"The city they landed in had been run through and destroyed by the demons…" Sandalphon's voice trailed off.

"Speak plainly, please, Captain," Gabriel said, seeing that Sandalphon was having trouble delivering his report.

"Our armies never made it there," Sandalphon finished, sadness and anger apparent in his every word.

Gabriel's face clouded over with a mixture of emotions. He was saddened by the thought of the frail humans below, who had been sworn protection by every member of the Seraphim. They had died alone, in the grip of their vile enemies. Any humans left were void of hope, with not one angel there for protection and comfort. The anger Gabriel felt coursing through his veins was the same as that of many other Seraphim: the angels were angry at themselves. They knew that the demons never should have been able to gain ground on Earth as they had done. The Seraphim had failed when mankind needed them most.

Gabriel would have asked how bad the damage was, but it was pointless; he already knew the answer. If the demons had run through the city unopposed, it was likely that its inhabitants had been massacred, with maybe a few captured for their heinous experiments. He hoped there were a few survivors; he had to believe there was still some good the angels could do, no matter how small the possibility might seem.

"Did Tabbris meet any resistance below?" Gabriel asked.

The Fallen | 85

"They ran across a small unit of dregs. They defeated them with no casualties. The ones that got away came back minutes later with an entire host," Sandalphon said, rubbing the thick black stubble of hair on his head. "Tabbris ordered the retreat as commanded, so as not to lose any warriors."

"At least they're all back safely," Gabriel said.

Suddenly there was a knock on the war room doors and Afriel came rushing in, straight to Gabriel, his eyes alight with pleasure. "Gabriel, the girl—she's awake," Afriel managed, trying to catch his breath.

The weight of this new development brought Gabriel to his feet, overcome with relief. *Finally, something good amid all the chaos,* he thought.

"Take me to her—I must speak with her at once," he said excitedly. "Captain Sandalphon, inform me when the other units return."

"At once, sir," Sandalphon replied, turning toward the balcony.

Led by Afriel, Gabriel hurried to the infirmary. He needed to find out what condition the girl was in and also brief her on Israfil's apparent vision for this "team," of which she was to be an integral part. His mind still reeled every time he said the word and thought of the members involved. Wondering how they were supposed to bring all the elements in place, he quickened his pace to match Afriel's.

Long minutes and many corridors later, the two angels finally reached the infirmary doors. Afriel stepped aside, allowing the All-Father's champion to enter first. The first thing Gabriel noticed was the number of warriors who were there. There were hundreds—some seriously wounded, others with minor injuries, and others dead. All showed physical indications of having been through hell and back.

Making his way through the sea of wounded, Gabriel felt pride at the sight of so many warriors still alive. Although they had suffered loss and defeat, they had served the All-Father with every ounce of strength they had. After a moment's pause, Afriel guided Gabriel to the female soldier's bed.

When she saw the highest-ranking angel of the Seraphim walking directly toward her, Zara gritted her teeth and did her best to stand and render the proper respect due to one of his station.

"Sit, sit," Gabriel said hurriedly, before Zara could fully stand. Looking at Afriel, Gabriel said, "Bring water and some food." Then he turned his attention to the young female sitting on the side of the bed. "You and I, we have much to talk about," he said. "Some things you're not going to like, and others you won't agree with. Regardless, I have thought through the entire situation a million times and I can't find an alternative or explanation." Gabriel paused for a moment to take a deep breath. "I'm getting ahead of myself, I'm afraid. First tell me your name and unit. Since you arrived back here you've been in a coma, and no one has recognized you. Thank the All-Father, Raphael was able to save you and treat your wounds."

Mustering the little strength she had regained, Zara lifted her head in pride, saying, "Captain Zara of the Twelfth Legion of Light, sir."

"Under General Wrenti," Gabriel finished. "We found his medallion tucked away in your gauntlet when Raphael was treating you. We've been wondering what force was powerful enough to stop the Twelfth."

"Here, Gabriel," said Afriel, who had walked in with a jug of water and a platter of meat, fruit, and bread.

"Thank you," Gabriel said, taking both items and placing them on the bedside table. Zara's eyes darted questioningly from the food to the water to Gabriel, and then back to the food.

With a smile and a slight chuckle, Gabriel said, "Formalities aside, Captain. Eat, drink."

Zara ate ravenously while Gabriel explained, to the best of his knowledge, everything that had happened to the Seraphim and mankind over the last couple of days. He also explained how Israfil's vision had shown him a glimpse of a team comprised of angels, fallen angels, demons, and a human girl. Zara's eyes were wide with questions as her mind absorbed everything she was being told.

When he had finished talking, Gabriel stood up to leave. Then, as an afterthought, he added, "When you're ready, head over to the war room so we can begin. We have much to account for and many plans to set in motion."

As he turned toward the door, he nearly ran into Raphael, who had been standing behind him with a vial of reddish liquid in his hand and a smirk on his face. Without a word he handed the vial to Gabriel and then went about his infirmary duties.

"What's this for?" Gabriel asked, eyeing the Seraphim healer.

"Drink it. You look like shit," Raphael replied as he headed toward yet another patient with a gash running across her ribs.

Smiling at Raphael's bluntness, Gabriel uncorked the bottle and drained the contents in two gulps. "Ugh," he said, wiping his mouth. But as foul as the red liquid tasted, Gabriel noticed its effects immediately.

The Fallen | 87

It rejuvenated his muscles and his mind, giving him a little more focus and energy to tackle the tasks ahead. Gabriel re-corked the empty vial, set it on the closest table, and walked to the door.

Upon entering the hallway, he noticed one of the palace guards running toward him at full speed. "Gabriel—Captain Sandolphon ordered me to find you. Raziel has returned with urgent information. Everyone is gathered in the war room, awaiting you. You must hurry, sir!"

Without a word, Gabriel was off, a blur moving down the hallway, his legs pumping. He could tell from the young angel's tone that this might be the critical information he had been waiting for—maybe some way to bring down the demons or retake the earth, something positive. The possibilities raced through his mind as he ran down the palace corridors.

Nearing the entrance to the war room, he saw that the doors were already open, and he heard loud, excited voices coming from inside. Bursting through the doors, Gabriel immediately took note of who was in the room: Sandalphon, Raziel, Metatron, Israfil, Abdiel… even Azreal was here. He also noted right away the dire, pleading look coming from Captain Raziel. Fire burned in her tear-streaked eyes.

"What is it? What news?" Gabriel asked, slowing to a walk as he neared his chair.

Raziel lifted her head to look Gabriel in the eye. Her face was a storm of conflicting emotions. One second she looked as if she were going to break into tears; the next, she looked like she wanted to rip the head off every demon in Hell and drink their blood, quenching her thirst for revenge. "We found a prison camp full of humans and angels in a canyon on Earth," she said. "The demons—they're ripping their fucking wings from their backs and burning them for all to see, Gabriel!" Raziel's voice cut through him; her every word resonated with the gravity of the Seraphim's situation. "The dark mages are turning the humans into some experimental form of demon to use against us, and there has to be at least a legion's worth of goat demons guarding the camp! We have to stop them. We need to assemble as many legions as we can and stop this right now, Gabriel!" Raziel didn't realize it, she was so lost in her frenzy, but by now she was practically screaming.

This was certainly not the news Gabriel was expecting to hear. His heart sank within his chest, and his stomach erupted in knots. In the blink of an eye, he felt his mood change from hopeful to vengeful.

Taking a moment to absorb Raziel's horrific news, Gabriel composed himself, arranging his thoughts. Vengeance would be theirs—but with rational logic, not raw emotion. Finally he spoke: "Sandalphon, I want two and a half legions ready to fly within two hours' time." He was giving orders by pure instinct at this point.

"Wait, Gabriel, there's more," Israfil said.

Turning his gaze toward Israfil, Gabriel asked, "What?"

"The vision has fled my mind's eye," Israfil said. "The human girl is gone, and with it the entire vision. Where once I saw clearly our lighted path, now there is only darkness. The only logical explanation is that the girl is lost to us. Perhaps she is dead, or maybe the demons have her and are blocking her from me. Either way… Israfil s voice trailed off.

"Fine, we stick with the last vision," Gabriel said. "Let me say this and be perfectly clear: as long as one of us breathes, this war is not over! We all swore the oath, and they are not hollow words. Mankind is not yet lost!" As he spoke, his eyes landed on everyone in the room, driving home the seriousness of his words. "We stick with the last vision Israfil had. We assemble the team and find the girl. Raziel, I'm going to need a descriptive layout of the land."

Grabbing a piece of paper and a feather pen, Raziel began to outline the camp's geographical position as well as mark it on the map spread across the table. Then, taking a deep breath to calm herself, she explained the layout.

"The camp is extremely well-hidden—we stumbled on it by sheer luck," she began, clearing her throat and taking controlled breaths to maintain her composure. "Here in the center is the camp itself," she said, pointing to a spot on the drawing. "Surrounding it on three sides are tall cliffs. Our archers could place themselves here, along the ridgeline. When we were there, there were no sentinels, but they could've changed that by now. From what I saw, the best way to approach this would be to have a half legion of archers posted on the cliffs, along with a half legion of infantry. Have the other legion and a half come straight across the valley floor, right through the front gates, where they enemy can see us coming. Roughly speaking, this is a case of 'You see us over here, and now our friends are gonna fuck you over here,'" Raziel said, her eyes steely.

"Very well thought out, Captain." This time it was Azreal who spoke, studying the layout and the troop placement. "Ideally, you'll have the archers fire down into the camp, expending two to three volleys. Before

The Fallen | 89

the demons can coordinate an offensive, you'll have the cliff force rain death from above, while the ground forces smash them from their fronts and keep them distracted," he said smugly. Then he turned to Raziel. "You are, of course, forgetting the fact that there are... how many mages in that camp?" He spoke to her as though she were a child.

"That's where you come in, Azreal" Gabriel interjected. "You'll lead the aerial infantry attack into the heart of the camp. Raziel, you will captain the archers until Azreal gives the word. I will lead the ground forces on the valley floor. Are there any questions?" No one spoke, so Gabriel went on. "Captain Sandalphon, you have your orders. The rest of you, suit up. We fly in two hours. Dismissed"

As the group dispersed to prepare for the upcoming assault, Azreal took one last, long look at the war room, with its high ceilings intricately carved so that when the sun hit directly overhead, its light was reflected throughout the room. His gaze went to the table, where he had sat and planned so many missions for the Seraphim, missions that because of him had been successful.

"I said we fly in two, Azreal" came Gabriel's voice from across the table. Without as much as a look or gesture to acknowledge him, Azreal walked straight to the door. *We'll see who flies in two hours,* he thought, and he walked out the door.

"Gabriel!"

The shout rang out form the courtyard. Gabriel knew that voice; it belonged to one of his oldest friends in the Seraphim. *Finally some good news,* he thought. His fiercest legion, Fury, had returned—their commander, Krillion, no doubt at the head. *Finally ...*

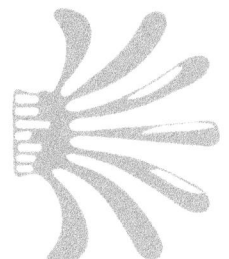 

Chapter 19

I OPENED MY EYES... At least I think I opened them. Once again, complete darkness—every direction an empty black.

This time feels different, though. It's quiet all around me. No fires burning, no people screaming.

No mutilated bodies scattered everywhere.

I don't know where I am, but I feel safe. There are no monsters here.

The last thing I remember was the lady grabbing me from my hiding spot, leading me away from the monsters. Then running from the alley outside my apartment to the park. That's where I found my .... I remember falling to the ground and screaming until my throat was raw and I tasted blood. I can still hear my screams, the pounding in my head, the beating of my heart.

Then someone behind me put a hand on my shoulder. Maybe a monster finally got me, and I'm dead? But if I'm dead, where's my mom? Shouldn't she be here with me?

Why isn't she here with me?

It feels like I'm floating on top of a warm cloud. I checked my pocket to make sure that I still have the picture of my mother, that I didn't lose it during the escape from our apartment. My memories and this picture are all I have of her now—all I have left of anything in the world.

The woman who dragged me from my apartment said there were other survivors, that I wasn't the only one left alive. Maybe someone will come looking for me.

Maybe I'll just stay here where it's safe. Just me... alone in the darkness.

Alone and safe.

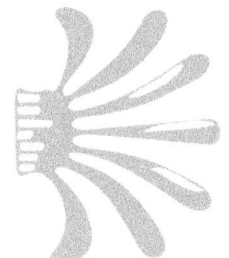 

Chapter 20

As Rai and Valafor approached the gates of Hell, they saw the massive form of Geryon manning his post as vigilantly as ever.

"What are we going do about him, Rai?" Valafor asked, pointing the blackened fingers of his right arm in the direction of the huge centaur blocking their way.

"If he tries to stop us we go through him, like we always do," Rai replied, securing his red mask across his face, exposing only his eyes and black ponytail.

Walking directly toward the gate, Geryon eyeing their every step, they stopped a few feet away and waited for the centaur to make the first move.

"Shouldn't you be on Earth with your legions?" Geryon asked accusingly, scrutinizing them both.

"We're here to"—Rai thought about his next words carefully—"have a little talk with Kobal."

Clearly suspicious of their motives in light of the war going on above, Geryon stepped aside. "You can pass," he said. As Rai and Valafor walked by, they heard a slight snort escape Geryon's lips, an almost threatening gesture directed squarely at Valafor.

"Shit," Rai said. He already knew what was about to happen.

"Something you want to say, big boy?" Valafor turned, baring his teeth at the huge centaur. Rai could already see Valafor's charred right arm begin to tense in preparation. Small cracks began to form in it as little pieces of crispy flesh started to fall away.

"What if there is, li'l demon, what are you gonna do 'bout it?" Geryon said, coming to stand directly in front of Valafor, arms folded across his broad, bare chest.

Knowing his friend wouldn't back down from any challenge, Rai stepped in to break up the two potential combatants. The last thing the duo needed was to fight their way through Hell all the way to Kobal's castle. "We don't have time for this, Val," Rai said in his ear. "Not here, not now. We have more important things to deal with first. If it makes you feel better, we can come back later—if we're still alive."

Never breaking his gaze from his huge adversary, Valafor began backing away, one slow step at a time. "Another time, then," Valafor said. He'd made his point to Geryon: the two of them were not finished.

† † †

Meanwhile, in the depths of Hell, sitting on his throne of smiling skulls, Kobal wondered how the takeover of Earth was coming along. It had been hours since he received news from any of the legions sent to Earth, and it had been a few days since he last talked with Leonard and Azazel, his most important generals in the war. He was starting to get bored—never a good thing for the master of hilarity.

He stood up from his throne and walked to the balcony overlooking his territory in Hell to survey the barren, burning land outside his castle walls. He noticed that the land was changing, a sign of Hell's dominance on Earth. Not a week before, his lands had been nothing but rock, fire, and ash. Now, with the victory on Earth almost complete, the two realms were starting to merge. Here and there across the land, Kobal noticed, little patches of grass and other vegetation were springing up through the rocky ground.

Of course, due to the pure evil nature of Hell, the plants immediately died, enhancing the landscape's deathly feeling.

Deciding that if something didn't amuse him within the next two minutes he was going to burst, Kobal stuck his head over the balcony railing and shouted at two of the golem guards on the ground. "You two—hey!"

Not the smartest demons in Hell's arsenal, the two lumbering mammoths started looking around for the voice they heard calling to them.

"Up here, dumb-asses!" Kobal yelled, waving his arms.

The Fallen | 93

Both creatures tilted their heads back, looking up at the master of the castle with blank expressions. A smile of satisfaction spread across Kobal's face. "Kill each other," he shouted down.

Without a moment's hesitation the two golems began pounding away at each other so as not to incur their master's wrath. Kobal was consumed by fits of loud, obnoxious laughter as his guards went about the task of destroying each other for his amusement. He was laughing so loudly, in fact, that he didn't hear the arrival of Mullin, who had teleported himself into the throne room.

"My lord," Mullin said, announcing his presence.

Startled, Kobal cut short his laugh riot and turned around. "Where is your master?" Kobal said, walking from the balcony back to his throne. "Why has he sent you here?" Kobal didn't like dealing with underlings—even this one, who would most likely take Leonard's spot at the head of the dark mages one day, if he survived.

"My lord," Mullin said, with a slight bow, "my master is currently occupied at the pens and has sent me in his stead to deliver news of an unexpected and disturbing nature."

As the master of hilarity and games, Kobal didn't like unexpected surprises unless he was the one doing the surprising. For just a second it seemed to Mullin that Kobal's posture and facial features actually took on a serious tone.

"Tell me your news, and be quick, apprentice," Kobal said with an air of authority not often heard from him.

"Roughly one day ago, my master detected a force on earth that was not foreseen prior to our invasion. It's a force that could upset our plans and bring ruin and failure to our armies," Mullin began. "I was dispatched to search this power out and bring it to my master for further investigation. I was successful in my mission, and between my master's powers and my own, we have subdued it in a spell of containment."

Kobal's eyes narrowed at this news. If this power was great enough to have Leonard send his prized apprentice to search it out, it must be great indeed.

"Lord Azazel and my master both await you at the pens to discuss this matter in its entirety, my lord," Mullin said, bowing one more time.

"Yes, yes, we should leave right away." Kobal's manner relaxed. "Just let me see to something real quick," he said, jumping up again from his throne and running to the balcony. He leaned out over the railing to see what had become of his current game. On the ground below, both golems lay dead. But it didn't appear they had killed each other. One lay on the ground with its arms and legs spread about it like a mannequin, dozens of cuts and gashes on its body. The other had a gaping hole through what used to be its chest.

Kobal was no fool. Whatever had killed his guards was probably loose in his castle right now, possibly looking for him. "Hmm … Mullin, gather up all the golems and skeletons around the castle, then send for the dregs." As Kobal spoke he stared down at the bodies, wondering who or what could have done this type of damage to his sentries. "After that, meet me in the throne room—and hurry. Time is of the essence. We have visitors."

Mullin didn't like taking orders from anyone except his own master, but this was one demon he was not about to cross. "Yes, my lord," Mullin said, and he vanished to complete his task.

Kobal wasted no time heading back inside to this throne, his twisted in a malicious smile at the prospect of adding a few more skulls to his grisly seat.

† † †

"You would think a demon of Kobal's stature would have more guards around," Valafor said, twisting his weapon arm back and forth. He'd had to dislodge it from the abdomen of the golem guard who'd had the unfortunate luck to meet the duo.

"I would venture to say that at this point it doesn't matter; he knows we're here. We've lost any element of surprise we might have had," Rai said, peering around the corner to view an empty, open hallway with massive double doors on the far end. "In any event, we have to make our way to the throne room. That's where he spends his days. Just be prepared for the worst, Val."

Valafor came to stand beside his friend and, looking down the hall from the opposite direction, said, "I knew what we were getting into back on the hilltop. I never liked Kobal, anyway—fucker thinks everything is so damn funny."

"We're clear. Let's go," Rai said, entering the vacant hallway. He held his sword in a reverse grip, with the blade running up the length of his arm past his shoulder.

Walking down the hallway at a brisk pace, eyeing every little nook and cranny in the event that their enemies try to get the jump on them, Valafor asked, "So what's our plan after this? Heaven and Hell are both going to be gunning for us. We're good, Rai, but not that good."

"Kobal has been lying to me as far back as I can remember. "As far as I'm concerned, he dies today… and after that, fuck it. Maybe we'll kill all the lords of Hell. There's none alive that could take down the two of us, save one. And when the day comes that I fill in the missing memories of my past, believe me—Lucifer and I will have words." Rai spoke in a hushed voice, playing with the idea in his mind.

All the lords of Hell? Valafor thought. *There's quite a few of them. No vacation time for us.*

They stopped a few feet from the main entrance to the throne room. "Ready?" Rai asked, looking at Valafor and taking a deep breath.

Blue light erupted from Valafor's arm, lighting up the hallway. In the glow, Rai could see Val's face spread into a malicious grin. "Hell yeah, brother!" Valafor replied, drawing back his weapon arm and striking the doors with a single, mighty swing that sent both of them flying off their hinges into the middle of the throne room.

Rai and Valafor ran in, weapons ready to kill anything within arm's reach. But the whole room was empty except for two figures on the far side—one sitting on the throne and the other standing beside him, arms folded inside the cuffs of his black robe.

Seeing his target in the flesh, gripping his sword with both hands, Rai was about to make a rush for his former master and end his lying, treacherous life.

Kobal wasn't known for his brute strength or fighting prowess, but for his ability to lure his prey and trap them like flies in a spider-web.

Seeing the two figures alone, Valafor unleashed a mighty beam of blue energy from his arm and shot it straight at Kobal. Just as the beam was about to find its mark, however, the robed figure lifted his hand, deflecting the energy so it struck the ceiling. Large chunks of rock broke free and fell to the floor, leaving a gaping hole in the roof of the castle.

"Enough," Kobal said. "What has brought you here, Rai? It's obvious that you want me dead. What I can't figure out is why." Kobal gave a derisive chuckle. Obviously he thought these two were insane to think they could kill him in his own castle.

Not letting his guard down, Rai stepped forward. "I'll make this quick, Kobal. I met an enemy commander on the field who claims to be my brother from heaven …. my twin brother." As Rai spoke, his eyes began to glow red with rage.

"Ah," Kobal said with a sneer. "So you finally know the truth you have always suspected, you wretch. I purposely sent you to fight him in the hopes of destroying any former ties that might still be lingering in the accursed realm of light. So you thought you would just come down here to make me pay, huh?"

"Rest assured, Kobal," Rai said, "your lies—along with your life—end tonight."

Kobal hopped over the back of his throne as if he were afraid they could follow through with their threat. "Ohhh, I'm so scared! Please, Rai, Valafor, have mercy on me … Oh wait." He gave a quick, wicked laugh. "Mullin, show them." Kobal moved back in front of his throne and pointed his finger across the room, mumbling incoherent words of magic.

Suddenly several golems surrounded the pair and dozens of dregs hung from the ceiling.

"Come get me, bitches," Kobal challenged.

They had been surrounded the whole time.

Reacting on pure instinct, Rai whipped his slender blade around in a wide arc, slashing the chests of the two golems closest to him. "It was the mage," he shouted over his shoulder to Valafor, bringing his sword back to guard. "He had a cloaking spell over the whole room!"

"Fuck it!" came Valafor's voice as another beam of energy shot from his arm, spraying the ceiling and burning a path through any dregs unlucky enough to be caught in its deadly blue path. "We knew this was going to happen. Let's just kill this bitch and get out of here fast!" He sprinted across the throne room.

Two of the slow-moving golems rushed toward Rai, intent upon smashing him on the floor with their great fists. Seeing this new threat in front of him, Rai leapt into the air, twisting and flipping his body as he jumped over them, his sword just a blur. By the time his feet hit the ground, both golems lay at Rai's feet, long gashes running from the tops of their heads down to their backs.

Scanning the room to find Val, Rai saw him clinging to the head of a golem with his left arm, punching it repeatedly in the face with his weapon arm. Every time face and fist met, blue sparks exploded in the air, showering the ground around the combatants. Three head shots later, the golem fell to the floor, motionless, with little more than a stump where its head had been.

"We need to get Kobal—that's how we end this!" Rai had to yell now to be heard over the screeching dregs that had begun dropping down from above to join the fray.

"I would love to help, but I'm a little preoccupied here," said Val, who was swinging violently, smashing everything in sight—golem or dreg.

Rai threw his body to the floor and landed flat on his back, holding his sword erect above him, as one of the dregs flew directly over him. The creature split itself in two on his blade, spilling its guts on the floor. Getting back on his feet, he saw Kobal through the mass of golems rushing toward him.

Kobal was sitting on his throne, watching the fight without a care in the world, as if no one had come to take his head.

More dregs flew into the room from the new hole in the roof, and the golems that remained were closing in quickly, cutting off any room to maneuver.

Valafor was fending off a whole host of dregs—punching, biting, kicking, doing anything he could think of to keep them away. Blurry energy showered the room every time it connected with an enemy, illuminating the cruel, determined faces of the dregs.

As one of them got in close, Valafor reached out and plucked the creature from the air with his left arm, bringing it to his mouth and clamping his teeth on its head, spilling blood and gray matter on his face. Spitting out a chunk of skull to the floor, Valafor threw the remaining corpse back into the cluster of airborne enemies, knocking many more to the ground.

Ducking the swing of one clumsy golem, Rai brought the hilt of his sword around, instantly crushing its face. Then Rai whipped his head around to check on Kobal's whereabouts, and his body went numb with cold. His sword fell from his fingers, clattering on the ground, and red lights streamed from the corners of his eyes as the realization dawned upon him: the mage had played his hand.

The next second, Rai's whole world exploded in an array of colorful lights and weird shapes as the golem's fist connected with the back of his head. Rai was out before he hit the ground.

Glancing around the room to see how Rai was faring, Valafor saw him on the ground, surrounded by golems. He ran to Rai's side, his eyes scanning the room, and realized at once that the battle was over. He saw Kobal and the mage still standing by the throne. *It's now or never,* he thought.

Shifting course and taking a hard left, Valafor ran straight for them. In his peripheral vision, he saw a massive clenched fist streaming through the air, on a collision course with his head. Instinctively he went into a somersault, jumping back to his feet and bringing his weapon arm straight into the face of another golem, taking its head clean off its shoulders.

His feet hit the ground hard and he continued running, weaving, and dodging, using all the strength and speed left in him to make it to the two figures at the far end of the room. Even if he fell in the end, he thought, he would take one of the two with him.

Seeing Valafor's progress through the slow-moving ranks of golems and the few dregs that remained alive, Kobal jumped up and ran straight to the balcony outside to escape. Simultaneously, Mullin had started chanting a teleportation spell. Just as Valafor was about to reach the mage, his weapon arm pulled back, ready to deliver the killing blow, the air around both of them crackled, and Valafor and the mage got sucked inside the spell. Valafor's last thoughts were that he and Rai had failed. *Oh well,* he thought. *It was fun while it lasted.*

Seeing that Valafor had disappeared along with Mullin, Kobal ran back into the throne room and straight toward Rai, who was still unconscious. Kobal didn't slow down but used his momentum to deliver a hard kick to Rai's motionless form. Wiping his mouth with the back of his hand and breathing heavily, Kobal glared at the limp body before him. "Come after me in my own castle!" Kobal yelled at Rai's still form. Then he turned to a waiting golem.

"Bring this garbage to the dungeon and string him up!" he screamed, seething with anger. "And don't be gentle."

This will be entertaining, he thought. Then he walked back to his throne, wondering what fate had befallen Mullin.

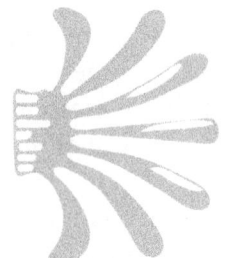 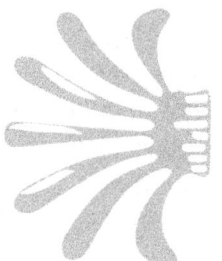

Chapter 21

THE WAR ROOM WAS SILENT.

All the chairs surrounding the great table were empty except for one. For more than a day now, Metatron had been sitting in a comatose-like state as he conversed with the All-Father about the events unfolding on Earth. His ability to transport his astral self to the All-Father's plane of existence was the only way the Seraphim could learn of the All-Father's will and fulfill his wishes for mankind.

Suddenly the eyes in his peaceful face opened, bursting with life, and the chest on his stone-still body started moving up and down to the rapid rhythm of his deep breaths.

Metatron had returned.

He flexed his fingers and wiggled his toes to get the blood flowing; they were numb from having been still for so long. Taking a second to collect himself, Metatron rose from his chair and stretched. Recalling the conversation that had just taken place with his creator, he walked to the balcony overlooking the main courtyard to find Gabriel and tell him of the All-Father's plans and desires for this war.

Gabriel would not be happy with their maker's decision, but he would accept it and fulfill his duty as the All-Father's chosen one.

Metatron felt a welcome breeze the moment he stepped from the war room walls, and he could hear loud voices rising from the courtyard below. Placing his hand on the balcony railing and peering over the edge, he saw Gabriel, Sandalphon, Cassiel, and the commander of the Fury Legion engaged in deep discussion. "Gabriel!" Metatron yelled.

† † †

Gabriel had been staring at his best commander, his heart sinking further into despair as Krillion reported that most of Fury Legion was dead, captured, or scattered on Earth. The only good news was that Krillion himself hadn't been killed. He was bruised and battered beyond belief, but not mortally wounded. Krillion was an icon to the younger soldiers—the physical, competent commander they all aspired to be one day.

Krillion stood among the other warriors, his broad frame dwarfing them all. He was leaning on his mighty war hammer, which was still covered with dried blood and bits of gore and flesh—reminders of the many demons he had dispatched on Earth.

"We already know about Rai," Gabriel said. "There is much we all need to discuss and very little time in which to discuss it. In two hours we launch an attack on the pens," he added, looking at Krillion and Cassiel.

"Gabriel," Krillion said. "You already know that I'm going with you. Rai is down there somewhere, and if he's at the pens, you'll need me to deal with him."

Staring hard at the exhausted angel standing in front of him, Gabriel thought about the pros and cons of allowing Krillion to fight alongside them in his condition. Certainly he was physically depleted; he had just been through hours of chaotic battle that his legion ultimately lost due to enemy reinforcements. And the fact that Krillion had met Rai on the battlefield might distract him mentally. On the other hand, he was part of Israfil's vision—in fact, he was supposed to assemble and lead this uncanny group of warriors. Plus there was no one Gabriel would rather have watching his back in the middle of a firefight.

"All right, Krillion," Gabriel said, his decision made, "get with Raph and get patched up, then hit up the armory. Meet me in the war room in forty-five minutes for a full briefing. And be quick—we fly in less than two hours."

As Krillion nodded, turned, and took flight toward the infirmary, Gabriel looked at Sandalphon and Cassiel. "Sandalphon, take Cassiel and the rest of her unit and get them treated and outfitted. For now they fall under you, until you're told otherwise." Both captains nodded and then left to assemble what remained of her unit.

"Gabriel!"

The Fallen | 101

Hearing his name yelled from the balcony, Gabriel looked up to see Metatron standing there, waving his arms. "Finally," Gabriel said under his breath. After so much bad news and defeat after defeat, the All-Father had finally stepped in. Surely his divine wisdom would see the Seraphim through this, their darkest hour.

His white wings stretched wide, Gabriel jumped up and caught the air among his feathers, flapping his wings vertically in order to gain height without propelling himself forward. He continued to gain altitude until he was perched on the railing, face to face with Metatron. "Tell me you bear good tidings, old friend. What's the All-Father's guidance on our situation?" Gabriel asked with an exhausted smile on his face.

Metatron's facial expression was impassive, as always.

"I have most assuredly brought tidings from the All Father, but whether they bode good or ill is entirely up to you and your interpretation of them," Metatron said in his monotonous voice. "There is one more member that will be added that Israfil could not have seen, though his power is great."

Gabriel's eyes narrowed at the prospect of this member who, for some inexplicable reason, Israfil had failed to see in his vision. Only one name came to mind... he knew this moment would become reality one day. "Kane," Gabriel whispered loudly enough for only Metatron to hear.

Metatron gazed at the ground and nodded in silent agreement. "The All-Father has said he will re-animate and bring him back to us. He will be part of the group, either as Earth's salvation or its destroyer," Metatron said. "The All-Father has declared that if the time of the angels is over, he will not let the Earth and mankind be subjugated to Hell's rule and influence. The light will not be extinguished quietly."

Gabriel hopped down from the railing and walked inside, followed by Metatron. "When will he be here?" Gabriel asked.

"I am already here ... chosen one," replied a cold and serious voice. Stepping from the shadows of the far corner of the war room to stand before Gabriel and Metatron was Kane.

Kane was a testament to the failed prototype of man that the All-Father and the angels had deemed too powerful to inherit the earth thousands of years ago, well before Adam and Eve, and had thus banished to Purgatory for all time. He was well-proportioned, around six feet tall and two hundred pounds. His head and body were a distinct shade of bright red and absent of all hair as a result of the immense power that constantly coursed through his veins. He emitted a reddish aura as a reminder of the awesome power he wielded.

There was a surreal calm about him that Gabriel found very unnerving. It was as if he were a child in an adult body—and in essence, he was.

Never having had time to fully develop his powers and mind before he was sent to Purgatory for all time, Kane was a massive X factor, with the potential to be as devastating to the angels as to the demons. If this was what the All-Father commanded, though, Gabriel would obey, praying they would not have to fight Kane as well.

Kane stepped forward and stopped short of the table where Gabriel and Metatron stood. He scanned the whole room top to bottom, taking in everything like a child, finally settling his eyes on the angels. Looking at the figure standing before him, Gabriel had wondered how things could have gone so poorly, so quickly, that the All-Father would have brought Kane into the fight. "Please sit," he said, motioning to a chair. Looking at Metatron, Gabriel also sat down, his hand resting on the hilt of his sword in case Kane attacked. "Kane," he began, "this is the situation: war has broken out on Earth and we are losing badly. Many of our warriors are dead or scattered down on man's Earth. We have suffered heavy—"

"*My* Earth, you mean," Kane said, cutting Gabriel off with a glacial chill in his voice. "Before your humans were a thought in the creator's mind, it was I who was destined to populate the planet and be his servant. After what all of you have done to me, why I should help you? What do I care about the weak creatures that now inhabit Earth in my stead?"

Gabriel knew this would come up, and for once he didn't have an answer. The bottom line was, yes, the All-Father and the Seraphim had decided that Kane was too powerful to remain on Earth, and so the All-Father had placed in him in a nether realm called Purgatory, an empty realm where his destructive powers would cause no damage to anyone or anything. Now, when things were at their worst, he had been brought back to do the Seraphim's job: protecting Earth and mankind from the demons.

Looking to Metatron and back to Kane, Gabriel said, "I'm going to be plain with you, Kane. We are almost lost. Hell's forces have overrun Earth; the merge between the realms has already begun. You are justified in your grudge against us—I understand that. But here are the facts: if the Seraphim fall and the All-Father is defeated, then you will surely cease to exist, just like the rest of us. Help us, and you will find your place on Earth, free of our influence ... forever."

Kane stared at Gabriel for a few seconds, considering his words, before answering. "What's to stop me from leaving here and making my own way in life, regardless? I am free now, and we both know that if what you say of the war is true, you don't have the resources to fight the demons and try to stop me."

There it is, Gabriel thought, *the threat I knew was coming.* "True," he said, "we wouldn't have the numbers to fight the demons and fight you, too. But, as I said, if we fall, it would only be a matter of time until Hell found you. Not even you could withstand the entirety of Hell's army on your own. Ally with us, and together we can stop them once and for all. Our backs are against the wall, Kane. Will you stand with us or against us? "

Kane was staring down at the engraved surface of the war room table, considering Gabriel's offer. Finally he was free of that infernal emptiness; he had the chance to lead his life free of any higher influence and decide his own fate. His eyes darted from Gabriel to Metatron and back to Gabriel again before he finally replied. "I will help ... for now. If you cross me, I will stop at nothing less than the entire destruction of the Seraphim. Once our work is finished, I will leave and you will not follow me. My life will be mine, and mine alone. Are we clear?"

Gabriel's eyes narrowed with rage; he was not one to be threatened or given ultimatums. Metatron placed a calming hand on his arm as a reminder of what was at stake and to place his ego aside for the sake of Earth and mankind.

"Yeah, we're clear, Kane," Gabriel said. "We're clear. We will wait until the rest your teammates get here, and you will be briefed on the final plans and brought up to speed with all that has transpired."

There were voices coming from the hallway outside of the war room, and Gabriel turned in his chair. A second later Krillion walked through the door followed by Afriel, who was trying without success to bandage a gash across the big commander's ribs. "Krillion, will you stop? I have to get this wound closed," Afriel pleaded, trying to tighten a knot to secure the bandage. Zara followed behind, along with the rest of the council, including Azreal.

"Okay," Gabriel said. "Everyone's here. I'll make this short because I already know the mixed reactions you all are going to have, and we've been over it already. Bottom line is, this is the All-Father's command, and we shall follow it through to the end. Remember, we have a battle to win. Israfil, if you would, tell them of your vision."

Israfil didn't take his seat, opting instead to stand beside Gabriel at the head of the table. "Here is the situation," he began. "Before my power blanked out, I saw the final hope for the Earth, mankind, and the Seraphim. It lies within a group that is to be assembled here and now: Krillion, commander of the former legion Fury; Zara, captain of the Twelfth Legion of Light; Kane ..."

All eyes in the room went to Kane, who sat unmoving and emotionless in his chair. All eyes except Azreal's.

Israfil continued. "Rai," he said, pausing again and looking at Krillion to see the big angel's reaction to this groundbreaking revelation.

Krillion's eyes narrowed. He shot Gabriel a look that asked a million silent questions regarding this unexpected member. Gabriel shook his head as if to tell him that it had all been worked out and he would explain later.

Israfil resumed. "There is a demon whose name I do not know, save that he wields a weapon of tremendous power on his right arm, an arm that is charred black."

Krillion's eyes lit up with recognition. "I know of this demon, Israfil. At the defeat of my legion, I was approached by my brother Rai and a demon bearing a weapon of that description. He is not one to be trifled with; he slew many of my warriors that day. And how exactly are they supposed to join with us when they both serve Hell?"

Israfil thought for a moment before answering. "Krillion, you understand better than most—it is not for us to sort out the All-Father's plan, just to have faith that this is the path laid before us. As his most trusted of all creations, it is our duty to carry out his will with our every breath."

At this Kane rose to his feet, and Gabriel rose with him, saying, "Kane, he didn't mean anything by it."

Turning to stare directly at Gabriel, Kane replied, "I know exactly what he meant by it. Let's just finish this up. The quicker we're done, the quicker I can leave your presence." Kane walked angrily to the balcony, within earshot of the assembly.

Sitting back down, Gabriel gestured for Israfil to continue.

The Fallen | 105

"Finally, there is a human girl on Earth who fits into this plan somehow. I cannot tell you any more except that we fear the demons have her, as my power of the divine vision has left me yet again. We must at all costs get her back for safeguarding and find out what role she plays in this."

"I know what her role shall be," Metatron said. "She is to be given the blessing of the All-Father. That is all I'm able to say for now, but if the demons do, in fact, have her, then it might be too late. I will focus my energies on finding this human child while the rest of you continue with Krillion and his mission."

"Okay, then," Gabriel said, turning his attention to the map on the table before them. "Raziel, you have been to these pens. Give us your strategy."

Standing up for all to hear her better, Raziel began describing the purpose of the camp, the lay of the land, and the best avenues of attack. When she finished, Azreal stepped forth with a smug expression, looking at the chosen group condescendingly. "And what of this so-called all-star team during the battle?" he sneered.

Gabriel stood up, feeling his temper about to get the better of him yet again. Azreal always had something negative to say, regardless of the situation. "They will be part of the ground forces with me. Don't worry, Azreal, you won't have any competition for your position in the upcoming battle," he said with a sarcastic smile.

Fingering the hilt of his sword, lips clenched tight, Azreal gave a forced smile and nodded. "As you command, Chosen One," he said.

"That's all," Gabriel said. "Everyone link up in the courtyard in ten." All the angels stood and proceeded to the courtyard except for Zara and Krillion, who exchanged glances and walked to the balcony. Kane was still there, standing by himself, watching the members of the Seraphim walk past him to leave. His face was filled with scorn and hate.

Not quite sure what to say to this new stranger who was neither angel nor human, Zara smiled slightly and approached him. "Hi, I'm Zara," she said, hoping that would be enough to break the ice.

Kane looked at her with a blank expression, although he was a tornado of emotions inside. He had made up his mind to despise the angels for what they had done to him millennia ago—but here stood a creature of unsurpassed beauty. Her black hair gleamed slightly purple in the light reflected from the roof of the war room; her skin was a beautiful shade of bronze that accentuated her exceptionally muscular body. She was a mystery to him. One second he saw in her a childish playfulness and kindness of heart; the next he saw eyes devoid of any feeling except for hate and rage.

Beside her stood one of the largest angels Kane had ever seen. He was easily a head taller than Kane and twice as wide. Strapped to his back was a war hammer that most angels couldn't even lift, much less wield in a fight. His short, spiked hair gave more definition to an already chiseled face. The parts of his body that were not covered in armor were covered in scars—some old, many new. He had seen battle recently and apparently had come out stronger than before. Kane didn't sense a specific power radiating from the large warrior, but more of a powerful presence.

Settling his gaze back upon the female, Kane replied, "I'm Kane. So… we are to be partners? I imagine Gabriel has filled you both in on who I am."

It was Krillion who answered. "I know who you are, Kane, and I know your story. If we are to work together, we should get any unresolved feelings out of the way right now. We all need to be on the same page; if there is any dissension among us, we will fail."

"I agree, but I wonder…" Kane began, looking at Zara. "Do you know what your leaders have done to me?" he finally asked, gesturing to the angels who were leaving.

Zara slowly nodded her head. "Yes, Gabriel told me what transpired," she said. "When it happened to you, I was just a few years old. And it was a terrible tragedy. But we need you with us, Kane, as an ally. Please."

Kane's gaze once more passed from Zara to Krillion, who stood with his arms folded over his broad chest. "We will be a team," Kane finally said. "I know it was not the two of you that voiced the decision to remove me from Earth. It may belong to man now, but once—for a brief time—it was mine." Looking up at Krillion and extending his hand, he added, "You have my word—whatever happens in the future, you can count me as an ally and a friend."

Krillion shook Kane's hand and smiled, showing his perfect white teeth. Then he breathed a sigh of relief. "Let's head to the courtyard where we can talk more and prepare," he said.

On that note the three of them walked to the balcony railing, where Krillion and Zara spread their wings, ready to float to the courtyard below. Zara stopped and glanced at Kane, confused. "Uh … Kane, do you need help down?" she asked.

As he detected genuine concern in her voice, a childlike smile spread across his face and the red aura that surrounded his body began to glow brighter. "No, Zara, I can manage."

Squinting at the light, Zara watched as Kane hovered in the air a few feet off the balcony and then drifted away from her. "Wow," she said, looking at Krillion.

"Didn't see that one coming'," Krillion said, and he jumped off the railing to follow Kane down to the ground.

Just as Zara was about to jump, she heard her name behind her. She turned to see Gabriel approaching her with a curious look on his face. "All went well with the introductions, I take it?"

"Yes, Gabriel, I think with a little work we'll manage fine," she said. "Besides, he's kind of cute … in a reddish way." With a wink and a smile, she leapt off the railing to find her teammates below, leaving Gabriel to survey the small army assembled before him. The horrors that were being unleashed by Lucifer's minions would come to a screeching halt soon, he thought. The pens were just the first step. The angels had made the first mistake by underestimating the demons, and it had cost them dearly. The second mistake would be the demons' thinking they would hold Earth.

"Gabriel," came the voice of Azreal from behind him.

"I told everyone to head to the courtyard too make final preparations, Azreal. I'm getting tired of you constantly challenging my authority," Gabriel said, watching his warriors below.

"I'm not here to challenge you—*Chosen One*," Azreal said, almost spitting the words. "There has been a change in the plan that wasn't mentioned earlier."

Gabriel didn't turn around. "And what would that be, Az?"

"You're not part of the plan."

Suddenly Gabriel's eyes grew wide with horror and pain as he felt cold steel slide in between his shoulder blades and wings and erupt violently from his chest. With one of his lungs punctured, he didn't have the breath to scream. The tip of the sword protruding from his chest was black as night and dripping with blood.

His blood.

Gabriel's vision blurred. He felt Azreal pull free the blade forged from black steel, and he collapsed to his knees on the floor of the balcony.

"Your reign as supreme archangel is over," Azreal said. "Now is the time for the age of death."

Azreal wiped his sword on Gabriel's armor and then sheathed it, glancing over the railing at the angelic force that would soon fall to Earth and its doom. Then, with a malicious smile, he spread his wings and jetted straight into the air, away from the body of Gabriel and the Crystal Palace.

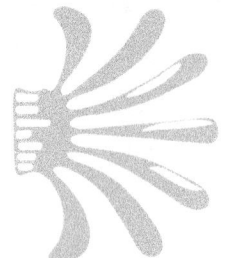 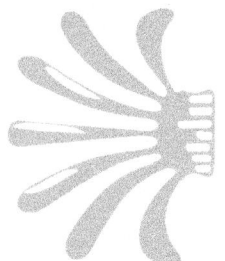

Chapter 22

THE CITY WAS DEAD IN every direction. No signs of life or movement anywhere. What once had been a thriving community of people with dreams, hopes, and ambitions now was a haven for demons—and worse—to roam.

The air around the entrance to a burned-out diner began to crack and sizzle with power. In a flash of blinding light, two figures now stood on the otherwise empty street. One wore a black robe that covered him from head to toe, including his face. The other was a massive demon with rippling muscles and a blackened right arm.

His body covered in fresh wounds, Valafor slumped to the ground, vomiting violently. This was his first time teleporting, and it had not been a good experience. Grinning, Mullin took a few steps back to put some distance between himself and the dangerous demon now on his knees before him. Teleporting could be very taxing on the body if you weren't used to it. "So tell me, Valafor," he said in mocking tones, "you thought you would just jump in my portal after me and kill me? Perhaps torture me? Minions of Hell call you one of the best, but if you're the best, then why are you on your knees before me, you filthy animal?"

Spitting out a mouthful of bile, his stomach churning, Valafor looked up at Mullin and smiled. Then, with a quickness that caught the mage off guard, Valafor lunged.

The mage instinctively started reciting an incantation that would trap and bind the demon—but he was too late. Before he could get the first few syllables out, Valafor had driven his powerful shoulders into the Mullin's abdomen, knocking him to the ground. Valafor stood triumphant over him, the radiant blue energy from his weapon arm lighting up the surrounding street. He could smell fear permeating the air around Leonard's prized pupil. Lying on the ground, Mullin wheezed and coughed.

Just then a hoarse scream pierced the air, and from around a nearby corner staggered a group of biters, looking at Valafor and Mullin with rage in their eyes and blood on their claws.

Valafor had heard of these creatures, humans who had been turned into hideous monstrosities, but he had never actually seen one of them in person. Looking at them now, stumbling toward him, he could see clearly the work of the dark mages. The creatures' bodies were charred black in some areas, the arms so long that their sharp fingernails scraped the ground. They had mouths like those of crocodiles, filled with row after row of razor-like teeth, ideal for ripping flesh from bone. Unlike their upper bodies, their legs were overly muscular. From the ravenous look on their disfigured faces, it was clear they had no preference in their choice of flesh, be it human, angel, or demon.

Bet these bitches can jump, was Valafor's first thought. With a quick glance down at Mullin, who was still gasping for air, Valafor decided the mage wasn't going anywhere for a minute.

Stepping over the still-reeling mage and standing before the biters, Valafor started plotting possible strategies and outcomes should they attack him. There were four of them and one of him. He had to act quickly lest Mullin regain his strength and start hurling black magic.

Judging from the biters' massive legs, Valafor decided that an aerial attack was their likeliest course of action. Just then, all four of them started shrieking and yelling in unison.

"Knew it," was all Valafor managed before the battle commenced.

The first biter jumped into the air, its distorted arms extending in order to find Valafor's body and rip it apart. Its eyes were locked on him as it flew through the air.

Bringing his weapon arm up, Valafor fired a beam of blue energy, blasting the creature in two. "One," Valafor said as both halves hit the sidewalk with a wet, slapping sound. The other three biters charged at once. As another one neared him, Valafor jumped up and over him, leaving a trail of blue light. As the biter's head went toward the sky, following the light to track his prey, Valafor brought down his right fist with the force of a thousand demons, driving it into the biter's chest. The impact was so hard that the creature's chest seemed to liquefy on the spot. "Two," Valafor said, his breathing heavy with exertion.

Risking a quick glance behind him to ensure that Mullin was still out of the fight, Valafor felt claws sink into his shoulder and hot blood pouring from yet another wound. He jerked his shoulder away to dislodge the creature that had done this, leaving bits of his skin and muscle clinging to the claws of the biter, who was yelling savagely and advancing again to finish the job.

It seemed to Valafor that the smell of his blood was igniting a primitive response in the creatures—an even more bloodthirsty frenzy. Rushing in before the biter could advance further, Valafor snagged it by the neck, lifting it from its feet, and spinning in a full circle to build momentum, he threw its body toward the final biter. The two connected with a sickening thud and then collapsed to the ground in a heap. Noticing that one of the biters was still alive and moving, Valafor walked over to the mess of tangled bodies and stomped on its head, splattering what remained of its brain onto the street before him.

"Three and four," Valafor said, turning back to Mullin, who was now on his hands and knees trying to get back to his feet. Valafor gave the mage a hard kick straight to his abdomen, sending him sprawling back to the ground, gasping for air. "What's up now, mage? Not used to physical contact, huh?" Valafor said in his rocky voice. He looked out at the again empty street, his mind racing. What should he do next? As far as he knew, Rai could still be alive. If that was the case, Kobal would be doing who knew what to him. In fact, Kobal by now would have put the word out on what the two of them had done, so all of Hell would be looking for them, as well as the forces of Heaven.

Valafor needed a plan and an ally, and he needed them now.

That's it! he thought. The angel commander, the one who said he was Rai's brother. Perhaps there was a remote chance that Rai's brother would help free him. *But how do I find him—and when I do, what's to stop him from killing me on the spot?*

Looking down at Mullin, Valafor began to form a most ludicrous plan: perhaps Leonard's little golden child could teleport him straight to the Crystal Palace, the bastion of the Seraphim. He thought over the insane strategy until he decided he had no choice. He had this one, remote chance—which would probably get him killed.

"Get up, mage. There's somewhere I need to be, an' you're going to take me there," Valafor said, pulling Mullin to his feet.

"Why should I help you, you piece of shit? You're a traitor to the realm of darkness," Mullin replied, still gasping.

Valafor's felt his blood pressure rise. He didn't have time to fool around with this pathetic mage. Every minute wasted could be Rai's last. Pulling Mullin's head very close to his mouth of razor-sharp teeth, Valafor hissed, "Here's how this is going to work. You take me to the Crystal Palace, you live. You don't, I start biting chunks of your fucking face off right now. Any questions?"

Feeling the heat of Valafor's breath upon his face and hearing the tone of his voice, Mullin knew this demon wouldn't hesitate to follow through on his threat. He thought it over, not that it was much of a choice. Finally he said, "I'll take you there, but know that the angels will tear us apart the moment we appear. You're sentencing us both to death."

"Let me be crystal clear with you on some things first, though," Valafor said. "One, if you do anything other than what I tell you, I promise you that I will kill you where you stand. Two, I have no other choice, as I will not leave Rai to the sadistic whims of your master. Are we clear, bitch?"

"Crystal ... and Kobal is not my master," Mullin replied.

Valafor's body tensed, weapon arm ready to strike at the first sign of betrayal, as Mullin began the incantation that would, he hoped, bring him to the commander of Fury Legion.

Valafor knew he was heading straight to his death, probably within minutes of arrival, but this was his and Rai's only chance. He tried to focus on the words that were coming from Mullin's mouth, but they sounded like gibberish. Then, in another flash of light, the street, the dead biters, and everything else around them faded away in to nothingness.

When he came to moments later, he seemed to be in a courtyard, the bright light of the sun blinding him. From all directions alarms blared; the call warning of intruders rang in his ears. *This is it,* he thought. He heard the sound of swords being drawn; he had to get his eyes adjusted and quickly. Angelic forms started coming into view all around him. He rubbed his eyes vigorously as his wider surroundings began coming into focus.

He saw some angels standing wide-eyed, mouths open in disbelief, others with swords drawn, sizing up the random demon that had shown up on their front lawn. Archers on the battlements above had nocked their arrows and were directing their gleaming, deadly weapons in his direction.

He saw Mullin, who was standing nearby, quietly pull a dagger from the hem of his robe as his lips started another incantation. "No way are you getting out of here alive, mage scum!" Valafor yelled, grabbing Mullin by his Adam's apple and pulling. Blood spurted over his hand as he pulled it back down to his side, complete with a chunk of Mullin's esophagus. The dying mage's hand immediately dropped the blade and went to the gaping hole in his neck, trying to force the blood to go back in. He collapsed to his knees in the dirt, still spraying the ground around him bright red, a look of pure fear and shock on his horrific face.

Valafor didn't waste another glance at the dying mage at his feet; he had more important matters to attend to, such as the two hundred angelic warriors who were about to gut him. Flexing his right arm, he brought forth its full power in hopes of stalling the oncoming force. He just needed a few precious seconds to think. Blue light poured from his arm, engulfing all the nearby angels and giving them slight pause. Who was this powerful demon that had appeared on their very doorstep?

Not knowing what else to do, Valafor started yelling. "Stop! I'm not here to fight you—I'm looking for the twin brother of Rai! The commander of Fury Legion!"

He was too late; a duo of angels sped through the air straight at him. Reacting with uncanny precision, he used his arm to throw up a force field, deflecting the arrows that would have killed him. They clattered to the ground at his feet, landing on the corpse of Mullin. Valafor took a few steps backward, sending a wave of blue energy toward the two angels, who had to take evasive action to avoid being hit.

Valafor knew his time was running out. Now warriors on the ground were starting to rush him, blades drawn.

Then a single, mighty horn rang out across the courtyard, stopping all the angels in their tracks. Valafor looked around wildly, keeping an eye on the warriors before him while trying to see who blew the horn that might have just saved his life.

A voice sounded through the courtyard: "Gabriel has been attacked! Gabriel has been attacked!"

A few of the angels took flight immediately, heading toward a balcony that overlooked the courtyard. The rest seemed ready to resume the attack on Valafor. "What the fuck is going on here?" he whispered to himself.

"Stand aside, let me pass!" a deep voice boomed through the crowd of warriors. Pushing through the angels still surrounding Valafor,

Krillion made his way to the front of the group, his massive war hammer in hand, ready to destroy the demon who'd had the audacity to defile the grounds of the fabled Crystal Palace with his presence.

Then he looked at the demon standing before him and recalled the battle his own legion had fought on Earth—fought and lost, due in part to this vile creature who was powerful enough to stop even his most veteran warriors. Even standing at his full height, Krillion had to look up to stare into Valafor's face. "What has brought you here, demon?" Krillion asked.

Still glancing around, running various options through in his head, Valafor decided it would be best to power down for the time being. He relaxed his right arm and the blue energy began to pulse less brightly, the cracks in his arm beginning to heal. "Are you the brother of Rai?" Valafor asked, trying to hide his sharpened teeth. They hadn't killed him yet—though not for lack of trying—but he didn't want to give them another reason to try again. "My name is Valafor, Rai's second in command. I have come seeking his brother for help," he said.

"Raziel," Krillion yelled.

"Yes, Commander," Raziel said, running up to stand beside him.

"Keep watch on him until I get back," Krillion asked. "If he moves, kill him." He turned to Valafor. "I'm Rai's brother, demon. You don't make any sudden movements or do anything stupid. You live and we talk; you do anything to provoke my warriors, and you die. Clear?"

That's ironic, thought Valafor. *I just finished giving Mullin the exact same ultimatum.* "Crystal," he replied.

Without wasting another second, Krillion extended his wings and took flight toward the war room balcony to see what had happened to Gabriel and, if possible, find his attacker. He found Gabriel unconscious on the stone floor. The sight of the All-Father's champion lying bloodied sent the big angel's heart into his throat as he tried to speak. "What happened? Who did this?" he asked, noticing the rise and fall of Gabriel's chest. They were weak, shallow breaths, but they were there, thank the All-Father.

Raphael was already there, on his knees in the spreading pool of blood, tending to Gabriel's wound, a massive gash that ran deep into his back.

It was Israfil who walked over to calm the big angel and explain. "It was Azreal. He stabbed Gabriel in the back and flew off to who knows where." The emotion in Israfil's voice was apparent. The Seraphim had

The Fallen | 115

been betrayed by one of their own. This was by far the most crushing blow the Seraphim had endured in the war—even more so than the loss of Armageddon. It meant that they were not just fighting the demons below, but their own brethren. '"What do we do now?" Israfil asked in a hopeless tone, his head hanging low.

"The attack goes as planned," Krillion said. "Now is not the time to be indecisive or show a divided front to our enemies. There is more news as well, Israfil. You should go to the courtyard with all haste. I think your vision just dropped in on us." As guards picked Gabriel up to carry him to the infirmary, Krillion's eyes followed the motionless form of his friend, the Seraphim's hope for victory.

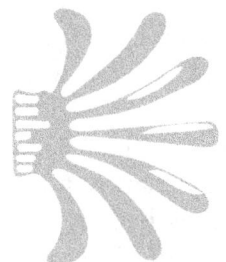 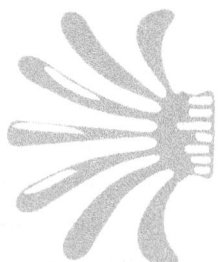

Chapter 23

"Let me through. Let me pass—quickly! Now out of my way, all of you!" Israfil demanded as he pushed his way through the swarm of angelic warriors still training their weapons on Valafor. Even though the demon had powered down both his arm and his temper, he was not liking this situation.

When he reached the end of the sea of warriors, Israfil stood face-to-face with the demon from his vision. He saw his massive muscles and rows of sharpened teeth and wondered how many angels had felt their tips sink into their flesh. He also noted the dominant feature that identified the demon in his vision: the deadly charred-black arm.

Seeing Captain Sandalphon standing at the front of the group, talking with Captain Raziel and Captain Cassiel, Israfil made his way toward him. "Captain Sandalphon, I need to speak with this demon immediately," he said. "Commander Krillion says the attack is to go ahead as planned. There will be some minor changes from the initial lineup, though."

"Right," Sandalphon said. "Is Gabriel going to be all right?"

Israfil looked downcast at the thought of what had happened to the leader of the Seraphim. "We don't yet know the extent of his injuries," he said calmly. "We do, however, know for certain it was Azreal, so henceforth we must assume that Azreal's loyalty lies elsewhere. For now, though, I need you to get everyone back and ready. You leave shortly."

Israfil wasn't a soldier, but Sandalphon had no problem with taking orders from a noncombatant who was an archangel of the Seraphim and a high-ranking member of Gabriel's council. "All right, men, fall back into formation. Once we get word from Commander Krillion, we fly!" Sandalphon yelled.

As the gathered warriors went to their designated spots and the archers on the battlements went back to scanning the horizon outside the palace walls, Israfil walked over to where Valafor stood. "You can relax demon. Fear not: I have foreseen your coming to us. Tell me, what is your name?"

Valafor, still unsure what to make of this little unarmed angel standing before him, eyed him thoroughly. This was defiantly not a warrior—perhaps a scholar or record-keeper. Demons had similar positions, but usually they were reserved for the disabled or disfigured. "Valafor," he said, finally. "Formerly first lieutenant under General Rai, until our departure from Hell's ranks." He spoke in slow, cautious tones.

"My name is Israfil. I am the angel of Judgment Day, and I have been expecting you … and Rai. It is my gift and my curse to have the power to see the Judgment Day. As of late my visions have become disturbing, and more recently they've gone entirely. Tell me how you came to be here at this moment." Israfil asked gently.

Clearing his throat so that his voice would not sound so gravelly, Valafor began describing the events of the previous few days, as well as his own background. "Rai and I have been friends since he was cast out of here with Lucifer," he said. "Since then we have had many battles and great victories. Together he and I were unstoppable—even your Fury Legion couldn't stop our attack. It was at the end of this battle that we ran down the Fury commander, an angel who wields a massive war hammer. Believe me, many of my legion fell under the force of his blows that day." Valafor's voice took on an almost respectful tone. "But we chased him down, bloody and beaten as he was. That's when he came out of nowhere, saying that he and Rai were twin brothers and all that. Before Rai could ask any more questions, more angels—not the ones from the battle—swooped down from the skies and snagged him right out from under us."

As Israfil listened to Valafor's tale, he began to wonder if the All-Father himself had played a hand in setting into motion this "chance" meeting between the two brothers.

"Afterward I told Rai everything I knew about him and his past," Valafor continued. "Needless to say, he got pissed—and believe me, Rai is not the one you want to piss off." The demon chuckled at the thought.

"So Rai decides he's done with Hell and me and him make our way back to Hell to give Kobal our 'resignation,' as it were. We knew it was going to be bad, but we didn't care. During the fight at Kobal's castle, we were overwhelmed and Rai was taken prisoner. Seeing that the fight was all but lost, I ran straight for Kobal. I decided I would at least take him with me before his golems and dregs got me. Instead the mage here conjured one of his teleportation spells at the last moment." Valafor gestured to the corpse lying a few feet away from them. "We ended up on Earth in one of the burned-out cities. That's when I forced him to teleport me here. I want to find Rai's brother to help me free Rai from Kobal."

"Krillion," Israfil said.

"Yeah, Krillion," Valafor nodded. "The way I see it, Hell wants us dead, you want us dead, all me an' Rai have left is each other, and with nowhere else to turn for help, I came here." Valafor took a deep breath as he waited for Israfil to respond to his request.

Israfil thought about the twisted fate of the only twins ever to grace Heaven. Theirs was a tale wrought of unimagined sorrow and shame. Separated by the horrible decision made by one of them through the influence of Lucifer, they fell—one to the light, the other to the darkness.

Israfil could tell that the demon before him was sincere in his request for help. *Angels and demons together.* Israfil pondered the concept silently. Finally, he spoke. "Before my gift of sight recently fell to darkness, I saw a premonition of a group of companions bound by the sole purpose of retaking Earth and halting the demon reign. As it stands, you are part of this team, Valafor—you and Rai both. You see, somehow, some way, it was preordained that you and Rai would leave the ranks of Hell—not so much to join us, but to undertake this task of immense proportions, as assigned from above."

Valafor was getting impatient. "Look, guy, I'm all about a good fight, but right now I have to get Rai out of Kobal's hands," he said. "I would imagine that if you're telling the truth, that also would be on your to-do list."

"We need to wait for Krillion to return. It seems there have been many unexpected surprises of late," Israfil said, glancing up toward the balcony that overlooked the courtyard. The image of Gabriel lying in a pool of his own blood, blood spilled at the hand of his own kind in merciless fashion, was still fresh in the angel's mind.

† † †

Back on the balcony, Krillion's mind raced as he plotted his course of action. "Raph, have some guards bring Gabriel to the infirmary," he ordered the palace healer, his role switching from friend to commander. "The rest of you, back outside—we have a battle to win." Things had just taken a terrible turn for the Seraphim, but they still had a job to do. Without as much as a glance behind him, Krillion ran to the edge of the balcony and flew down to the ground below, followed by the others. Upon landing, he headed straight for Israfil and Valafor. "Where is Rai?" Krillion asked Valafor.

"He is being held in Kobal's castle, most likely for entertainment purposes until Kobal has had enough," Valafor said. "Then he will be killed. Will you help me free him? If not, I need to know now so I can at least go back by myself."

Krillion turned to Israfil, putting a hand on his shoulder. "Raziel will lead the attack on the prisoner camp," he said. "I will take Zara, Kane, and Valafor to go get Rai. Once that is complete we will make our way to the pens. I know this may not be the best course of action, but you know as well as I do that in order for your vision to become reality, my brother must live."

Israfil didn't like the decision, but he knew there was no option left to them. He nodded. "I shall tell Raziel to fly on the camp," he said, and then he turned and left.

"Come on," Krillion said to Valafor. "Let's go meet your new teammates."

† † †

"Below on Earth, in the realm of man, there lies a camp where atrocities are being committed against our brethren," Raziel said, her voice commanding. "Angelic wings are being torn from the backs of our comrades, and the sons and daughters of the All-Father are being subjugated to the experimental desires of the dark mages. This day we shall end the tyranny of the vile creatures below. To the skies—and to victory! For the All-Father!"

In a heartbeat, the sky filled with angelic warriors intent upon exacting revenge on those who had ravaged and destroyed everything in their way, those who had burned the world. Now was the time for the

Seraphim to prove their worth, to uphold their sworn oath. This would be the beginning of the end of Hell's reign on Earth. It would be known as the flight of the Seraphim.

Once the warriors had cleared out, Zara and Kane started walking toward Krillion and this new ally. "Zara, Kane," Krillion began, "this is Valafor. We have all talked about this unlikely alliance, but our purpose now is greater than Heaven or Hell. We either work together or we fall separately."

Zara scrutinized the demon standing before her, impressed at his physical stature and the intimidating aura that surrounded him. She could tell that this creature had immense power at his disposal. Reflecting upon all that Krillion had said earlier, she offered her hand in friendship to Valafor.

Valafor was still uneasy about the concept of teaming with the warriors of light, but he realized he had no choice but to go along with the plan. His first priority was to free Rai. After that—who knew. Looking at the delicate hand extended before him now, he grasped it gratefully in his own, careful not to crush it.

"If we are done here, Krillion, I believe we have some important work ahead of us," Kane said, not wanting to bother with introductions. "The longer we delay here, the worse off your brother will be."

The prospect of finally being reunited after so long with his brother brought a gleam to the big angel's eyes. "Yes, you're right, Kane. We should make all haste to Kobal's castle. Valafor, can you fly?" he asked.

Valafor looked at the big angel with a cocked eyebrow and replied, "Does it look like I can fly, big guy?"

Krillion smiled and motioned to Kane, who with a mere thought and a slight gesture lifted Valafor off his feet to hover in the air.

"Looks like you can now," Zara said with a grin.

"Let's go," Krillion said. "Valafor will fill us in on the full situation on the way to Hell. We must be ready for anything that Kobal might have waiting for us."

† † †

Israfil was left to ponder the meaning of everything that had transpired in the last hour. There were the addition of Valafor and Azreal's mysterious betrayal and defection. The attack on the slave pens were in motion, and the rescue party to retrieve Rai from Hell had just left. All that remained for the angel of Judgment Day was to attend to Gabriel and look for a new vision of the future. He had to find out why his eternal gift had suddenly failed him.

What had happened that had caused Judgment Day simply not to exist? Had they lost already, or was this team the answer they had all been looking for? What if they succeeded where the Seraphim had failed? And, most important, what part would the human child play? The answers to these questions and many others had to be found, and fast.

Mankind's last hope was airborne, heading to the worst possible spot anywhere. The team was nearly complete; their first mission was to free their last remaining member. If this newly assembled array of warriors failed, mankind and the Seraphim would perish beneath Lucifer's boot.

Grabbing a bucket of water and a couple of rags from a nearby table, Israfil walked up the stairs and turned left to the hallway that led to the now-empty war room. Walking over to the place where Gabriel had been stabbed, Israfil knelt down and started cleaning the blood off the stone floor. He was thinking of all that had transpired and all that was to come.

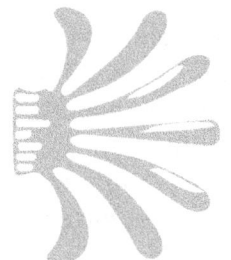 

Chapter 24

Soaring through the dark skies, thinking of the plan he had just set into motion, Azreal gazed down to Earth below. Even with no sunlight, his sharp eyes could make out the floor below him through the grayish darkness.

Having been to Hell on several occasions, he knew exactly what that realm looked like, what to expect, and how to get there. In fact, Earth was very much starting to resemble Hell. Every day that Hell remained in control of Earth, the two realms merged just a little more. By now large patches of grass and trees had disappeared, replaced by barren, dead ground and sharp, jagged mountains. Here and there on Earth's floor he saw the orange glow of small geysers shooting out flames. Every now and again he also saw small hordes of demons destroying buildings or torturing some humans they had found—not his business for now.

With Gabriel out of the way, he was free to enact the rest of his plan.

Being the angel of death for so long had warped Azreal's mind and his way of thinking. He felt that he should be the rightful ruler of all Heaven, possibly even greater than the All-Father himself. Azreal's pride and ego devised his plan, his arrogance drove his black sword into Gabriel's back, and his conceit would rally all the angels to his side in their darkest hour. After they realized that he was their only hope for surviving this war, he would deal with the demons and their lords one by one, thus claiming the Earth in his name.

Now, where is that opening? Azreal asked himself, scanning the landscape before him.

"There it is," he said, and tucking his wings, he shot down to the ground below. To someone without Azreal's knowledge or celestial gift, it would have looked like he was free-falling straight to his death, and that he would be no more than a stain on the ground after he hit. But instead of hitting the ground like a bullet, he passed through it and began the journey to the heart of Hell. Passing layers of dirt and rock, feeling the air getting warmer, he sped downward. After a few seconds, he emerged from a hole and crawling down out of a ceiling.

He was back in Hell. The smell of fire and brimstone hit him in the face, and from every direction he could hear the screams of the tortured. After getting his bearings, he spotted Kobal's castle in the distance and started making his way there.

As he neared the castle, Azreal heard more screams—not an uncommon sound in Hell, but there was something different about these. They didn't sound like the regular screams of agony that usually came from Kobal's castle. When he reached the front door, Azreal landed in front of two golems standing guard there. "You know who I am," he said. "You will let me pass." One of the lumbering golems stood aside; the other opened the giant door, allowing Azreal entry into the castle.

It was easy enough to guess where Kobal would be. All Azreal had to do was follow the screams erupting from the dungeon below. Taking his first left down an empty hallway, he descended a set of spiral stairs leading to the lower level of the castle. From there he could easily tell which room Kobal would be in, for his high-pitched laughter echoed all across the lower level. Azreal stopped at a large oak door and pushed it open, scanning the whole room.

It was the torture chamber. The metallic smell of blood overwhelmed his sense of smell, and he saw who was screaming. He couldn't believe it.

Rai, who had been a member of the Seraphim millennia ago, was chained to the wall opposite him. Azreal recognized him instantly, for they had fought in many battles together, and in the end they fought each other briefly during Lucifer's last stand, until Rai's muscle-bound brother interfered.

Along with Rai there was Kobal, who was holding a small knife in one hand and a clear bottle with green liquid in it. Judging from the number of little cuts and gashes all over Rai's body, Azreal guessed that Kobal was rubbing the liquid on them to cause more burning or infections.

A few golems stood in the corner, watching silently. In the very center of the room was a table with all manner of rusted, blood-covered tools used to inflict excruciating pain by all means imaginable.

Chains and shackles hung from various spots along the walls of this evil room, rotting flesh still hanging from them. The smell of death hung in the air, filling Azreal's nose every time he breathed.

"I'm surprised you're actually getting your hands dirty," Azreal said.

Kobal stopped what he was doing and looked back to see who had spoken to him in such an impudent manner. When he saw Azreal, his eyes lit up. "Azreal! Excellent. Have you completed your part?" he asked in his obnoxious voice.

"Yes," Azreal said, walking over to stand in front of Rai, who was bleeding from what had to have been a dozen different cuts. "You've seen better days, haven't you … Rai?" Azreal asked sarcastically.

At the sound of his name, Rai lifted his head to see who was speaking to him. Rai didn't know who this person was, but judging from the wings protruding from his back, he had to be an angel, part of the Seraphim—which meant that Rai had probably known him long ago. "Why don't you let me down and I'll show you a better day, you fuck," Rai said through bloodstained teeth.

Azreal backhanded Rai across the face, spraying the wall with fresh blood. Then he studied Rai closely. "You know, I never liked you, even when you were one of us," Azreal said. "Since it looks like you're going to be down here for a while though, I'll let you in on a little secret—not that you'll know what I'm talking about. Gabriel has fallen, and soon what's left of the Seraphim will be under my control … except for your brother Krillion." Rai's eyes grew wide with recognition. "Ah, you remember him, huh?" Azreal said with a sneer. Then, turning to face Kobal, he said, "So tell me—what happened here to have Rai hanging in your dungeons?"

"Well, that is an absolutely hilarious story," Kobal began. "Rai and his furry little buddy actually had the balls to come to my fucking castle and try to kill me." As he spoke he walked over to Rai, grabbed him by the chin, and slammed his head against the wall with a sickening thud.

In agony now, gritting his teeth so he wouldn't make a sound, Rai felt a trickle of fresh blood run down the back of his neck.

"Not so badass now, are you," Kobal said with a shrill laugh. "Even though his friend got away, thanks to Mullin's teleportation spell, there's still plenty of fun to be had with Rai here," he added, giving Rai a mocking slap in the face.

With a burst of energy stemming from pure rage, his eyes glowing red at the corners, Rai tried in vain to lunge at Kobal, to rip his throat from the rest of his body. "Let me off this wall, bitch—I'll give you something to smile about!" he screamed.

Laughing hysterically at the futile gesture, Kobal backed up a few feet, out of range of the chains that bound his captive. For now, all Rai could do was slump back against the wall in defeat and humiliation.

"So, Azreal—tell me all that has happened above," Kobal said, still smiling.

"Here's the situation," Azreal said, turning to face Kobal. "Gabriel has two plans in motion right now. One is a full-on assault of your pens. The other is a strike force that's been put together through the divine vision of Israfil. Apparently, Rai and his friend—"

"Valafor," Kobal cut in.

"Whoever. Apparently they are both to be part of this elite force to retake Earth. If I were you I would kill this little bitch quickly. Israfil's vision has never been wrong, and there's no reason to feel it would be wrong now. Also, you should warn your forces in the pens about the oncoming assault so they can stand ready for it."

Looking at Azreal as if he were an idiot, Kobal said, "If I kill him now, then fun time is over. No, he shall live a little longer. Perhaps his friend will come back to claim him, although I doubt that." Kobal started to laugh thinking of the ridiculous battle that had taken place just hours before, in his throne room. "As for the pens, they are more than prepared to handle a few angels. Leonard and Azazel are both there, with a legion of goat demons and a handful of dark mages. No, no—I think they will be fine."

"For your sake, they had better be," Azreal said before turning to leave. He took one last glance at Rai, who was hanging from the wall, most of the fight drained from his body. "You should kill him, Kobal," Azreal said simply, shaking his head with an arrogant grin. Then he walked out the door.

As he made his way back through the hallway and up the stairs to a more pleasant area, Azreal began thinking of the next stage in his devious plans. Yes, he had aligned himself with Hell, but in the end it would be neither Hell nor Gabriel who would emerge as the victor. Eventually he would kill Kobal and the rest of the demon lords across the land and retake the Earth under his name. Those whom he deemed unfit to live under his specifications would be hunted down and exterminated.

It was a dangerous game he was playing, he knew that, but he was the angel of death, and his power in battle was unmatched.

As he stepped outside past the golem sentinels, Azreal surveyed the landscape. There wasn't much to look at in Hell. Everything was mostly dry, jagged rock, with some geysers of flame and the occasional small demon running around, doing whatever. To look around, you certainly wouldn't think that there were hundreds of thousands of demons inhabiting the place.

He looked up to find the highest point of the castle, somewhere he could be alone to sort out his thoughts. Spotting the perfect place, he effortlessly unfurled his white wings to their full span and began to flap steadily, gradually gaining altitude. Seconds later he landed on the highest balcony, where he could see for miles around. Off in the distance he saw hordes of demon soldiers, probably marching up to Earth to reinforce the forces already in place.

No doubt about it, Azreal had his work cut out for him. Now he just had to find a way to deal with Krillion's little band of warriors.

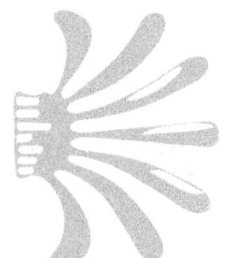 

Chapter 25

NERVOUS AND EXCITED, SHE COULD hear her heart pounding over the noise of the rushing wind in her face. A million thoughts raced through her mind—the main one being that their plan of attack on the pens had already gone to shit, and they hadn't even begun.

First the attack on Gabriel had taken him out of the fight and delivered a massive, demoralizing blow to the Seraphim. Then all their heavy hitters headed to Hell to free commander Krillion's twin brother instead of flying to help free their brethren and the humans from the pens. Due to these unforeseen disasters, she had been placed in charge of the assault. Captain Raziel—leading the forces of the Seraphim to battle.

The plan was a simple one: eliminate the enemy on contact and save as many captives as possible, human and angel. And in a way it made sense for her to lead the charge. After all, it was her scout group that had initially found the camp during their trip to Earth to do recon and search for survivors.

The last time she laid eyes upon this unholy area, she had wanted to rush down to the compound and kill every demon in there with her bare hands. Now she and her brethren would have their chance to mete out swift vengeance together. For what seemed like ages, the warriors of Heaven had been dealt crushing blow after crushing blow, defeat after defeat falling upon their burdened shoulders. Now was time to turn the tide, time to strike back at the very personification of evil. Still, as much as she wanted to fly full-strength toward their unsuspecting prey and rend flesh from bone, she knew that would be a mistake. It would only exhaust her troops before the fight even started.

Raziel stretched out her wings and began to descend in a graceful circle. Following behind her, a legion and a half began their silent descent, too.

Once on the ground, Raziel looked around to assess the situation. Earth wasn't much to look at anymore. The longer the demons stayed there, the more their evil and hatred killed everything good and pure. By now the ground was bare of all life, plant and animal. This particular area had become a dismal land of blackened rock, and nothing more.

Motioning the other captains forward, Raziel knelt on the dusty, hard ground. She picked up a rock and began to sketch a rough outline in the dirt. It was the final attack plan.

"The pens are located here," she said, drawing a square. "Cassiel, you'll take your archers up here, along this ridgeline. Remember, you'll get off three shots at most before the mages below act, so make them all count and pick your targets wisely. Captain Sandalphon, you will be with me, leading the charge through the front gates." She drew arrows indicating the planned path of the ground forces. "Cassiel, as soon as the mages get involved, drop bows and rush them for close combat. The more distance between you and them, the deadlier they are to your unit. They have to be taken out as fast as possible." Raziel then turned to Tabbris. "Your job will be the hardest. You will take two dozen of your best warriors with you and make your way here," she said, pointing to a square at the far end of the camp.

"What's that?" asked Tabbris, kneeling next to Raziel and studying the diagram.

"That," Raziel said, choking back tears and trying to repress her memories of what happened there, "that is where the angel prisoners get their wings ripped off. We're not going to save all of them, but if we can stop one more from being tortured, then we'll take it. After that, see what you can do about unlocking the prisoners in the cages surrounding the fire in the center of the camp."

Raziel looked around at the warriors on either side of her, wondering if this would be the last time she talked to any of them again. This was it, then—the final push of the Seraphim to restore some small amount of light to the earthly realm.

"Any questions? No? All right, we attack on my signal. You all have fifteen minutes to get into place. May the All-Father watch over us all," Raziel said, standing up. Then she walked over to the captain of the guards, leaning her head in close to him. "Captain Sandalphon, can I talk with you a moment?" she asked in soft tones.

Sandalphon was always looked upon as a father figure by the younger warriors, someone they could talk to if they needed it. And right now, Raziel needed it. "Sure, child," Sandalphon said as he led her a little ways away from the group. Once they stopped, he looked deep into her eyes and said, "You're scared, aren't you?"

Her eyes wide, the burden of leadership apparent on her young face, Raziel responded with a slight grin. "Am I that transparent?"

"Lass, I've seen the look you now wear a hundred times," Sandalphon said. "Yes, we have a tough day ahead of us, and not all of us are going make it through. But you were placed here to lead this battle by Commander Krillion, which means he saw the strength you have inside you." He clasped her arms in his hands. "Just follow your instincts and keep your mind focused, girl. All will right itself before this battle is through."

Raziel wrapped her arms around his waist in a tight hug. "Thank you," she said. Then, letting go and stepping back from the veteran captain, Raziel looked up into his face. She saw the fierce determination implanted there from years of battle and hardship.

"Let's do what we came here to do, girl," he said. And they walked back together to begin the attack.

† † †

Captain Cassiel rounded up her half legion of archers and flew up and around the far outskirts of the camp, well beyond the view of the camp's occupants and the range of the illumination pulsating from the inferno burning in the camp's center. Once atop the ridge, she gave the signal to hover. Floating in the air, their bodies wrapped in the cloak of darkness due to the absence of the sun, the archers scanned the floor below them. Cassiel immediately saw what she was looking for.

There were three lookout points on the ridgeline, each manned by two goat demons. That meant the demons really didn't think an attack was imminent.

Now all Cassiel had to do was eliminate them in the next eleven minutes and get her men set up and ready for the call to arms. Signaling forth twelve of the scouts closest to her, she instructed them to fan out to each observation post and fire directly into the guards' necks.

Four warriors, four arrows—two per neck as a fail-safe. They had no room for error. To lose the element of surprise would be exceptionally detrimental to the angels' victory. "Retrieve your arrows and make sure they're dead. Go, you have two minutes," Cassiel whispered.

Moments after the scouts disappeared into the darkness, Cassiel heard the sound of bowstrings snapping and the guards' bodies falling to the ground. She gave the signal to spread out along the ridgeline, and her archers landed with a silent, deadly grace. Their feet touched earth, and they dropped to their stomachs and began inching their way to the edge, where they could peer down at the camp below.

Even though she had been told of the horrors that went on in the camp, she discovered that hearing the tales and seeing the sights were two entirely different things. Within seconds of looking down, Cassiel was consumed by a whirlwind of emotions. Sadness, despair, hopelessness, anger, and rage radiated through her. Her stomach was in knots at the sight of so many humans and fallen angels treated with so little dignity. For a split second, she wondered how the All-Father could have allowed this atrocity to happen.

The humans and angels were housed in numerous cages that formed a horseshoe shape in the very center of the small camp. In one corner of the compound was a holding pen full of creatures that resembled humans but whose proportions were all wrong. "Monsters," Cassiel whispered under her breath. Looking toward the front of the camp, she saw what must have been the main body of Azazel's legion. She guessed that there were six to seven hundred crowded around the inside of the gate, while another two hundred or so were walking around the camp, eating, drinking, or having a good laugh tormenting the prisoners.

Then her eye fell on the hellish bonfire at the dead center of the camp, and her pulse raced uncontrollably. She knew what fueled the grisly flames, as well as its symbolic meaning to the surviving prisoners, humans and angels alike. All she could do at this point was hold her anger in check and wait for the signal.

† † †

"Raziel, all troops are ready for the charge. All we need is for you to give the command," Sandalphon said with an air of confidence, steeled for the upcoming bloodshed.

"One more minute," Raziel responded. "I want to make sure Cassiel has her men in full position. I don't want anything to go wrong here."

Despite Raziel's nervousness at being in command of such a major operation, Sandalphon noted that she was handling herself as though she had been doing this for years.

"Horn-bearer, on my mark," Raziel ordered. "Captain Sandalphon, relay to the warriors to ready weapons and prepare for a full frontal assault."

"Blades out," Sandalphon shot down the line in hushed tones.

Raising her arm and taking one last look at Sandalphon, who gave her a wink and smile, Raziel threw her arm down in a slashing motion, giving the signal to the horn-bearer to announce their presence.

† † †

Looking to her left and right up on the ridge, Cassiel saw her archers were ready and just as eager to spill demon blood. She leaned toward the warrior on her left. "Nock arrows, down quivers, and stay alert," she whispered. As her command was passed down the line in hushed tones, she silently pulled one of three arrows from her quiver and gracefully unlatched a quick-release strap, pulling her quiver from her back and laying it on the ground.

It was deathly quiet as the archers lay flat upon the ridge, soon to rain cold, steel death down on their hated enemies. Time slowed to a crawl; the seconds seemed like hours. And then Cassiel heard it.

From off in the distance came the sweetest sound she could hear, a sound that sent shivers down her spine, tingling every nerve in her body. The call to battle! Instincts and training taking over, Cassiel jumped to her feet followed by the hundreds under her command. "Fire!" she yelled with all the air in her lungs.

Inside the camp on the ravine floor, hundreds of demon eyes looked around in wild amazement at the single note that echoed through the still air. The demons that looked up at the dark sky could just make out the silhouettes of the deadly arrow shafts cutting through the air, on course to fulfill their destiny.

"Battle positions! We're under attack!" a goat demon yelled.

Scurrying around like ants, the demons ran to draw their weapons and seek shelter from the hail of death speeding their way. The noise was deafening as hundreds of arrows streaked through the air, whistling their song of destruction.

All around the compound, encaged prisoners looked up to see what the commotion was about. It didn't take long for it to dawn on them that the camp was under attack, that their angelic brethren had come to save them from this nightmarish place. Their spirits brightened and morale restored, they knew retribution would be theirs this day. They rushed forward to the rusted cage bars with renewed energy, yelling and trying unsuccessfully to pry open the doors, the noise adding to the demons' shock and horror. The distorted, buzzing screams of the dead and dying could be heard from all directions as arrows found their marks, puncturing skin, muscle, and cartilage. Dozens of goat demons fell in the first volley, with many more wounded—and by the time that volley was complete, the next was well under way.

By this time the element of surprise was gone and the demon captains had begun to pull their troops into ranks to find and eliminate this unseen foe. All over the camp, the sky was exploding in a series of red bursts as the second volley was reduced to mere ashes that fell harmlessly on the demon soldiers below.

Looking down into the camp, Cassiel saw right away what had happened: the masters of the dark arts had stepped in to take firm control of the situation. "Shit," she said.

The number of dead and wounded had not been as great as Cassiel had hoped for, but she had a new mission now, and that was to find and destroy the dark mages. A quick scan of the compound revealed three black-robed demons standing on top of the infamous building in the far corner. She didn't know how many there were in all, but these three would be a good start. "To the building!" she ordered, dropping her bow, drawing her sword, and pointing to their destination.

A high-pitched, gut-wrenching scream from the front gate drew her eyes to the opposite end of the camp, where she saw Raziel leading the frontal assault. Some warriors had stopped to tear down the gate to allow more of them to pass through at once, while most of the others opted to fly up and over the walls themselves. From the few seconds she watched, she already knew it wouldn't be an easy victory. The goat demons had awakened from their initial shock and organized to fight the threat pouring over their walls.

They met Raziel's force with a clash of sword and blood.

Not wasting any more time, Cassiel leapt off the ridge. She folded her wings to her sides, allowing gravity and momentum to take her to a speed at which the mages would have difficulty hitting her with any hurled projectiles. Her warriors followed close behind her. Soon she was within seconds of reaching the top of the building; she would unfurl her wings at the last possible second to slow her descent. By now her sword arm was shaking, it wanted to spill demon blood so badly.

Suddenly, in a flash of light, a massive red dome appeared over the entire rooftop, forming what appeared to be an impenetrable wall.

"Fly through—smash it! We must kill them," she yelled over her shoulder, never taking her eyes off her prey below. Flying as one, hundreds of angel warriors, including Cassiel, smashed against the sides of the red dome. But instead of breaking through it to their targets inside, their bodies crumpled and began sliding down the side of the dome, the impact shattering their bones and faces, spraying blood in all directions. All air forced from her lungs, her vision blurred, Cassiel could barely manage to control her wings enough to catch slight air current and slow her plummet to earth.

The warriors a little ways behind her, as well as those in the last row, saw their brethren crumple into heaps of flesh and armor upon the red dome, and they slowed in time to avoid impact. They immediately took defensive measures and reached out to grab the wounded angels from the air and help them to the ground.

Cassiel felt like she'd been tumbling head over feet forever before she felt a strong pair of hands grip her tightly. Seconds later she was on the ground, coughing and gasping for air. Although her eyes were still blurry from the initial impact, her hearing was good enough to discern what was going on around her. A foot away from her she heard something she was glad she couldn't see: not all the angels had been able to save someone, and the wounded angels in free fall began to hit the ground with sickening thuds. Rubbing her eyes vigorously, she heard the first body hit, heard the bones crunching, heard the final moan escape the lips of the warrior who wouldn't arise to see another morning.

"Regroup," she coughed, still trying to suck in air. "We have to go in through the building itself."

As her breathing returned to normal and her vision cleared, Cassiel saw that all across the camp, Raziel's ground forces were engaged in a brutal battle with the hordes of Azazel's goat demons. Swords struck metal and demonic organs, and screams of the dying filled the air as demon goat horns pierced angelic flesh. The ground was quickly soaked red with blood.

"Quickly, we have to get inside," Cassiel said to the warriors still with her. At her command they ran straight into the eerie, dark building—and stopped dead in their tracks. Cassiel noticed three things immediately. The first was the dead angel with no eyes and two gaping holes where her wings used to be, suspended from chains attached to the ceiling. The second was the smell of blood and decaying flesh. And the third was the ceiling, which was covered with hundreds of dregs.

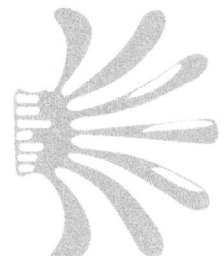 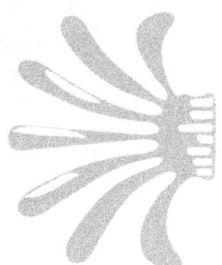

Chapter 26

"So this is Hell?" Zara asked, looking around as she walked through the dismal land.

"No, this is merely the first layer of Hell," Valafor replied. "Think of Hell as an onion: there are layers upon layers to it. Right now we're going through the gates to the first layer. Kobal's castle is located farther in and farther down."

"All right, hold up a minute, guys," Krillion said, turning around to face the group assembled before him. "Valafor, as none of us has ever been here before, you need to fill us in on exactly what we can expect."

Valafor laughed. "Well, you see the big thing in the distance over there?"

Squinting, Zara said, "Oh, you mean that huge mountain?"

"Yeah, that's not a mountain. That's Geryon—he's the guardian of the gate. Before we even get into Hell, were going to have to deal with him, and he don't like me," Valafor said with a chuckle, rubbing his blackened right arm. "Once that's done with, we might run across a few minions, but they shouldn't be a problem. Most of the forces should be up on Earth right now. Inside the castle itself, Kobal has golems and dregs everywhere. That's when the real fun starts."

"Enough talking already. Let's just go get your brother, Krillion," Kane said, looking bored.

"All right, Val," Krillion said, "You know this guy up here? What's the best way to take him out?"

"There's only one way to handle Geryon," Valafor said, flexing his right arm so it erupted with tiny cracks and shot an astounding blue light in all directions. Zara could only stare in amazement as she felt the awesome power radiating from him. *No wonder we lost,* she thought.

"All right, then," Krillion said, un-strapping his massive war hammer.

Zara followed suit by brandishing two slender, short swords, which she twirled with ease, weaving a deadly pattern in the air.

"We do this quick and fast. Let's go!" Krillion said. And they turned and walked in the direction of the mammoth figure off in the distance.

† † †

Geryon was manning his usual post as guardian of Hell. It was a position that had been appointed by Lucifer himself, and one that Geryon took very seriously.

As he was sliding a sharpening stone with concise strokes up one side of his massive claymore sword and down the other, he glanced up and saw four figures walking across the land straight toward him. Dropping the stone to the ground and resting the weight of his sword upon his left shoulder, he walked over to stand directly in front of the towering gate.

Geryon recognized Valafor immediately, but the other three were new to him. The wings on their backs told him two were angels; the third looked human, but with a strange red tint. When the four were within hearing distance, Geryon called out, "So the little demon come back to play again." He spoke with a sneer, goading Valafor to finish what he'd almost started the last time they met.

No words came from the four figures, who now stood just a short distance away from the mighty centaur; instead a massive beam of blue energy shot forth from Valafor's right arm, streaking through the air straight at Geryon's chest. Caught off guard, Geryon clenched the hilt of his sword and gritted his teeth, taking the full brunt of the blast. A cloud of smoke arose from his body, and the smell of burned flesh filled the air. "That's not going to stop him," Valafor remarked as the smoke began to drift away.

And he was right. Geryon emerged from what remained of the smoke cloud with his massive claymore gripped in both hands. His chest was singed where the blast had hit him, but he looked otherwise unaffected—besides being royally pissed off.

"Go!" Krillion yelled, rushing Geryon with his hammer poised, ready to strike down the behemoth creature. Kane took flight to get an aerial advantage, but as he gained height he saw a dozen screeching dregs racing his way.

Running full-speed to keep up with Krillion, Zara grabbed the blade of the dagger strapped across her chest and whipped it in the direction of their foe. Flying end over end, the dagger found its mark deep in Geryon's shoulder—but if he felt it, it didn't show. Instead, when Krillion was within striking distance, Geryon reared up on his hind legs, clasped his sword in both hands, and raised it above his head, ready to cleave Krillion in two.

Krillion held his hammer crossways in front of him, blocking Geryon's sword with the handle. For all Krillion's size and power, the kinetic force unleashed as the two weapons met rattled his teeth.

"So tell me while I kill you all," Geryon snarled, bearing his great weight down upon Krillion, "What would angels be doing in Hell with a demon?"

Zara saw her opening clear as day. As Geryon was engaged with Krillion, she let loose her wings, flying fast and low to the ground straight toward her target. Speeding through the small space between the battling figures, she raked one of her short swords across the rib cage of the huge centaur, drawing blood.

Meanwhile, Valafor ran behind Geryon and hopped onto the massive horse body. "I'll tell you what we're doing here, horse," Valafor yelled as tried to pull back Geryon's huge arm to take some of the strain off of Krillion, who was slowly lowering to his knees. "But first … you … have to die!"

High above the ground, Kane was having troubles of his own. As the first of the dregs closed in on him, he pointed his arms in the direction of the oncoming demons and let loose a burst of red energy, cutting through the dregs' bodies as though they were made of paper.

But two dregs managed to latch onto his back, clawing and biting the much larger Kane, trying to bring this new foe down. Slowly the weight began to take its toll on him, and he began to lose altitude. As more and more dregs piled on top of him, their plummet became faster and far more dangerous. A bright red aura emanated from Kane's body, slipping out through the mass of leathery wings and tangled limbs until it looked as if a giant ball of fire were hurtling to the ground.

Disoriented, Kane tumbled head over feet, gaining ever more speed on his deadly descent. He struggled in vain to free himself; with every second that passed, he felt new bites and cuts on his body. Finally, in a state of complete panic, he began to flail his arms and legs like a madman, trying to knock the determined creatures off him. Through the mob of their small bodies, he could see that the ground was fast approaching.

Zara was circling through the air, heading back into the fight with Geryon, when she saw Kane falling fast. Tucking one wing close against her back, she veered off in his direction, praying that she wouldn't be too late.

She hadn't known Kane very long, but when she first laid eyes on him, something struck her deep in her heart. As she gazed deep into his eyes, she saw a man torn, a man consumed by a tornado of emotions. Here was a man who had never had the chance to see where his destiny would take him. Instead, Gabriel and the council had decided to place him in Purgatory, for fear that his kind would become too powerful and destroy the Earth. Once promised the world, Kane had been ripped from his short existence on Earth, never having known love or acceptance. His was a bitter fate that Zara would have wished upon no one.

Zara saw past all of that, though, into the heart and soul of the man himself. Something about Kane intrigued her to an extent that she wasn't ready to lose him—not if she had any say in the matter.

Valafor had by now given up on Geryon's right arm and wrapped both his hands around the centaur's massive neck, pulling with all his might. Finally Valafor wrenched the centaur's thick neck back, giving Krillion the chance to regain his footing and assert his power over Geryon. "You will never beat me!" yelled Geryon. The centaur was trying to reach behind him to pull Valafor off, but all he received for his futile effort was repeated blows to his head from Valafor. Meanwhile Krillion took a small step back from Geryon and then rushed in close again, this time ramming the head of his war hammer straight into the centaur's gut.

The combined assault by Valafor and Krillion sent Geryon into a primal rage. The human side of him lost over to the base urges of survival from his animal side, and it seemed to Krillion and Valafor that the centaur's strength increased drastically.

"Away from me!" snorted Geryon as he backhanded Krillion, sending him sailing through the air. Krillion landed hard a few feet away from the fight. Then, moving impossibly quickly for a creature so big, Geryon snatched at Valafor, who was trying to dig his claws into his thick neck. The centaur yanked Valafor off his back as if he were a child and held him by his left arm, letting him dangle high in the air. "You are dead, scum!" Geryon said, drawing back a clenched fist to unleash the full force of his mighty strength directly into Valafor's face.

Struggling to free himself from the centaur's monstrous grip, Valafor aimed his weapon arm at Geryon's face and grinned. "Don't count on it, bitch!" he said. The energy he released blasted Geryon point-blank in the face. The centaur dropped Valafor, who fell to the floor and rolled away.

As Geryon put his hands to his face, screaming in pain and thrashing wildly, Krillion was just rising to his feet. "Valafor, you good?" he asked, running over to help his new and unlikely teammate.

"We need to finish this now," Valafor choked, shaking his arm to restore blood to the weakened limb.

The pair ran full-speed at Geryon, Krillion's war hammer raised up and Valafor's blackened arm shooting beams of blue light everywhere.

Just then, Kane and his dreg passengers hit the ground with enough force to leave a huge crater and send tremors rippling in all directions.

With no thoughts of her own safety, Zara flew right into the dust cloud that had erupted from the fresh, gaping hole in the ground. As she neared the center of the crater, she saw Kane trying to rise to his feet, one of the dregs still clinging to him. Soaring past Kane at a sharp angle, Zara plunged her sword into the dreg's soft neck. Its head hit the ground before its lifeless body did, squirting blood all over Kane.

Shaking himself off, trying to clear the cobwebs from his vision, Kane limped over to a dreg that was still alive but unable to move, moaning in pain. Placing his hands on both sides of the demon's head, Kane focused, allowing his uncanny power to surge through his body and arms and into the head of the immobile dreg. Shrieking in agony, the dreg writhed, trying feebly to get away and kicking small dust clouds in the dirt. A second later its head exploded all over Kane's arms and chest, spraying its dark red liquid that covered everything within a two-foot radius.

As Kane breathed in huge gulps of air, trying to calm his body from its adrenaline rush, he looked around for Zara, who was hovering in the air, looking down at him with concern. Focusing his energies once more, he propelled himself into the air where she was waiting for him.

"You should be more careful, Kane—I might not always be around to save you," Zara said playfully.

The two of them locked eyes, oblivious to everything going on below them. Kane's heart was beating a mile a minute and his face darkened as if he were blushing. As he reached out to take Zara's hand in his, the silence was broken from below by savage screams of outrage and pain. Looking down, they spotted Krillion and Valafor running side by side toward Geryon, who was still clutching his smoking face.

As the duo ran, Valafor took a half step and leapt into the air, while Krillion charged straight from the ground.

"We have to go," Kane said, watching the battle rage.

He felt warm lips on his cheek as Zara kissed him quickly and then shot to the ground, pulling another dagger from her belt. Stunned, Kane placed his hand on his cheek, his heart pounding. He had never been kissed before. Strange new thoughts and emotions took hold of him as he watched Zara's body speed toward the massive figure of Hell's guardian. Then he shook his head to clear it of all thoughts besides those of battle, and his arms shot out to either side of his body as it became a streak of red, heading to help finish this fight.

Krillion, meanwhile, had quickly covered the ground between himself and his foe, bringing his massive hammer up and over his right shoulder. Then he swung with all the force he could muster in the hopes of bringing the monstrous beast to its knees. As the head of his hammer hit Geryon's chest, Krillion heard the snap of bones and cartilage and then a small hissing of air. Geryon fell to one front knee, unable to breathe properly with one collapsed lung, and Valafor again jumped on his back and started ripping and clawing at him like a beast caught in the grip of madness.

Just then a blade flew just inches over Valafor's head to sink into Geryon's shoulder blade. Following close behind was Zara, who flew low to plunge both her short swords deep into Geryon's rear hamstrings, crippling his back legs. Meanwhile Kane landed near the centaur's front leg, which was still partially upright, and gripped it with both hands. Glowing bright red, Kane pulled with all his strength.

"Krillion," Kane grunted through his exertion.

Dropping his hammer and running to Kane's side, Krillion also wrapped his massive hands around the leg. Sweat formed on the brows of the two combatants as they continued to pull. A popping sound followed by a ripping noise was all they needed to renew their energies, as the leg slowly started to detach from the torso of the horse body. Loud, bloodcurdling cries erupted from Geryon's mouth, piercing the air as, with a last surge of power, Krillion and Kane ripped the huge leg from his gargantuan frame. Veins and arteries stretched between the severed leg and the torso, bright red and dripping with blood. Finally, Geryon's screams became weak, pitiful moans, and his body slumped to the ground on its side.

Valafor jumped off Geryon's back and stood covered in sweat and breathing heavily. Zara came to land next to him, her swords drawn in the event that the monster still wasn't done. She let her arms relax from the weight of her swords, and blood began dripping down the polished metal.

So many injuries at once had left Geryon's body in a state of shock. Muscle spasms rippled through him like little waves hitting the beach. Krillion's team stood before the monstrous centaur, this guardian of Hell, victorious. Then he walked over to retrieve his hammer, grasping it directly under the head, and returned to stand before their fallen enemy. "For Rai," he whispered.

Krillion brought the hammer straight up in the air and down onto the skull of Geryon.

"Holy shit—that was intense," Valafor said, a smile of satisfaction on his face. "Hope everyone is all right, 'cause we still have to deal with Kobal and his lackeys."

"I'm good," Zara said. She was standing a few feet away from Kane, staring at him with wide blue eyes, trying to wipe some of the blood from her twin blades.

The red aura around Kane had dimmed considerably; the bite marks and cuts on his body were clearly visible. "I got a little torn up, but nothing major," he said, trying to shake off bits of gristle and blood.

"Okay, Valafor, you take point. We need to make up time due to this setback," Krillion said. "Follow me and stay alert—two angels and a red man are going to have a hard time blending in around here."

"For all we know, word is already out about me," Valafor said with an evil chuckle. As he walked away, he relaxed his right arm; its blue energy slowly started to fade as the weapon sealed itself, locking the deadly power within.

The group followed Valafor past the gate and the mutilated corpse of its guardian. "Just a little longer, Rai," Krillion whispered to no one in particular, surveying the desolate land stretching before him.

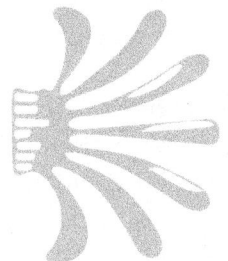 

Chapter 27

ALL AROUND THE CAMP, THE minions of Azazel were in a confused frenzy. They'd been shocked to see the enemy army flying toward the front gate, weapons drawn, from the seemingly empty landscape, while deadly arrows flew at them from above. The precious seconds Cassiel bought with her efforts were all Raziel and her warriors needed to breach the outer walls and front gate and enter this hideous compound of nightmares come to life.

After the first fatal minutes, however, the demons began to grasp their situation and launch an organized counteroffensive.

These insights and more were racing through Raziel's mind as she parried with a goat demon that smelled like it had never had a bath or even fallen into a pool of water. Being much smaller than her foe, Raziel had to rely on her speed and sword skills to stay alive and one step ahead of her opponent. Ducking a clumsy sword slash to her chest, Raziel jumped backward into the air, allowing her wings to momentarily suspend her as she threw her blade straight into the face of the vile demon before her.

Her aim was true; the sword found its mark, burying itself at an angle between the demon's eyes and down the side of its snout. Continuing to hover, Raziel studied the whole battle scene; finally she spied the infamous building at the far end of the camp where her brothers and sisters in arms were being mutilated and tortured.

"Tabbris!" she yelled, scanning the crowd for him.

She spotted Captain Tabbris a little ways away, on the sidelines of the main fighting. He and his two dozen warriors were attempting to sneak undetected around the melee and carnage. Their job was an especially important one: they were to make their way to the building and free whoever was in it, and then find a way to unlock all the cages, freeing the captured angels and humans trapped inside them to bolster their ranks. Even though the angels had lost the initial war and Hell dominated Earth, it was still their sacred duty to protect and shield the humans from the influences of Hell's minions.

"Tabbris, fly now!" Raziel yelled, and pointing toward the building. Seeing Raziel hovering above the battle, Tabbris couldn't make out what she was yelling, but he understood what she was pointing at and took action. Twenty-five angels at once jumped into the air, speeding straight for the building at the far end of the camp. Seconds later they had landed in front of the hideous structure, allowing their senses to absorb everything around them.

The limp bodies of their fellow angels lay scattered about the tower, their facial expressions a mix of pain and confusion. Their limbs were twisted in such an unnatural way that Tabbris's men could hardly bear to lay eyes upon them. Pools of blood had formed around the unfortunate angels who had fallen to their death, and blood still gushed from their eyes and mouths. Here and there among the disfigured bodies, bones poked through skin like spikes, causing such swelling and discoloration that their fallen comrades looked like they had been there for days instead of minutes.

"Captain Tabbris!" one of his men called. "Do you hear that coming from inside?"

It was hard to hear anything with the sounds of battle and screams everywhere, but as Tabbris neared the door, he heard all too clearly the unmistakable sound of dregs and the battle cries of Cassiel's archers. "This is it men," Tabbris said. "Once inside, our mission comes first, Cassiel's group second. Stick together, look out for one another, and pay attention to the space above us. Any questions?"

Without another word, they dashed through the door and into a scene of carnage and chaos. Angels and dregs everywhere were engaged in a symphony of death. Bodies covered most of the floor, but upon closer inspection the angels determined that they were dregs, with only a handful of angels scattered among them.

"There in the center, Captain," one of Tabbris's men said, pointing toward the female angel who hung suspended from the ceiling.

"She's dead," Tabbris said. "We can do nothing for her." Then, with renewed purpose, Tabbris yelled, "Spread out! Help Cassiel's men! We will not lose this fight, men!" With a mighty war cry pledging his allegiance to the Seraphim and the oath, Tabbris led his men into the thick of combat, joining Cassiel's archers to end the life of all dregs in the building.

Knowing that Tabbris was on his way to his target, Raziel had to retrieve her own weapon from the goat demon's cloven head and make her way back down to the fight. From the air, she couldn't tell which side was winning. Her warriors were everywhere, fighting with an intense passion that burned in their souls, fueled by the loss of the Earth and the devastation the demons had wrought upon mankind and the Seraphim. Taking in one last lungful of clean air, Raziel tucked her wings to her side and rocketed back toward her men and their fate.

Spying a goat demon who was ready to run its sword through an angel sprawled on the ground, Raziel angled her body and wings to head in their direction. With no sword or other weapon available to her, she had to improvise and quickly. The second before impact, she pulled her head up, flung her body back, and stuck both her legs out, landing a powerful kick directly to the spine of the towering demon. She heard and felt the snap of its spine in multiple spots as it let out one last buzzing death scream. Breathing heavily, Raziel never slowed for a second. She flew to the warrior on the ground and knelt down beside him. "Are you okay?" she asked, calm but assertive.

The warrior was clearly shaken up but began to nod his head before yelling, "Captain, look out!" He pushed Raziel out of the way just as a massive spear slid past her and into the soldier's rib cage. Raziel landed on the ground with a hard thud, the air knocked from her again. She could only gasp and watch as the warrior who had just saved her life was lifted into the air on the tip of a spear wielded by an unusually large goat demon.

"Azazel," Raziel said through gritted teeth. She felt anger form in the pit of her stomach, renewing her limbs with unholy energy. One of the most primal forces anywhere in the universe is unbridled, raw rage and hate, and she was about to unleash it all upon the lord of the goat demons.

Standing here before her was a living breathing, testament to why she became a soldier in the Seraphim: a physical being upon which she could unleash all her fiery emotions. As Azazel stood towering over her, staring down and mocking her with his vicious, yellow grin, he drove the opposite end of the spear into the ground with the young warrior still impaled upon it. The warrior screamed in pain, trying in vain to free himself. His body slowly slid down the shaft until it lay pinned to the ground.

Raziel's face flushed with anger, and she rolled out of the way of Azazel's massive hoof as he tried to stomp through her chest. Finishing her roll a foot away, she came up in a crouch, reaching for a discarded spear lying in the dirt near her. "Today, you die, Azazel!" she yelled, flinging the spear at him with all her strength. Her aim was straight and true, but this wasn't just any demon she was fighting: it was Azazel, lord of the goat demons. With one muscular, long arm, he batted the spear away, sending it sailing. Then, arching his back, he let out a mighty roar heard by all over the din of battle.

Raziel took a nervous step backward, unsure of what her next move was going to be. Her mind raced through endless scenarios and their probable outcomes. She had no weapon at her disposal: no sword, no spear, not even an arrow.

Without warning, Azazel leaned down, exposing the gnarled, twisted horns that protruded from the top of his head, and rushed full-force in Raziel's direction. With no other immediate option, Raziel retreated into the throng of warriors still battling around her, hoping to stall and buy herself some time. Her plan was partly successful; she was able to bob and weave her way through the crowd. But Azazel was close behind, clearing a path through angels and demons alike to get to her.

Two Seraphim warriors near Raziel saw Azazel chasing her and came to the aid of their captain. They flanked Azazel, intent on slowing him down, even if it cost them their lives. Both wielded swords dripping with fresh blood from their fallen foes. Their chests heaved from the exertions of battle, sweat covered their brows, yet they stood in the path of this monstrous creature, a tribute to the iron will of the Seraphim.

Time slowed to a crawl as they watched this lord of demons plow through anything and everything to reach their captain. Seconds before the inevitable collision, the warriors exchanged salutes and charged, blades high, ready to give the ultimate sacrifice to their order.

With no mercy or hesitation, Azazel's horns pierced the breastplate of the first angel, breaking through ribs and organs, and then he threw his head back to send the dead warrior sailing to land into the dirt. While Azazel's upper body was exposed, the second warrior seized the opportunity to capitalize on his friend's death. "Die, demon!" the soldier yelled as he brought his sword up, slicing through the tough, hairy hide of Azazel's chest. A trail of blood dripped down the demon's torso.

Adrenaline pumping through his veins, the scent of blood in his nostrils, Azazel never felt the ghastly slash. "You dare to strike me, you fucking wretch!" Azazel snorted in rage, looking down at the angel who had the gall to attack him. "Tonight I will feast upon your bones!" he yelled, walking methodically toward the soldier.

Even in the face of such an intimidating foe, the angelic warrior wouldn't back down. With a final surge of energy and courage, he charged Azazel, sword raised. The demon laughed and caught the angel's wrists in his hairy hand, lifting him off the ground. He watched his captive squirm for a few seconds, and then he reached down, grabbed one of the angel's legs, and lifted him over his head. Consumed by primal rage, he ripped the angel's body in two, throwing the pieces in separate directions, where they hit combatants from both sides.

"Now where's that little bitch?" Azazel said to himself, looking around to see where his prey had run to. The hunt was on. The animal in him would not be sated until Raziel died by his own hands. With a quick scan of the crowds, he spotted her running in the opposite direction. "Playtime," he said aloud, following her with his beady eyes. Then he began thundering after her.

† † †

Across the camp, Captain Sandalphon was leading a group of about thirty angels. A veteran of many battles and campaigns, Sandalphon was in his prime: he was just as much at home here, in the height of battle, as he was back at the Crystal Palace.

He and his men were pushing back a number of demons, who were scattering in all directions from the onslaught of Sandalphon's angelic warriors. "Keep pushing, men! Don't stop till we cut them all down!" Sandalphon yelled, rallying his troops to even greater feats of strength. Fighting past the cages which held the prisoners, he wanted nothing more than to stop and free them—but orders were orders, and his was to ensure the victory of the Seraphim at all costs. The constantly moving battle had brought them to an unusually large clearing in the center of the camp. Ever vigilant from years on the battlefield, it did cross Sandalphon's mind that this space was strangely empty, but he let the thought slip away as his warriors pressed their advantage over their enemies.

The noise was deafening as holy swords continued to pierce demon flesh and the howls of death and destruction rolled through the camp. Then, directly behind the few remaining goat demons, there was a massive explosion of smoke that stopped Sandalphon and his men dead in their tracks. As they coughed and covered their eyes, Sandalphon's first reaction was to step back and regroup in case the demons had enough courage left to charge them through the smoke screen. "Hold," he yelled, coughing and waiting for the smoke to clear. "Defensive positions!" The warriors did as they were instructed.

Then a slight breeze passed them, blowing the dust and smoke away to reveal a sight that sent ice running through the veins of every angel present. While a second ago there had been nothing but empty space around the warriors of light, now there were four figures dressed in black robes. Next to them, floating a few feet off the ground, was a black ball that looked to be made of moving liquid.

But what really captured Sandalphon's attention was the fire burning brightly behind the cloaked figures and the mysterious ball. Prior to the mission, all the warriors had been briefed on the horrors that went on here, and when they saw the fire they all knew immediately what it was and what it represented.

The remaining goat demons laughed in harsh, buzzing voices at this new turn of events. Not only was the angels' offensive push completely stopped, but now they had the master of the dark arts standing next to them.

"Leonard, you snake!" Sandalphon yelled. Here before this small, exhausted group was the master of the dark arts himself. He and his breed had been responsible for countless deaths of humans and angels throughout the ages.

Sandalphon was always confident in his actions, and he wasn't going to second-guess himself now. "Charge—kill them all!" he ordered, and his men reacted with solid discipline, yelling and positioning their swords for killing blows.

A spidery, incoherent sound escaped Leonard's lips, and from the ground directly under the first group of advancing angels burst a wall of hellfire that set ablaze all those unlucky enough to be caught in its deadly flames. The panicked warriors threw their weapons down and began to scatter, trying to douse the unholy flames that ate their flesh and consumed their will to live.

Sandalphon had no choice but to leave them and press his attack. "Fly high and strike down!" he ordered, taking to the skies to pass over the wall of flame. The remaining angels gained height, ready to exact revenge for the brutal deaths of their comrades, and awaited orders. On the ground on the far side of the flames, the ten or so remaining goat demons were now ready to square off against the angels who had almost killed them.

With four dark mages beside them, their courage restored, they gripped their swords and stomped the ground with their hooves in anticipation of the victorious bloodbath they knew would follow. From the ground they yelled their taunts, daring the angels to come down and face them.

Without hesitation, Sandalphon gave the order, and firelight danced on the ground all around the demons, gleaming off two dozen swords rushing to toward them.

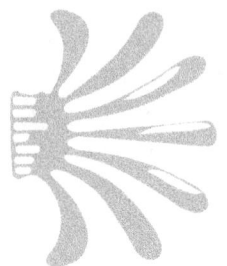 

Chapter 28

HOLDING HIS HAMMER FIRMLY UNDER the head, Krillion and his team made their way through the fiery depths of Hell toward Kobal's castle to free Rai.

The atmosphere in Hell was the very opposite of the blue skies surrounding Heaven and the Crystal Palace. This was nothing more than a baron wasteland of untold horrors. Still, for a land so very dead, it was also very much alive. Screams of pain and agony echoed from all directions from the unfortunates who spent eternity here.

Stopping by a large pillar of rock spiraling up from the ground, Krillion called a halt in their journey through the hot wasteland. The rest of his team caught up with him and gathered around to hear what he had to say.

Krillion stared at each one intently, remembering their victory over the monstrous Geryon. He had to admit that for such an unlikely group, thrown together at the whim of Israfil, they possessed some serious firepower when they combined forces. "All right, guys, here's the lowdown" he said. "We're standing virtually right on top of Kobal's castle. We need a full plan of attack. The last thing we want is to run in half-cocked and end up like Rai." At this he looked at Valafor. "Kane, I need to know what you're capable of in the event that things go south and we need a quick egress. Also if any of you have any doubts about Valafor, now is the time to speak up about it. But after seeing him and fighting alongside him against Geryon"—Krillion paused at this statement, looking at Valafor again and extending his hand—"he has my full trust and confidence."

Staring at Krillion's outstretched hand, Valafor processed a flurry of thoughts: Rai and his turning away from Hell; the fact that he was thrown into a suicide mission with a handful of angels; and Kane, whatever the hell he was. As Valafor brought his gaze level with Krillion's, his mouth spread into a wide grin, showing rows of sharpened teeth, prime for rendering flesh from bone. "We'll see what Rai has to say. Until then you have my word: I'll watch all your backs in the upcoming fight," he said, accepting Krillion's hand in temporary alliance.

Looking pleased, Krillion pulled his hand away and turned his attention to their mysterious companion. "Kane?" he said.

Kane was standing near Zara—a fact that didn't go unnoticed by Krillion. "As far as I know, the only limit to my power is my imagination," Kane said in his monotonous voice. Some of the eyes in their little group widened at the prospect of having so much power their disposal. "The only problem that I've noticed," he said, "is that the more I exert myself, the more drained I become. In essence, I think I'm slowly burning my body out with each use." Kane's voice dropped considerably, adding an almost threatening tone to his next comment. "It seems that in his infinite wisdom, your All-Father had a built-in fail-safe in case I ever became too powerful."

Krillion noticed a sorrowful expression creep up and mar the smooth face of Zara, who was still standing next to Kane. But he had no time to dwell on the implications. Right now, he was utterly focused and insanely driven to save his brother. Krillion addressed the group. "Plain and simple, then, when we reach the castle, we storm it by brute force; we let them know we're here. Anything that gets in our way, we mow down without mercy or regret. Kane, as soon as we have Rai, you teleport all of us to the surface, preferably to the pens, where the battle has undoubtedly already begun. We still have a duty to help our brethren achieve victory. All I ask of any of you is that you don't stop fighting until we've won or we're all dead."

"One more thing," Valafor said, his raspy voice capturing everyone's attention. "Kobal's castle is guarded by golems—large, powerful creatures with a ton of strength but not a lot of quickness or brains," he said, tapping his own temple. "In ones and twos there no big deal, but when in large numbers they have a tendency to overwhelm their enemies in a brutal manner. So don't let them corner you." At this he peered around the rock pillar, looking down at Kobal's castle. "Kane, come with me for a second," he said. "There's something I've been thinkin' about and want to try."

Azreal sat atop the highest point of Kobal's castle, feeling the hot wind rushing through his hair. The sword by which he earned his nickname, the angel of death, sat resting comfortably against his shoulder. Scanning the horizon, Azreal pondered his next move. First he had taken Gabriel out of the picture, and by now the rest of the Seraphim should have realized by his absence that he had committed the violent act. Now all he had to do was remove Kobal from the game while in the presence of his fellow Seraphim, so they would turn to him to lead them through this, their most trying time. Granted, there would still be some warriors loyal to Gabriel, but that was nothing he couldn't handle.

As he contemplated his situation, little figures off in the distance caught his eye. After a few minutes the figures came into sharper focus, and Azreal was taken aback by what he saw. "Well I'll be damned," he said out loud.

Sure as hell, Krillion himself was making his stealthy way across the barren landscape, accompanied by three others, most likely the rest of Israfil's precious team. Now the question arose, Should he tell Kobal or sit back and watch this unforeseen turn of events play out?

After a few moments Azreal stood up, deciding that it would be better for now to keep Kobal as an ally until the time to play his hand presented itself. Grabbing his sword, he stepped off the edge of the tower and fell straight to the ground, gaining speed along the way. Moments before impact, his wings shot out to either side of his body, allowing him to land gracefully. Then he turned and walked into the castle to inform Kobal of this unexpected intrusion.

When their small group was close to the outer walls of the castle, Kane and Valafor glanced at each other and Kane began levitating. As Kane focused his energy, weaving his uncanny power between his hands, a small red globe began to materialize. On the ground below, Krillion and Zara flanked the group, serving as lookouts for approaching demons as their teammates brought their plan to life.

As the red ball of energy grew in size in between Kane's hands, Valafor's blackened right arm burst to life, emitting blue energy in all directions. When the red globe grew to the size of a small boulder, Kane gave it a shove and Valafor, below, aimed his weapon arm and unleashed a torrent of energy that hit the globe and was absorbed, the colors clashing in a potent, swirling mass of devastating energy.

"Golems on the left—let's speed it up, guys," Zara said, pointing to the castle. Golems were heading toward them from the castle, intent on protecting their master from the interlopers.

The globe was radiating an immense amount of power. Valafor and Kane continued combining their powers to supersaturate it, and when it was filled to the point of exploding, Kane gave it a forceful push to sending the swirling, multicolored orb hurtling toward the castle wall. There was a brief calm as the few golems standing outside stared in awe at the globe flying overhead. Then it smashed squarely into the wall. The resulting explosion was so great that the castle wall came crashing down like a house of cards on a windy day. Large chunks of rock and debris shattered everywhere, ripping into the golems as though they were made of paper.

Hovering in the air above the destruction, Kane marveled at how well Valafor's plan had worked. Not only had the enemies outside the castle been reduced to a near unrecognizable state, but now there was a brand-new door into the castle itself.

Taking advantage of every second of the confusion, Krillion called a charge through the hole and into the castle, praying they were not too late. As they started running toward the gaping hole, dregs shot forth from it, screeching their rage at the beings responsible for the devastation around them. Since he was already airborne, Kane decided they were his, and he angled right for them, his red aura growing brighter by the second.

"Zara—with Kane. Meet up inside. Go," Krillion ordered. Without a word, Zara burst into a dead sprint and jumped, pushing off the ground to gain the few feet of altitude she needed to unfurl her wings and join the oncoming battle above.

Valafor and Krillion ran side by side past the remains of the broken wall, hopping over random pieces of debris in the process. "Stay with me at all times," Krillion said. "We must not show a divided front!"

"You got it, Krill," Val replied.

As they neared the hole in the castle, two golems hopped out of the opening. Raising his weapon arm, Valafor let loose two blue beams which hit both golems square in the chest. Without missing a step, Krillion ran directly into the castle and then stopped short, not knowing where to go.

"Follow me. We have to find the stairs down to the dungeon. That's where Rai will be," Valafor said, passing Krillion and turning down an empty hallway in search of the stairwell that would lead them to his best friend. Krillion rounded the next corner to find Valafor standing a few feet inside a large room. As Krillion came to stand beside his teammate, a shrill laugh rang out, echoing across the room.

"Oh look, Azreal, the little monkey has come back—and he brought a friend," Kobal said, taunting Valafor.

Krillion followed the sound of the voice until his eyes found Kobal sitting atop his throne of demented, smiling skulls. He had a fairly humanoid form compared to most other demons. His skin was dark, but it was his face that caught Krillion's attention: it appeared to have been mutilated, carved into a frozen smile. Kobal sported a dark-green mohawk that extended from the top of his head down his back in a ponytail. Next to Kobal stood Azreal. Krillion's blood boiled over at the sight of the traitor standing before him; his tactical prowess was overtaken by vengeful madness.

Directly surrounding the throne itself were golems and grisly skeletons, fallen warriors of times past, resurrected by Leonard to serve Kobal for eternity.

"Azreal, you're dead bitch!" Krillion shouted, pointing his hammer at the angel of death. His eyes were murderous.

"Let's go," was all Azreal said, ominously quiet.

His mind clouded by an unsurpassed rage, Krillion ran straight toward the traitor responsible for bringing down Gabriel. Nothing would stop him from crushing Azreal's head.

† † †

Outside the castle, the aerial battle was fully engaged. Zara was flying back and forth between the dregs, using her deadly twin swords with uncanny precision to sever heads from shoulders and limbs from bodies. There were a few dozen dregs in all, but as long as they couldn't use their strength in numbers, they weren't much of a threat.

Meanwhile Kane was soaring through the air, leaving a trail of bloodied, lifeless dregs in his wake. Out of the corner of her eye, Zara saw a dreg flying directly behind Kane, intent on bringing him down to the ground. Battle instincts assuming command of her motions, Zara reached to pull a dagger from her belt, intent upon ending the dreg before it could reach Kane. Her hand hit empty space as the realization hit that she had never retrieved her daggers from their fight with Geryon.

"Shit," she scolded herself, altering her flight. She had no choice but to try to intercept the dreg before its lethal claws found their mark in Kane's back.

As she flew around the outskirts of a castle tower, her wings propelling her to maximum speed, she realized that she wouldn't make it in time and that Kane still did not know he was being trailed. Pushing her wing muscles to the point of failure, she yelled as loudly as she could between deeps breaths. "Kane!"

No response. He was so absorbed in the fighting that he was oblivious to her pleas. Then it happened: the dreg slammed into Kane hard, knocking the wind out of him and providing an opening for the rest of the little beasts to take full advantage.

It didn't take long for the dregs to see this opportunity and capitalize on it. Once again, Kane was fighting off too many dregs while trying to keep himself airborne. And Zara was still pushing herself to make it to him before they began to plummet. Just a few more seconds and she would be able to—

From Zara's left came a force that sent her hurtling through the air, completely away from Kane; she had been so absorbed in saving her teammate that she didn't see a dreg closing in on her from the side.

Kane had no choice: grabbing as many dregs as he could, he shot himself through the air toward the castle at an alarming speed. He spotted an existing hole in one part of the ceiling and headed toward that.

Extending one wing out to her side, Zara was able to stabilize her body and regain control of her flight. Turning her head, she saw her attacker flying straight for her again, its outstretched arms ending in savage claws. The dreg's mouth opened in a desperate wail of anger and bloodlust, dripping saliva from the corners of its lips. Then it charged with a fresh burst of speed.

Zara met the creature head-on, plunging a bloody blade through the foul demon's gut. Within minutes, its high-pitched screams faded into moans. Zara kicked the dying creature off her blade and it fell onto the tower beneath her, rolling off to land in a distorted heap of limbs and organs. Looking around, Zara realized there were no more enemies in her way. She turned her head in a panic, looking for Kane, and by the grace of the All-Father saw his faint red energy trail. Taking a deep breath, she followed it into the castle.

Inside, Krillion was lost in a rage, his eyes bloodshot with hate, swinging his hammer around with the full force of his mountainous muscles.

The skeletal warriors that surrounded the throne were more grotesque than threatening. Due to the unnatural reanimated state of their bones, they didn't move fluidly, which made them easy for the duo to eliminate.

"Krillion—on your left!" Valafor yelled, jumping away from a rusty sword that barely missed his chest. But in his bloodlust Krillion didn't hear his teammate or notice the golem looming up to him. "Krillion! On your fuckin' left!" Valafor yelled again.

Krillion was weapon-locked with a skeleton wielding a spear. Letting go of his hammer with one hand, he clenched his fist and sent it straight into the dead warrior's face, which exploded in a small cloud of dust. As the skeleton's body fell motionless to the floor, Krillion gripped his hammer tight and slammed it into the abdomen of the approaching golem.

Azreal was watching this impressive display of skill from Krillion, the notoriously unstoppable angel, when the throne room went red and Kane and a host of dregs shot through the hole in the ceiling.

Right before they hit, Kane stopped in midair, sending all his passengers crashing to the ground with such force that their bones snapped. Kane floated above the throne, looking down upon Kobal, Azreal, and the few minions still alive as if they were nothing more than insects and he was an evil ten-year-old with a magnifying glass. "Valafor, go find Rai," he said. "We'll wrap this up." Kane was burning brighter by the second, the air around him crackling with energy.

As Valafor turned and ran to find Rai, Zara came through the hole, shooting past Kane like an arrow, heading straight for Azreal. Her twin blades, smeared with the blood of fallen foes, were trained on his blackened heart. "Zara, no!" Kane screamed, but he was too late to stop her. With a quickness that defied the eyes, Azreal drew his infamous sword in his right hand, parrying both Zara's blades simultaneously while spinning his body around and catching a handful of her black hair in his left hand, jerking her to the ground.

Zara's swords flew from her hands, clattering to the stone floor several feet away. She hit the floor hard with Azreal still holding her hair. He had his sword in a reverse grip, daring Krillion or Kane to step forward.

Kobal was up and jumping around, laughing at this new turn of events; the few skeletons and golems that were left retreated as Kane's power started pulsing out of him in waves. Kane had no love for the Seraphim for what they had done to him, but the sight of Zara being held at the whim of this single renegade angel buried his concern about expending his power.

† † †

Valafor exited the throne room and sprinted down random hallways, looking for a way down to the dungeons. As he rounded a corner, he came up behind a skeleton guard who was standing in front of a door on the left side of the hallway. Without missing a step, Valafor brought his weapon arm down through the skeleton's shoulder, straight through its ribs, and down through what once was its abdomen. The guard crumpled into a heap in seconds.

Valafor moved to the solid wooden door, slowly turned the handle, and pushed the door open, peering down a dark stairwell into the unknown below.

"Jackpot," he whispered.

He proceeded cautiously down the winding steps, guided only by the light from his arm, trying to be as quiet as possible in the silent passage. He didn't want to run headlong into the darkness in case the bottom was crawling with golems or dregs or whatever Kobal had lurking about.

Once he reached the bottom he found a single hallway, its only visible door on the far end about twenty feet away. The hallway was clear except for a few fading torches that provided minimal lighting. Walking quickly down the hall, his guard up, Valafor made it to the door unchallenged and unchecked.

So far so good, he thought as he inspected the door briefly for traps. *Okay, let's see what's behind door number one.* He tensed his right arm, increasing the size of the cracks and output of energy. With his right foot propped behind him, he sent his left foot crashing into the door, right below the handle. It gave way under the first blow and shot open, splinters flying in all directions.

The whole scene hit him at once: the table with the rusted, crude instruments of torture; the chains and shackles clinging to the walls; and, on the far wall, Rai.

The room was empty of all enemies; the only two beings in the room were Valafor and Rai. He ran to his friend with a smile of joy at seeing his friend still alive. "Rai, wake up," Valafor said, gently shaking his shoulder.

Rai's eyes slid open and he slowly raised his head, thinking it was Kobal back for more "fun." When he saw Valafor his eyes opened wide. "Val," Rai said, his voice raspy from dehydration. "What are you doing here? What happened to you?"

"No time—we have to go. No telling what's happening to the rest of the guys upstairs," Valafor said. He gripped the shackles binding Rai's hands and broke them apart, allowing them to clatter to the floor. "Listen, Rai, I know you're pretty banged up right now, but you need to get it together. When we get out of here we'll have Zara look at these wounds on you, but I'm not going to lie to you, were in for a fight again. Azreal is upstairs right now, probably trashing your brother."

At the mention of his brother, the start of all his confusion and eventual break from Hell, Rai's eyes lit up with an intoxicating energy. "Krillion is up there ... fighting ... Azreal?" he asked, looking at the ceiling.

"Yeah, and not for much longer if we don't hurry," Valafor said. "Come on, man." Valafor guided Rai's body toward the door. He could tell by the small streams of red radiating from the corner of Rai's eyes that the rage was returning to him.

Stumbling, getting feeling back into his numb legs, Rai grabbed his long, slender blade from the table nearby. He followed Valafor out the door and down the hallway that would lead them back upstairs and, he hoped, to a brother still alive.

† † †

"Kill them! Kill them all, Azreal!" Kobal screamed, jumping up and down on the throne.

"Fight or silence your tongue, fool," Azreal spat back.

As Kane continued to burn brighter, the room was awash in red energy that had caused the few remaining golems and skeletons to flee moments before.

"Let her go, traitor!" demanded Krillion as he charged the dais where Azreal stood, still clutching Zara by her hair and immobilizing her completely. Fast as lightning, Azreal delivered a knee straight to her stomach, forcing all the air from her lungs and sending her into fits of coughing. He left her curled on the ground, her arms wrapped around her midsection, and hopped off the dais with a graceful leap to prepare himself for Krillion's attack.

Krillion's hammer met Azreal's blade in midair. Azreal ducked down into a crouch, spinning on his foot and effectively sweeping the legs out from under Krillion, sending the big warrior to the hard stone floor. Then Kane let loose with multiple bursts of energy directed into the ceiling directly above Azreal, bringing large chunks of jagged rocks down upon him.

Azreal was no rookie fighter, though, and he hadn't earned his reputation by being defeated with so simple a tactic. Using his wings to propel him further and faster than his legs could, he dodged the falling debris; instead they almost hit Krillion, who rolled out of the way at the last second.

Kobal was jumping up and down on his throne, cursing Kane for destroying even more of his castle. "Kobal, shut the fuck up!" Azreal commanded, pointing his sword at the demon master of hilarity. Kane again let loose with a barrage of blasts, this time to the floor around Azreal. Each time the energy struck, huge craters appeared in the floor, followed by clouds of dust and tiny projectiles peppering the walls and combatants. "Damn you," Kobal yelled, shaking his fist at Kane as if that would have any effect whatsoever.

Just as Azreal leapt into the air to deal with Kane, Valafor and Rai emerged in the throne room doorway. Seeing Azreal flying straight for Kane, Valafor unleashed one solid, massive beam with the intent of obliterating Azreal for good.

Kane saw the blue energy heading his way and flew out of the line of fire, which caused Azreal to follow suit. The beam instead connected with another section of the ceiling, this time over the Kobal's throne, abruptly bringing the roof down on his head. Kobal struggled to his knees and shook chunks of rock and dust from his head and shoulders. "Azreal, to me!" he yelled. "We are leaving!"

Kobal began weaving a circle pattern in the air with his fingers, and a portal materialized in front of him. Taking one last look at his throne room—now in utter ruins thanks to these fools—Kobal leapt into the portal and vanished.

As Azreal neared the portal he stopped and turned, looking at the motley crew all around him. Floating in the air mere feet before the portal, his sword clenched in his hand down by his side, the angel of death's eyes burned through every one of them. Had he enough skill, it was very possible he could take out Israfil's entire team single-handedly—but right now time was not on his side. Without a word, Azreal slowly took his sword and cut through the air, left to right, in front of all of them, indicating that this fight was not over. Then he turned and flew through the portal, which zipped shut as he passed.

Kane flew down to attend to Zara, who was now beginning to get to her feet. Meanwhile Krillion and Rai saw each other. Retrieving his hammer from the nearby pile of debris, Krillion walked over to his brother, who met him halfway. The two stood staring at each other for long seconds before Rai finally spoke. "So what now?"

"Now we have a job to do—brother," Krillion replied with a melancholy look. It had been so long, and he had missed his brother terribly through the ages. Although Rai didn't know it, it was Krillion who had defeated him during the battle of Lucifer's last stand. Krillion knew he would have to tell him that sooner or later.

"Valafor," Krillion said, "you have about five minutes to explain everything to Rai and for the two of you to come to a decision. After that we leave, together or separately." Krillion hoped Valafor and Rai would remain with the group, but he knew that if Rai didn't, Valafor wouldn't abandon him. The team would be broken. Giving the two room to speak, Krillion turned to check on Kane and Zara.

"Hey, girl, that was a nasty blow you took back there. You okay?" Krillion asked, falling into his old role of commander of Fury Legion. He'd forgotten that he didn't lead an entire legion anymore, but rather a small team ordained by the All-Father with the sole purpose of retaking Earth by any means necessary.

"Yeah, I'm fine, but by all that's holy, that son of a bitch hits hard," Zara said, trying to lighten the situation.

Krillion looked at Kane next. "Kane?"

Rubbing his arms to get rid of some of the tension in his muscles, Kane looked up at Krillion. "Yeah, I'm good. Just a little tired." He was still breathing heavily, his physical exhaustion obvious.

"What's up with those two?" Zara asked Krillion. She nodded at their other teammates, who were talking by the pile of rocks that used to be part of the ceiling.

"Right now they're deciding whether they want to stay with us or not," Krillion said.

"But if they leave, then Israfil's vision is empty and we've lost," Zara replied quickly, her eyes growing wide with worry.

"I know, girl, but they have to want to stay of their own accord—we can't make them. And they need to hurry; we still need to head to the pens and pray that there's still enough of us left to fight and win up there. Kane, you're going to have to teleport us in a minute. Zara, you stay by Kane's side when we get there in the event that the strain is too much." Kane looked at Zara, who looked back at him—infatuated, intrigued, and smiling from ear to ear.

Kane glanced over at Valafor and Rai. "Here they come," he said, walking to meet them.

"Valafor has explained everything to me," Rai began, adjusting his black ponytail. "There is a lot I don't know, and apparently I haven't made the best decisions through the years. For now we will help you, but when this is over, you and I will have a long talk."

Krillion beamed with happiness that he hadn't felt in the years—not since losing his brother. Krillion was the elder by a few minutes, but the two of them had always had an unbreakable bond. Even back when they fought each other on the battlefield, there was something that made Rai stop fighting at the sight of the huge warrior commander on the far side of the field.

Extending his hand, Krillion awaited his brother's approval. Seconds passed as Rai looked down upon the hand offered him. Rai was no longer an angel of light, but rather one of the fallen. His skin had taken on a darkened shade; his once elegant white wings had turned the color of midnight. While he still had his angelic facial features, they were now marred by traces of the red power that came out of his eyes when his rage took over.

Still staring at the hand of the brother he couldn't remember, Rai shifted his sword from his right to his left and grasped the hand firmly in his own. Krillion and Rai gazed at one another with pride before letting go. The team was just about complete; all they needed was their final member, the human girl.

"Kane, when you're ready," Krillion called. Zara was attending to Kane's wounds, and when Kane heard his name, his head shot up and he glanced in Krillion's direction. *If he wasn't already red,* Krillion thought, *you might think he was blushing.*

"No time to rest," Krillion said. "Once we touch ground, we spread out. If it doesn't belong to the Seraphim or mankind, cut it down. No demons live by the end of this day." The angel hoisted his mighty war hammer, looking at Rai and Valor on his left and then Kane and Zara on his right. "Let's go," he said, and the team disappeared in a flash of red light.

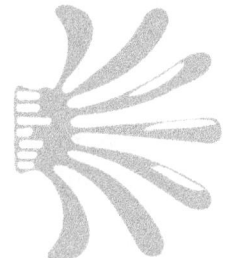 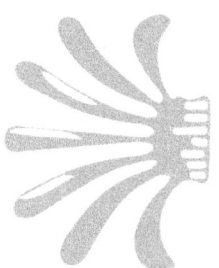

Chapter 29

THE BATTLE INSIDE THE DARK tower was intensifying as Cassiel's men hammered away at the demonic dregs. The archers had no choice but to fight the flying demons so they could proceed to the rooftop, where the three dark mages had already caused who knows how much damage to Raziel's unit outside.

"Captain Cassiel!" a familiar voice rang out as Cassiel severed the head of a bloody, screeching dreg in front of her. Turning around, she saw one of her sergeants flying toward her. "Captain … Captain Tabbris and his men are here behind us and have joined the battle," he said, pointing down to where Tabbris was engaging the dregs on the ground floor.

Seeing that her unit had the situation well in hand here, she looked at her man and said, "Report to him that we're fine, that there's nothing he can do here, and to carry on with his mission."

The sergeant nodded and dove straight down to the floor, avoiding any dregs that could intercept him. Landing right behind the rushing angels, he called out, "Captain Tabbris, sir!"

Pulling his sword from a twitching corpse on the ground, Tabbris turned his head to see the sergeant standing there, his chest rising and falling sharply. "Captain Cassiel reports that we're set here and to proceed with your original orders, sir."

"Okay then," Tabbris said with a smile, slapping the sergeant on the shoulder. "Men, fall back outside!" he shouted.

Cassiel watched from above as Tabbris and his warriors headed to the open door leading to the onslaught outside and plunged head-first into the chaos. She was hopeful that they would free as many prisoners as possible, but she knew it was a nightmare out there, chaos at its worst.

Returning her focus to her own problems, she scanned the area and noted that there were hardly any dregs left inside to deal with. She began looking around the big room for a way to the roof, but there were no stairs or anything similar around her. The whole building appeared to be just one huge room that was about seven stories tall. "Damn," she said, still trying to find a way up. "Sergeant!" she yelled, beckoning to her second-in-command. He flew to her side, and she instructed him to go to the door and see if the dome was still intact on the tower roof. If Cassiel was right about the mages, then the red dome would have to be down in order for them to participate in the battle outside.

The noise in the room had dimmed, as all the dregs were either dead or dying. It was a small victory of sorts, but Cassiel's forces still had to complete their mission, and that meant the deaths of more of her archers.

Moments later the sergeant ran back through the door. "Captain Cassiel" he yelled. "The dome is down, but they are up there hurling fire and lightning all over the place!"

Without hesitation Cassiel gave the order: "To the roof, warriors of light! Kill those bastards by any means necessary!" Soon the inside of the building was quiet except for the final, pitiful moans of the dying.

Cassiel descended to the door below and stepped outside. She was surprised to see how much the battle had intensified: all over the camp angels and demons were killing each other in an onslaught of merciless violence. Already her unit was flying up the sides of the building to destroy the mages on top and end the devastation they were inflicting. "Fly to the back side—try to take them unawares!" Cassiel ordered over the sounds of screams and clashing metal. Within seconds she and her archers would be at the top; whatever fate awaited them, they would deal with it in kind. They had to win this battle at all costs; failure was not an option.

When Cassiel cleared the top ledge, she realized the situation couldn't have been more perfect. The three magi were turned away from her warriors. The element of surprise was theirs, and she was not about to lose it. As they hovered there, staring down at an enemy utterly oblivious to their presence, Cassiel had an idea. She gave a silent signal for anyone with a dagger or similar weapon to move in front with her. Some fifty warriors floated near her, deadly projectiles in hand. "We throw, we rush," Cassiel whispered, and the warriors around her nodded. Drawing her arm back, she loosed her dagger, and the fifty others followed suit. As soon as the daggers left their hands, they charged, screaming oaths of allegiance to the Seraphim.

Tabbris and his two dozen men exited the building and entered the fray outside. They stayed close to the walls, trying not to get into the actual battle itself. All around them were hundreds of combatants, each consumed with bloodlust and convinced that his or her side must dominate Earth.

From Tabbris's view, the demons fought with the confidence of having won the initial war over the Seraphim, while the angels fought with the ferocity of a bear that had been backed into a corner.

It was bloody. It was loud. It was war.

Try as he might, Tabbris couldn't find the cages in the midst of all the fighting. He ordered his troops to form a small, semicircular defensive perimeter, while he took to the air to get a better view. Once he was above the heads of his comrades, he saw them: directly in the center of the camp there was a line of cages set in a circle around a blazing fire. Having been briefed back at the Crystal Palace, he knew exactly what the fire was and decided not to dwell on it or let the symbolism behind it consume him.

He saw that there was a small group of goat demons and a few mages right by the fire, looking up at something in the sky. Following their sight line, Tabbris saw Sandalphon and his men bearing down upon them, as well as the dying wall of flame. The bodies of unfortunate brothers and sisters who were caught in its fiery embrace had been left to wither in agony.

Returning to the ground, Tabbris called his troops. "We'll make a beeline to the cages that way, through the battle," he said, pointing. "Avoid the fighting if possible. Captain Sandalphon is over there. We'll unlock the cages, then help him. You ten will provide security for us as we unlock the cages. Let's go."

Running at full sprint toward the fire, his men behind him, Tabbris felt the adrenaline rushing through his veins. Finally they hit the battle, running past everyone, friend or foe, to make their way to the prisoners. Upon reaching the first cage, Tabbris saw that the captives were angels—

wingless angels. They had the look of dying creatures, probably from starvation and the hopelessness wrought by unimaginable torture.

The ten designated guards formed a semicircle around the door of the cage about ten feet out, swords brandished, eyes darting everywhere, trying to ensure that no demons slipped past to get an easy kill on their captain while his back was turned.

"Everybody back!" Tabbris yelled, and he began to hack at the first lock with his sword. After just a couple of swings, the lock was barely attached to the frame. With one solid kick from an angel warrior, the lock fell to the floor and the gate flew open. "Remember your oath, for mankind and the All-Father!" Tabbris yelled.

The wingless angels ran past the warriors, shouting with pride and freedom, heading straight into the fray, heedless of the fact they had no weapons or armor. Some stopped to pick up weapons from fallen combatants; others simply jumped onto the closest demon, punching and kicking, doing as much damage as they could.

"Shift left!" Tabbris ordered. With one fluid movement, his security guards stepped left to the next cage. As Tabbris approached it a shout rang out behind him. "Look out—incoming!" Tabbris turned his head and his eyes grew wide, his jaw agape in surprise and fear. Then he screamed and fell to the ground as a huge fireball flew over his head, smashing into the top of the cage and tearing it open like a tin can. On all fours in the dirt, Tabbris peered past his men and saw the owner of the fireball, a black mage who stood across the camp by the fire. He had seen them freeing the prisoners.

Tabbris watched as the mage's mouth began moving to send another spell his way. Then, in a splash of bright-red blood, organs and bone fragments exploded from the mage's chest, followed by the metal tip of a sword. Then the sword was retracted, and, dripping gore, the mage fell into a pool of his own blood. Behind him stood Sandalphon.

"Go!" he yelled to Tabbris.

"Watch out!" Tabbris warned, pointing toward a creature behind Sandalphon.

Sandalphon barely had time to pivot out of the way of a pair of gnarled, grisly looking horns that missed impaling him by just a few inches. He spun around, grabbed one horn with his free hand, and, using the demon's own momentum, brought the creature to the ground and ran his sword through the back of its neck. Then, nodding his thanks, Sandalphon turned and ran back to help his own men.

Shaking his head to clear the cobwebs and the ringing from the impact of the fireball, Tabbris got to his feet and turned back to the cage. Already the prisoners inside were helping each other scale the bars to the open ceiling above. Looking down the row of cages, Tabbris saw that he had about twelve more to go before his mission was complete. "Shift left!" he yelled. This time only eight warriors shifted.

† † †

Startled by sudden yelling and screaming behind them, the three mages on the rooftop turned just in time to see a barrage of daggers and knives heading their way, closely followed by their owners. One of the mages tried to cast a spell to ward off the deadly blades, but just before he finished, metal kissed flesh as the blades found their home. The mages fell to their knees, their bodies covered in daggers, and Cassiel's group landed right on top of them, slashing and hacking with already bloodstained swords.

Seconds flew by as the angels continued to mutilate and desecrate the dead bodies. Blood sprayed up and everywhere, coating them all in sticky wetness, as swords fueled by anger, rage, and sorrow continued to fell blow after blow.

"Stop!" Cassiel finally yelled. "They're dead. It's over." The angels slowly returned to their senses. "Sergeant," Cassiel said, breathing heavily, "get me a count of how many we have left." Then she walked to the edge of the rooftop to get a view of the entire camp. She could see Tabbris rushing from cage to cage, freeing humans and angels. She also saw Sandalphon in the center by the fire, and a huge black blob floating above the ground next to it. Fire and lightning smashed into Sandalphon's men as they continued their ruthless attack on Leonard's troops.

Across the field she saw Raziel, who was running through the throngs of warriors. She appeared to be running from something or someone. "Azazel," Cassiel said, as her men came to stand next to her.

"Captain Cassiel," her sergeant said. "We're just standing around—three to four hundred of us."

"Right," she said. "Now who do we help?" In the second it took her to ask this question out loud, a portal opened up right by the fire, where Sandalphon's men were fighting. Through the portal came none other than Kobal himself, followed by ... "Azreal!"

The Fallen | 167

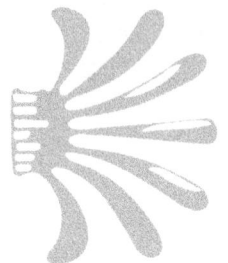 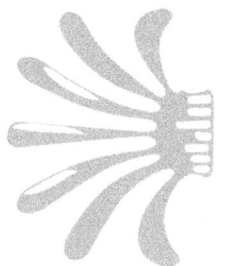

Chapter 30

ALISHA LAY IN THE STILL darkness, alone but unafraid. She wasn't sure how much time had passed since she had awakened there. She didn't even know where *there* was. All she knew for certain was that, for the time being, she was alone. Alone and safe.

She didn't have to hear the screams of the dead and dying night and day, or see the horror-filled faces as humans were cut down like grass on the streets outside her mom's apartment. The creatures from her nightmares, which had haunted her for so long, were nowhere to be seen here.

She vividly remembered the park and the grotesque statue that towered over even the tallest of trees. The vision had burned itself into her mind, a monument to the demons' reign on Earth and the unimaginable evil they represented. Any time she thought of her mother's face, forever twisted and contorted in eternal pain and suffering, she would pull out the photo of them in the park ... the photo taken before the light of the world was extinguished, before mankind was scattered to the winds of fate, on the brink of utter annihilation.

Alisha lay there in her dark, safe prison and recollected everything she'd borne witness to over the last few days.

Sure, the warriors of eternal light had descended upon Earth, intent on fulfilling their sacred duties in the All-Father's name. They were the Seraphim, and they had but two purposes, unbeknownst to Alisha or most humans on Earth. One was to be subservient to the All-Father and fulfill his will. Although he gave humans free will to live their lives as they saw fit, he put the Seraphim in place as a fail-safe to help guide his children and ultimately defend them from the forces of Hell, even at the cost of their own lives.

Through millennia there had never been a challenge that the Seraphim had not accepted and overcome, even when there was civil unrest in Heaven and Lucifer took a third of its warriors with him in an unsuccessful coup.

Now, from their celestial realm, the angelic warriors had seen the dark portals materialize and open all over the planet. They had seen the plague of the underworld scour the Earth, killing at will and running unchecked. And they had answered the call to arms in the defense of mankind.

The Seraphim had launched full-scale counterattacks all over the planet with the intent of once again driving the evil forces back to their dark realm. But things hadn't work out the way they planned. As angel met demon in the cities, woods, and fields across Earth, swords clashed against swords, and blood flowed on a scale never before seen or even imagined.

For the first time since their creation, the Seraphim lost.

Alisha thought back to that fateful day—it seemed so long ago—when the sun darkened, never to shine again. She had seen the portals open, had seen the denizens of Hell pour through them with malice, had seen the wholesale slaughter.

She had watched the most beautiful creatures she had ever laid eyes on descend from the skies, swords brandished, screaming war cries, ready to sacrifice their lives so that man might live on. She had seen them fall, killed brutally and without mercy, mutilated almost beyond recognition, their heavenly features forever scarred.

As she thought about everything she had witnessed, she stared hard into the vast darkness surrounding her. Was it her imagination, or was there a faint orange glow appearing from the darkness in front of her? Shifting her body so she was kneeling, she extended her arm toward the small amount of light that had begun forcing its way through the darkness. Her hand struck a wall of sorts, and it dawned on her that she wasn't floating in oblivion, but trapped in a prison of some kind.

When she had awakened in the dark however long ago, she had decided not to explore. She was happy and at peace knowing that there was nothing in this place that could hurt her.

But now, her curiosity piqued, Alisha reached out with both hands to touch the wall. It was solid, but at the same time it felt like she could push through it. As she started pushing through the substance that served as her prison walls, her hands sank just a few inches before ripping through to the other side. She could feel heat on one side of her hands and a breeze hitting them one the other. She pulled her hands back inside and placed her forehead against the wall of muck. Closing her eyes, she began to push her head through to see what was on the outside. As her face touched the black wall, she took a deep breath and held it, and then she started pushing her face through harder, bracing herself on her hands and knees.

As her face sunk in, the orange glow emanating from outside got brighter; soon she could tell that it was the light of a fire. She also heard random sounds, but they made no sense to her. She could vaguely make out silhouetted shapes running and flying in all directions as the black wall thinned and stretched before her.

Finally her head broke through and reality slapped her hard in the face. She was back in the real world.

The demons from her nightmares were everywhere, fighting angels. There was a massive fire right next to her, surrounded by cages. Some of the cages were open, while others were still locked tight, with angels trying to open them and free the inhabitants.

Fire was everywhere, illuminating the battleground. Lightning hurled from above arced through the air, destroying everything in its wake. There were dead bodies everywhere, too—some covered with bloody gashes, some horribly burned, the flesh blackened and peeling off in layers.

As Alisha looked around in horror, taking in the carnage she'd thought she was free from, a black-robed figure nearby looked directly at her, pointing a finger that extended from the cuff of its robe. Its hand was covered in scales, like a lizard's. A black cowl shrouded most of its face, and Alisha heard a guttural sound erupt from its hidden mouth.

There was a flash of blinding light as Alisha scrambled to get back inside the prison—to once again escape the demons surrounding her.

She fell back against the far side of her cage and tears made their way down her cheeks to the corners of her mouth. She choked away the salt as she began to cry harder, realizing that her worst fears were again reality.

She had to figure a way to escape, to elude the creatures once more and find a new hiding spot. She began frantically clawing at the opposite wall, trying to make a hole so she could run away. She didn't know where she would go; all she knew was that she had to run, run as far and as fast as she could. After so many seconds that seemed to drag on, she had made a hole just large enough for her to climb through. She scrambled to get her legs through the opening that was already beginning to close around her, and then she found herself free of the darkness and cast once again into reality—free of the darkness and falling straight to the ground below.

Alisha landed hard on her shoulder and glanced up to see the black ball just floating there, a few feet above the ground. It didn't look that big from the outside.

To her left was one of the creatures she had seen before—it looked like a goat—and she realized that it had spotted her lying on the ground. Thinking her easy kill to satisfy its bloodlust, it lowered its head, showing a set of huge, gnarled horns dripping with blood and bits of flesh from previous enemies. With a high-pitched scream, Alisha got to her feet, knowing she wouldn't be able to outrun this massive demon hell-bent on gutting her with its horns. She just needed to find help or a place to hide. She ran through the throngs of angels and demons, a bloody massacre playing out before her very eyes, until she saw a small clearing free of people or creatures. She took off for the spot in a dead sprint.

As her legs pumped to put distance between herself and the gruesome death giving chase, she saw the oddest group she had ever seen materialize from thin air. One was a huge male angel with spiked blonde hair, carrying a hammer bigger than she was. Next to him was a female angel with beautiful wings that she unfurled as she drew two swords. There was a red-hued man who instantly fell to his knees, gasping for air, and the girl angel took a protective stance in front of him, guarding him from immediate danger. There was also a demon with them—a tall, hairy demon with a wide mouth full of sharp teeth and an arm that looked burned. From his arm came a blue light that pulsed around and through everything.

Last there was a tall angel—only he looked different from the rest. His wings and skin were black, and his long black hair was tied into a beautiful ponytail. He held a long, slender sword that looked like it could cut through silk. Something about him left her frightened, yet calm. She noticed that red beams shot out about two inches from the corners of his eyes.

With the demon behind her and closing in fast, she had no choice: she ran to the angel with the black wings, hoping he would protect her from what would certainly be her death. As she neared him, she heard the howl of a wild animal behind her. Reaching out her trembling hands, she grabbed the dark angel's leg and tucked herself in tight. Placing a protective arm around her, he said, simply, "Get behind me."

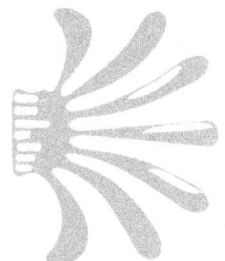 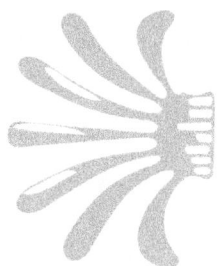

Chapter 31

IN A FLASH OF BRIGHT red light, Krillion's team appeared in the pens just in time: all the major players had finally entered the battle in one arena.

After the successful rescue of Krillion's brother, Rai, the team had fought Azreal in Kobal's castle—proof beyond doubt that Azreal was in league with Kobal and responsible for the attack upon Gabriel. But before the fight could reach its bloody ending, Kobal and Azreal had jumped into a portal and escaped. Now, having abandoned the castle, Krillion's team followed right behind them, intent upon ending both thier lives.

Within seconds of the group appearing in the pens, Kane fell to his knees, exhausted. Zara wasted no time coming to his defense. Any demon that wanted Kane would have to deal with her and her twin blades first.

Valafor clenched his weapon arm, sending blue beams of energy throughout the chaos of the battle around them.

Krillion stepped forward to the head of the group, war hammer in hand, ready to give orders. It was immediately clear to him that Raziel could use their help. Though it didn't look as if either side had an advantage, the Seraphim's heavy hitters were about to tip the scales in their favor.

As Rai's eyes adjusted to his new surroundings, the first thing he saw was a red-haired human girl about eight or nine years old, darting straight for him like an arrow. Panic and pure horror spread across her face like wildfire. Looking past the mortified child, Rai saw her fears made flesh: one of Azazel's goat minions was on her trail, hunting her down like an animal and closing in fast.

Holding his slender blade so the sword lay parallel to his arm, Rai waited. As the child closed the distance between them, Rai noticed dried tears streaked across her face. If he didn't act in her defense, she would die. When she reached Rai she wrapped her arms around his leg and pulled herself close.

The human girl clinging to him for her life sparked a fire inside of Rai. A small part of his former, "divine and compassionate" self combined with the darkness in his soul, and his rage came to life as a separate entity, completely overwhelming the fallen angel. "Get behind me," he said, gritting his teeth. He guided the human girl a few feet behind him, never taking his eyes off his advancing prey.

The goat demon, seeing this band of newcomers appear from nowhere, never faltered. Instead it let out a mighty bellow that echoed throughout the camp. Behind Rai, the girl cringed in fear. Rai's eyes began to glow red, a sign that he was losing control to the rage inside him, his rage at the idea of this little girl succumbing to the darkness.

The demon came closer and closer, kicking up billows of dust as its hooves dug into the ground, searching for more traction to propel itself faster. Rai bent his knees, crouching ever so slightly. Within seconds, the demon would be on top of both of them. Timing was critical.

Gripping his sword hilt so tightly that he could feel its ridges dig into his hand, Rai waited. At the last second, just as he was about to be impaled upon the nasty, bloodied horns, Rai ducked, pivoted on the ball of his foot, and brought his blade around in a wide arc, slicing through the demon's back.

Rai completed his pivot to stand upright once more, his sword positioned for another strike if needed. Turning quickly toward the girl, he saw her standing a little ways back from him, trembling in fear and staring at the two pieces of the demon now lying in the dust, forming pools of blood.

"Come with me," Rai said, gripping her arm and leading her away from the carcass.

† † †

"Spread out! You know what we have to do here," Krillion ordered.

Valafor, ever happy to be in a fight, no matter the odds, ran and jumped onto the back of a goat demon that was parrying blows with a female warrior. Valafor used his right hand to punch straight through the back of the demon's head, spraying the female angel with guts and gore, and then as she went bounded away as she went after him, yelling that he was on her side.

Looking down at the girl while keeping an eye out for enemies, Rai asked, "Are you okay?"

By now the girl's tears had subsided and her breathing was returning to normal. Though she was clearly still shaken, she responded in hushed tones, "Yes."

"Listen," Rai said in a calm voice, "I have to leave now to—"

But before he could finish his sentence, she wrapped her arms around his waist, pleading, "No, please, don't leave me! Please don't leave me all alone! They'll find me and kill me. Just like they killed my mom and everyone else! You have to stay with me!"

Shit, Rai thought, trying to sort out a dozen options that came to mind. Looking around the battlefield he saw Krillion running into the fray, swinging his hammer and yelling like a madman. To Rai's left, Kane was still on the ground recovering, while Zara was busy fending off numerous foes around him. Valafor had long since disappeared into the crowd.

As much as Rai wanted to leave this girl and join the fight, something inside him wouldn't let him leave her to the evil surrounding them all. But before he could figure out what to do, he realized that two goat demons had spotted them. "Run over to the wall, little one. Try to stay low and out of sight," Rai said, giving the girl a slight shove in the opposite direction and never taking his eyes off the charging demons.

"But I wanna stay with you! Please don't leave me alone. If they get me, they'll kill me. Please!" Again the girl begged with all her heart, her eyes overflowing with fresh tears; the prospect of being alone in this nightmarish reality was too much for her.

"I promise no harm will come to you, child, but you have to go now," Rai said, trying to keep his voice calm. The goat demons were almost on top of them now, their primal rage and power evident in their every step. Howling with the glory of battle, their adrenaline and animal instincts took over, giving them even greater speed and strength.

Pushing the girl well out of the way, Rai positioned his feet to balance his body weight so he could anticipate the demons' moves and act in kind. As the girl started taking small, backward steps away, sobbing hysterically, Rai made the first move.

As the demons closed in, Rai jumped into the air, twirling his body to the left. His foot connected squarely with the jaw of the first demon, the force of the impact and the shift in momentum causing the creature to drop to one knee in the dirt. Rai knew that he had barely stunned it and it would recover in a second, but that should be all the time he needed to deal with its counterpart.

The dark angel landed back on the ground and spun with such speed that the girl had trouble following his motions. His eyes scanned the area for the other demon. Suddenly he saw his prey rushing him from the side. Too late to fully react, Rai tried dodging the massive, hairy fist that was swung with deadly accuracy, ready to separate his head from his shoulders. The end result was a glancing blow to Rai's shoulder. Still it sent him spinning to the floor; his sword flew from his hands to lie a few feet away.

The girl gave a high-pitched cry of terror as her champion fell to the ground.

Rai tried in vain to rise, and pain shot through his arm as it hung limp at his side. Kneeling and clutching his arm as the feeling slowly returned to it, Rai searched for the girl and spotted her cornered against the wall where he had ordered her to stay. He had promised her that no harm would come to her, and, fallen angel though he was, his word was still his life.

"Hey, bitch—over here!" he yelled, trying to get the attention of the goat demon seeking to satisfy its bloodlust with the human girl.

Fortunately for her and Rai, the goat demons were as stupid as they were big. The demon looked around to see where the voice had come from, turning its huge, masculine body to reveal bare patches of skin along its torso. *Scars from previous battles,* Rai thought.

As he regained his footing, Rai glanced at his sword, which was lying on the ground nearby, and realized that it was too far for him to reach in time. His mind raced as he tried to form a plan of attack.

Suddenly, from his left, a beam of solid red light shot forth, whizzing past the black wings of the fallen angel and blindsiding the unprepared demon. It hit the demon in the side, sending it sprawling to the ground, its hair and muscles smoking.

Not about to let this opportunity go to waste, Rai dropped to the ground and rolled for his sword, the impact on his shoulder sending waves of fresh pain shooting through every nerve in his body. Then, sword in hand, Rai sent it sailing through the air in a straight-line shot.

As the demon rose to its knees, clutching its charred side, the sword hit its jaw, passing through flesh, bone, and cartilage to stick out the back of its skull. The demon collapsed, incoherent moans emanating from its blue lips. Rai made his way over to the demon, put his foot on its lower jaw, and using both hands, pulled the sword free.

Spotting the girl again, Rai also saw Kane rising to his knees, supported by Zara. A faint trail of red could still be seen hanging in the air from his energy. With a nod of thanks and respect to Kane, Rai hurried over to the girl. "Come, you have to get somewhere safe," he said, looking around for a place to hide her.

† † †

Else-where in the pens, another blood hunt was still in progress.

Terror and panic filled Raziel's mind, and her heart was racing to the point of explosion. He was still after her. No matter where she ran or tried to hide, he would find her and kill her.

She had witnessed so many brave warriors fall in her defense, trying to protect their captain from the lord of the goat demons, but to no avail. He was huge, evil personified, and very much real, and Raziel had to find a way to stop him or else she was sure to die a grisly death.

Her natural instinct was to ascend into the sky to stay beyond his reach, but here in the midst of the ground battle, with combatants everywhere, she had no room to fully unfurl her wings. And besides, Azazel was never far enough behind her to allow her a moment to breathe. He had long since thrown away his weapon; he relished the thought of killing her with his bare hands and horns. There was a reason he was the lord of the goat demons: in that crude world, the leader is simply the best at mortal combat. For millennia, Azazel had led the clan, knowing that no other goat demon would be stupid enough to face him in combat in order to challenge his leadership.

Without hesitation or mercy, Azazel continued to cut a swath of destruction through the angelic ranks, trailing the female warrior who had so far eluded him.

He was a force of nature and pure, primal rage.

Raziel stumbled over the body of a fallen demon, and for a just moment she lay in the dirt, trying to catch her breath and cough out the dust she had inhaled. From behind her she heard the screams of more of Azazel's victims as he ended one life after another, all in pursuit of her. Rolling onto her back, gasping for air, she saw him holding another angel by the neck several feet off the ground. The demon looked straight at Raziel, and with a cruel smile he tightened his grip on the angel's esophagus, crushing his throat and letting him fall to the ground.

Then he walked methodically toward Raziel, his mouth open, white froth seeping out of the corners, and he spoke to her in a high, buzzing voice that was filled with a mixture of hate and joy at having finally cornered the angel who had dared defy him. "You are the one who led the charge here," he said, his chest heaving. "Before I kill you, tell me your name so that all may know your folly at trying to best me."

Forcing herself to her feet despite the fear coursing through her body, Raziel stood proudly, staring Azazel in the eyes. "I am Raziel, the angel of mysteries. And your reign of terror on Earth is over, demon!" As the last word escaped her mouth, she lunged forward, ready to claw his eyes out with her bare hands if necessary. Just as her fist connected with his jaw, he caught her in midair with his hands, one hand on her right arm, the other on her left wing. Laughing and mustering all his immense strength, he snapped the wing at the base, as if it were a twig. Raziel let out a scream of pain.

Suddenly the head of a huge war hammer passed by her body, striking Azazel in the rib cage. As his bones snapped and his lungs expelled all the air stored in them, Azazel dropped Raziel to the ground, clutching his broken ribs. Raziel landed hard, her world a red blur overcome by darkness and pain. The last thing she saw before oblivion took her was Krillion punching Azazel in the face repeatedly with his bare hand.

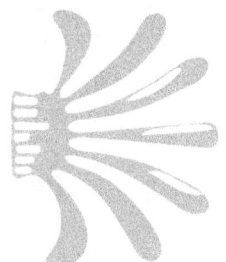 

Chapter 32

As Kobal exited his teleportation portal, the last thing he expected to find was a bloody battle being waged on what he was now calling his Earth.

Everywhere he looked, the remains of angels and Azazel's goat minions littered the ground in a gruesome fashion, proof of the angels' determination to win. Kobal wasn't sure, but it seemed to him that there were more of Hell's forces dead than Heaven's.

For the first time since meeting him, Azreal didn't see a smile upon Kobal's face.

"Now is the time to fight, you fool!" Azreal said. "I told you to kill Rai when you had the chance, told you the dangers associated with letting Krillion get Israfil's team together!" He spat out the words and assumed an attack posture, sword in hand.

"Azreal, I tire of your useless banter. As of now our deal is concluded," Kobal returned, looking casually around the battlefield.

Azreal couldn't believe that this insect of a demon would dare betray a deal with him, the angel of death. He turned to see Kobal spinning around and around, looking for a way to escape. He grabbed Kobal by his shirt and pulled him in close. "You dare presume to tell me what is what of our deal, you filthy wretch?" Azreal yelled. "Give me one reason why I shouldn't end your miserable life right this second, demon scum!" Spittle flew from his mouth with every word.

Gripped by fear, Kobal began swinging his arms in the vain hope of hitting Azreal hard enough to force him to release his steadily tightening grip. Instead, Azreal tossed Kobal to the ground and stood above him, sword poised and ready to plunge into the master of hilarity.

But as Azreal's sword began its deadly descent, a broad-headed, double-bladed ax shot underneath Azreal's blade, stopping the blow before it could land. Shifting his eyes to the handle of the ax and following it upward to its owner, Azreal saw one of Azazel's minions standing before him. The goat demon had come to defend Kobal and end Azreal's life. Kobal seized this exceptionally opportune time to scamper away from the angel of death, crawling away on all fours and disappearing into the chaotic crowd.

Azreal jumped straight into the air, landing on the head of the great axe. Then, bringing his sword around him, he leapt again, this time flipping his body in a wide, twirling arc backward over the demon. He landed with his feet back on solid ground and his back to his foe.

A thin line of red began to spread from one side of the demon's neck to the other. As the line grew deeper, its severed head fell from its shoulders, and the body slumped to its knees and fell forward.

"Time to end this charade," Azreal said to himself as he started after Kobal.

Before Azreal had taken his first step, he saw Cassiel and a host of angels at her command flying straight toward him. If they knew that he had slain Gabriel, his plans were already doomed to fail. As he stood there, looking up at the semi-darkened sky and watching the light of the main bonfire glint off the warriors' armor, he detected anger in their voices. Obviously they had learned his dark secret. He would have no choice but to kill them all.

He would forsake his oath and spill the blood of his celestial brethren.

"Let it be," Azreal said aloud, and he expanded his wings and slowly flapped to rise and meet the challenge racing toward him. "The time of the Seraphim is over! Hell will fall, but it will be to my sword. Hear me now, children of the All-Father!" Azreal yelled so all could hear his decree. "The Earth and mankind shall be mine, now and forever to be remade … in my image!" He twisted the hilt of his infamous sword at a precise angle, and red-hot flames erupted from the edges of the blade, illuminating the sky in a lush orange glow.

All around, angels, demons, and humans paused to take in the horrific site above.

Most angels had never seen Azreal in full death mode. His skills were so great that he rarely brought his sword to life. The sight of the angel of death in his full glory froze even the most stalwart veteran warrior.

"Don't fear him, men! Slay the traitor!" Cassiel yelled, urging her remaining warriors into a battle they most likely would not live through.

As Azreal's sword wove a deadly pattern in the air, the trail of flames left in its wake gleamed off the faces of the incoming angelic warriors, illuminating their anger at the sight of the traitor before them. Then steel met flame as swords clashed, sending sparks to the ground below.

On the ground, Sandalphon's men were hard-pressing the attack on Leonard and the few remaining goat demons. As Sandalphon felled one of the mages, he was distracted by the sight of Tabbris freeing prisoners in the distance. The battle was raging all around him, and he noticed a great many events transpiring.

The first was that the black ball hovering above the ground a few feet from where he had been fighting developed a mysterious hole in the side. He watched the hole grow larger until a human child emerged from the blackness within, her face alight with fear. Then he saw her take off running with a goat demon hot on her trail.

Farther away, by the side wall of the camp, he saw Krillion appear with Zara, Rai, Valafor, and Kane. As far as he could tell, the team of Israfil's vision was complete and intact.

As he watched these events unfold, a small lightning bolt struck his leg, singing clothes and skin together. Grunting in pain and falling to the ground, he saw Leonard standing a few feet away, his scaly hand outstretched, still pointing in his direction.

Leonard walked over to Sandalphon until he was standing directly over him. Then, looking down, he said, "Game over." As spidery words of dark magic escaped his mouth, a fireball began taking shape in his hand, growing bigger by the second. Every syllable uttered from his vile tongue brought more flame and heat to the fireball.

Sandalphon could feel heat radiating from it and hitting his face in waves. He tried to get up and fight or, at the very least, crawl away and put some distance between himself and Leonard. But due to the damage to his leg, he was unable to move.

Just as Leonard finished his spell, a beam of blue light arced past, squarely connecting with the fireball, and the two powers cancelled each other out in a mighty explosion of sparks and embers. Leonard looked shocked as he searched for the source of the beam. He turned his head to look around, and a blackened hand shot from beyond the range of his vision, slamming into his face hidden deep within his hood.

Dropping to one knee, lost in a haze of red and the smell of his own blood, Leonard was aware of the hovering black ball disappearing into nothingness.

Above the lord of the dark arts stood Valafor, his hairy chest heaving. Leonard stared at him, about to curse his existence, and Valafor raised his weapon arm, a small smile spreading across his face. There was an explosion of blue light.

Valafor directed a continuous stream of energy into the demon's face, tearing away pieces of skin and bone. The power of Valafor's weapon arm was so great that Leonard couldn't even scream in pain as his hood was blown back and his reptilian features bared to for all to see. Then, within seconds, Leonard's head was completely obliterated; all that remained was a body cloaked in a black robe and a small, ghastly stump.

Walking over to where Sandalphon lay, still struggling to rise, Valafor extended his large, sweat-covered hand to the captain of the guard. Sandalphon grabbed it, grunting in pain, and was pulled to his feet. "Never thought I would be alive on the day demons and angels worked together," Sandalphon said, wincing as he shifted his weight to his uninjured leg.

"Remember, Captain," Valafor said in his rocky voice, "it was not my idea, but rather the Seraphim's. An' just so we're clear ... I don't fight for the light. I fight for Rai." Without another word, Valafor turned and joined what was left of the battle.

Sandalphon stood by the fire in the center of the compound, testing his leg and allowing his eyes to follow Valafor for a moment. "Dark times, dark allies," he said to himself, shaking his head. Finally he decided that he was good enough to resume the fight.

Just as he bent down to retrieve his sword, a deafening scream from above caught his attention. Streaking through the air off to his left were Cassiel and her remaining archers, their bows replaced by swords.

Ahead of her flew Azreal, and his flaming sword danced with the promise of imminent death for all.

Gritting his teeth, pushing past the pain of his wounds, Sandalphon leapt into the air to help his young captain and her legion from a most certain outcome.

† † †

Their weapons had long since been discarded. Both combatants, battered and bruised, were now fighting with their bare hands. They rolled on the ground among the weapons and the bodies of the dead and dying, oblivious to everything but their goal: the demise of the opponent before them.

Azazel's hand connected squarely against Krillion's face, snapping his head back. Grunting in pain, Krillion brought his head back up with surprising speed and power, smashing Azazel in the face with his own forehead and then using momentum to roll the goat demon off him and onto the ground.

Rising to his feet, Krillion stood before Azazel, the lord of the goat demons. His chest was heaving, sweat coated his muscular frame, and there were cuts all over his body that either were bleeding or had turned black from dried blood. Krillion stared at his ancient enemy, hate in his eyes.

When Azazel tried to get up, Krillion delivered a swift kick to the side of his elongated goat snout, sending him back to the dirt. The fight was over: Azazel was too weak and beaten to mount any type of defense, much less offense.

Krillion knelt down by the lord of the goat demons and looked into his swollen, bruised face. Then he grabbed him by the neck with one hand, while his other sought out the gnarled horns that had been used to kill so many Seraphim that day and during battles before. Without a word he grabbed hold of one horn, feeling his hand wrap around fresh blood and small pieces of flesh attached to this gruesome instrument of death. Then he snapped the horn off at its base, sending fresh waves of pain coursing through Azazel's body.

Tightening his grip on Azazel's throat to hold him down, Krillion brought forth the ugly, twisted horn for Azazel to see. As Azazel's eyes widened in shock, Krillion drove the horn straight into his forehead. The horn broke through the thick skull and found its way deep into the brain of the vile creature. With little more than a pitiful moan, Azazel's head slumped over.

The lord of the goat demons was finally dead. Krillion wondered how many lives he had saved by destroying this evil enemy. He stood up slowly, still not taking his eyes off his fallen adversary. He noticed that the sounds of fighting had dimmed considerably.

He looked around to take in the battle scene and saw Raziel lying on the ground a little ways away from him. He'd been so caught up in his fight with Azazel that he had completely forgotten her.

"Raziel!" he said, rushing to her side. He dropped to his knees again, and lifting her upper body in his massive, blood-covered arms, he put his ear to her mouth and watched her chest for any signs of breathing. To his relief she was alive, but barely. One of her wings had been viciously mutilated where Azazel had snapped it.

Looking around, still holding Raziel in his arms, Krillion saw an angel nearby, pulling his sword free from the body of a dead demon. "Hey!" Krillion yelled.

The young warrior looked around for the source of the commanding voice. Seeing Commander Krillion, his eyes lit up with hope and excitement, and he ran toward them. "Yes, sir," said the warrior, showing strict military discipline even in the middle of the battle.

Krillion positioned his arms under Raziel's back and legs and lifted her from the ground. "Are you hurt?" he asked the warrior.

The young warrior shook his head. "No, sir, just a few cuts and bruises," he said, displaying his arms and legs.

"Here is what I need you to do then," Krillion said. "Gather a few more men and search the battlegrounds for the wounded. Find a centralized location away from the remaining fighting, and start saving the ones you can. If any enemy happens upon your position, cut him down without hesitation." Handing over the limp body of Raziel, Krillion added, "And be quick." Then he left to find his weapon and finish the fight.

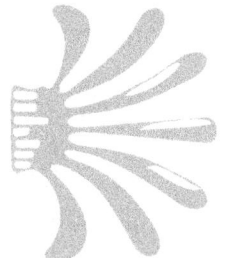 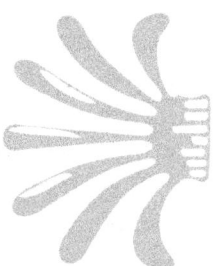

Chapter 33

Rai was pulling the girl at a brisk pace along the outer wall surrounding the pens, still trying to find some safe place for her amid the chaos, when he noticed that all around them the fighting was dying down. There were some minor pockets of resistance here and there, but for the most part it seemed the Seraphim had won this day.

His spied Zara and Kane off in the distance, along with a small group of freed humans and mutilated, wingless angels. Then he returned his gaze to the young girl in his charge. "We must, hurry little one," Rai said to her in a soft, calm voice.

She nodded in compliance. Even though she had stopped crying, there were dried tears as well as random splatters of blood streaking her young face. In fact, she was covered in dirt and blood, and her clothes had holes all through them, each a testament to her frightful experiences over the last few weeks.

† † †

As Rai neared Zara, he saw that she was attending to Kane, who was lying on the ground, looking like he had been through hell and back. Around them lay the bodies of countless demons, still glowing with a slight tinge of red.

"Rai," Zara said, standing up. She glanced behind her dark ally, and seeing a young girl holding firmly to Rai's hand, she gave him a quizzical look.

"She ran to me when we first appeared here," he explained quickly. "Azazel's minions were going to kill her." He glanced back at the fighting that was still taking place. "I need you to watch out for her and keep her close. I'm not sure, but I don't think they were going after her as a random kill. And I have to go; Val and my brother are still out there somewhere."

Rai bent down, putting himself eye level with the girl, and ran his fingers through her tangled red hair, pushing it behind her ears. "Child, you must stay here," he said. "My brother and friend are still out there fighting—do you understand?"

Once more she looked deep into Rai's gaze, her innocent, sea-blue eyes catching his red ones. She nodded her head. Giving a quick look at Zara, who was standing beside him, Rai guided the girl away from him and turned and started running across the open courtyard, his slender blade in a reverse grip up beside his body, to find Valafor and Krillion and put an end to the day's conflict.

"What's your name, sweetie?" Zara asked the little girl who was watching her champion charge across the pens.

"Alisha," she answered shyly. The girl looked up at the angel speaking to her and noticed how her black curls hung heavy, matted with blood and sweat. Her breastplate was dented in numerous spots and dug into her skin, causing further damage to her battered body. "Will he be okay?" Alisha asked, looking into Zara's blue eyes.

"I haven't known Rai that long, but from what I've heard and seen, he'll be just fine, hon. And my name is Zara," she added.

Taking the girl's hand in hers, she led the girl over to Kane, who was just now getting to his feet. Looking around at the gathered group of freed humans and angels, Zara felt her leadership instincts take over. She had to get the freed prisoners out of danger in case more portals opened, bringing enemy reinforcements.

As Zara was debating how to accomplish this, another human female darted toward her, hopping over dead bodies across the battlefield. By the time she reached Zara, she was panting heavily. "All the wounded are gathering over there on the far side," she reported. "The angel in charge has set up defensive positions, and every able body not fighting is to help with the wounded and security."

The girl looked no older then twenty-five. She had piercings in her ears and nose and cropped, jet-black hair with three white stripes. Her clothes were torn and tattered, and she had several gashes across her arms and legs, probably from some type of torture the demons had put her through.

"Let's go, everyone. Quickly now," Zara said to the group, which had huddled around her among the bodies of the dead. "Kane, go with them and take this girl with you," she said. "I'm going to find Krillion."

Kane lifted his head to look at her. The red tint of his body had faded to a slight pinkish tone, his eyes were sunken in, and he looked like he could barely fight a bug, much less a demon. "I can still fight, Zara," he gasped, choking on the words. Clearly he had severely overexerted himself between the battle at Kobal's castle and teleporting the group to the pens.

"No, Kane, I need you to take this girl and make sure she stays safe," Zara said, pointing to Alisha.

Then Zara walked over to him, cupped his face in her hands, and pressed her lips against his. Her lips were dry from fighting in the dust of the pens. "Go—I'll be fine, I promise," she whispered in his ear before turning to make her way into the final fight. She ran a few feet and then leapt into the air, her wings speeding her to her companions.

Kane watched Zara depart and then looked down at the girl, who was staring at him intently. There was a solemn look on his face as he stared back at the brave child before him. *Perhaps I should let go of my hatred for the humans,* he thought. Maybe it was best for the planet that the humans had inherited the earth instead of him. Without another word, he took the girl's hand in his and began to follow the group headed for the makeshift defense that had been set up for the wounded.

† † †

Across the pens, Tabbris's sword found its mark deep in the throat of a demon. With a spurt of dark-red blood, he yanked it free and stood there, panting for air. By the time he and his men had finished opening all the cages that held more than a hundred captives, he had only three of his original two dozen warriors left. Then he did the only thing left to him: he joined the fight.

Standing there now over his latest kill, it began to dawn on Tabbris that they had won. There was only one battle still being fought in the skies above. All that remained in the unholy camp were the sounds of the dead and dying.

"Captain, what now?" one of his men asked, coming to stand beside him. "Do we join the last skirmish or tend the wounded, sir?"

"Tend the wounded, and search out and kill any live demons that may be among the bodies," Tabbris replied. Then he noticed something moving in the fading light of the fire, creeping through the still darkness, apparently oblivious to all. "What is that?" he asked, pointing his sword in the direction of the shadowy figure.

From the darkness, out of reach of the quickly fading light, came a streak of orange light that zipped past Tabbris, connecting with the chest of the warrior standing behind him. The unsuspecting angel burst into flames. Screaming in fear and panic, he threw his sword down and began running in frenzy until two humans grabbed him and threw him to the ground, patting out the flames and scarring their hands in the process.

"Destroy it!" Tabbris yelled, running toward the shadowy figure, sword raised high. His final two angels followed close behind him, the clank of their metal armor making the creature pause. Then, as they closed the gap, Tabbris and his men heard hideous, morbid laughter erupt from the shadows in front of them.

"You little birdies think you have won the day here? All you have done is delay the inevitable," the voice rang out. "Heed my words well, bitches of the Seraphim: I will return for you and the rest of your damned order." Again the high-pitched laughter pierced the air, and the smell of fire and brimstone was overwhelming.

By the time the smoke had cleared seconds later, the shadow and the voice were gone, and all was quiet again.

"Who or what was that, sir?" one of the warriors asked Tabbris.

"I don't know," he replied. "When this is done, I'll report it to Captain Raziel. Personally, I'm glad it's gone for now." Tabbris gave a sigh of relief, thinking of the flame that had killed his man. "Now, let's get back to work," he said, turning back the way they had come.

† † †

Azreal's skill with a sword was known throughout all three realms. Angels revered it, demons feared it, and humans wrote stories of it. In Earth, Heaven, and Hell, his reputation was well-deserved. Azreal had always been the wild card Heaven could play against the forces of Hell— and upon Earth if the All-Father so desired it. But never did the warriors of Seraphim believe that one day they would have to fight him.

A paralyzing cold ran through the angels' veins as their fear made their sword arms limp and heavy. As Azreal's sword caressed the air, leaving trails of flame and smoke and burning bodies in its wake, Cassiel pushed her men harder. "Hit him fast, men—all angles!" she yelled, flying close enough to parry blows with the angel of death.

With a mere twitch of his wrist, Azreal batted Cassiel's sword off to the left. He followed with a deft strike with his sword hilt to the side of her head, sending her spinning out of control to the ground below. Fortunately, for the second time that day, there were warriors there to catch and steady her, and she avoided plummeting to the body-littered ground below.

As Cassiel was being carried to the ground, she saw Krillion approaching from one direction and Rai from the other. "Put me down over there," she told her rescuer. With a nod of his head, the angel banked hard to the right in a low, downward spiral and descended to the ground. As soon as he alighted and Cassiel got her footing, she stumbled toward Krillion, waving her hands to get his attention.

Krillion ran toward Cassiel, war hammer in hand, covered in dank blood. Everywhere he saw the carnage wreaked by Azreal; bodies of the dead still burned with flames meant for demon flesh. "Cassiel, call off your men. Fight's over," Krillion said, wiping the sweat from his brow and looking up as another warrior fell victim to Azreal's fiery blade.

"Rai!" Krillion called to his brother, who was across the battlefield, also staring up at Azreal.

Hearing his massive brother beckoning him, Rai nodded and made his way over to Krillion, walking over the bodies of the fallen—angels, demons, and humans—their faces forever frozen in pain from having experienced such violent deaths. "We going to try this again?" Rai asked, still looking toward the dark sky.

"We have no choice … brother," Krillion responded, the word feeling right even after so long. "One way or the other, this ends today."

Rai rested his long, slender blade on his shoulder to rest his arms, and small beams of red shot out inches in both directions from the corners of his eyes. Then he unfurled his black wings in anticipation of the rematch that was soon coming. "Where's Val and Zara?" he asked, his eyes never leaving the sky.

"Right here, boss," boomed a hoarse voice, and Val ran up to stand behind his closest friend.

"Took you long enough," Rai said with a grin, still staring at the sky.

"All present and accounted for, sir," Zara said, landing a few feet away from the angel commander, taking daggers she had retrieved off the fallen and securing them in various spots on her ruined armor. At first glance, Zara looked as if she might collapse from the number of injuries covering her body. Putting the last blade in place, she glanced around at the remains of the pens.

The unholy fire in the center had been reduced to smoldering embers with no fresh fuel to feed its hunger. The dead lay scattered across the ground in hideous fashion, limbs contorted, some with the eyes still open. Some bodies were so burned by the legendary sword of Azreal that their own friends and comrades hardly recognized them. Those not yet in the throes of death's unforgiving embrace struggled to check on their comrades.

Humans and angels worked side by side to overcome the horror that befell Earth weeks ago during Hell's initial invasion. They worked to stem the tide of darkness that had nearly extinguished the light of Heaven and exterminated mankind. They worked to forever drive back the demonic legions from the realm of Earth.

"What do we do about him?" Zara asked, her eye catching the flaming trail of Azreal's sword as he swung it without mercy, striking down yet another angelic figure.

"You have to stop him, Commander!" Cassiel said through bloodstained teeth. "He's killed too many of our own, and with what he's done to Gabriel... End this now, please!"

"Where's Kane?" Krillion asked, never taking his eyes off the sky.

"He's in the defense perimeter with the rest of the warriors and humans who are unable to fight," Zara said. "He has a human girl with him. We believe she's the one from Israfil's vision."

"Rai, Val, you guys ready for this?" Krillion asked.

"Oh yeah," Valafor answered, a malicious look in his eyes. The blue energy from his arm was pulsing out in waves, hungry for death and violence.

"Rai?" Krillion said, looking at the brother he had lost so many years ago. Rai didn't say anything but merely nodded his head, the red beams from his eyes giving Krillion all the answer he needed.

"Cassiel, make your way with the others and pull back to the outer part of the camp. If we fall, run. Get as far from him as you can. Do you understand?"

"Yes commander," Cassiel said, and she turned and made her way to the survivors, calling back her few remaining warriors.

"One way or the other, this ends today," Krillion said. Then, brandishing his hammer, he knelt down, took a deep breath, unfurled his wings, and leapt into the air.

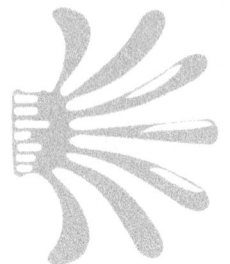 

Chapter 34

Kane and Alisha made their way through the dark pens, which were deprived not only of sunlight, but also of the light from the bonfire that earlier had illuminated the camp. The two made their way through the throngs of dead, heading toward the security of the defense perimeter.

Through the haze of exhaustion, Kane noticed that many of the captive humans and angels had survived. They were now running all over the area with makeshift torches, looking for more survivors and killing off dying demons. There were shouted orders and requests for help from every direction. Seeing the humans and angels standing together now, unified by a common cause and common foe as well as their will to carry on their legacy through the ages, Kane realized that Gabriel and the council had been right for exiling him. The power granted him by the All-Father surely would have led to the destruction of Earth.

Stumbling over the armor of a slain angel, Kane fell to his knees in the mud and blood, and Alisha caught him under his arms to help support his weight. As they neared the makeshift entrance, spotted only by angelic guards with torches retrieved from the fire, a man approached them wearing the ripped remains of priestly garb. "Oh my," he exclaimed upon seeing the small child and the red man. "Come, my child, let me help you with your burden," said the priest, gently placing one of Kane's arms around his own neck and helping him to the ground.

"Thank you," Kane said through gritted teeth. "What is your name, human?"

"Paul … and it is I who should thank you and your friends, red man. If not for you, we would all be slaves of the demons," the priest responded. "A. J.!" the priest called behind him as he began evaluating Kane's injuries.

"Yes, Father," said a woman's voice through the darkness.

"Bring water, my dear, quickly," the priest said over his shoulder, focusing his energies on his two new charges. Seeing no visible injuries to the red man other than exhaustion, Paul turned his attention to the girl, so young and frightened, and his heart immediately sank. *This girl has seen and experienced things no child should ever bear,* he thought, his once-solid faith shaken to its core. *Have strength, Paul,* he said to himself.

The child sat before him on a bare patch of ground, surrounded by the dead and dying. Her shoulder-length, flame-red hair was streaked with blood, both dried and fresh, and he couldn't tell if the spots on her face were freckles or more blood. Her clothes were tattered and hung loosely around her slender frame, each rip and hole telling a story of her ordeal since the invasion began. What he noticed most, though, was the girl's eyes—blue-green eyes devoid of all emotion except fear and horror, and perhaps something much worse. Caught by her hypnotic gaze, the priest felt a single tear escape the corner of his left eye.

"All-Father, in your blessed name, how could you allow this atrocity," he whispered under his breath.

As Alisha sat on the ground, her eyes darting back and forth from the priest to the distant dark where her protector, Rai, was, she felt waves of nausea flow over and through her. Her eyelids began to flutter as her body fell backward and began shaking violently. Again the darkness had come to claim her.

Tired of the constant struggle for survival, Alisha allowed the darkness to consume her, praying this time would be a permanent end to the horrific trials of the last few weeks. She felt herself sinking into oblivion even as hands gently shook her. It was the priest. "Child, stay awake!" he cried, gripping her by the shoulders. "You must keep your eyes open!" That was the last thing she heard before, yet again, her world caved in upon her.

Within seconds that felt like an eternity, Alisha's eyes shot open. It was still dark out, but there was a faint light coming from somewhere, illuminating her surroundings.

She found that she had the energy to sit up. Rubbing her eyes as they adjusted to the dim light that enveloped her, she realized that she was sitting on the living room carpet back in her mom's apartment in the city. Something was different this time, though. She walked to the window and cautiously stole a glance outside.

The city was intact. There were no demons, no fires, and no dead bodies anywhere. The constant screams of pain and fear were no longer happening, although she still heard them clearly in her mind. The streetlights gave off a small glow, enough to show her the clean, bare sidewalk below.

"A dream," she said aloud.

"This is not a dream, child," said a voice from behind her.

Turning quickly, she saw a man sitting on the couch behind her, dressed in a black, hooded robe tied with a simple beige sash. She was certain he hadn't been there seconds before. He stood up and gracefully pulled back his hood to reveal one of the most beautiful faces she'd ever seen.

Alisha noticed many things at once.

This man's clothes were complete and intact. They had no rips or bloodstains, nor was his face dirty or smudged with ash from the fires outside. And she realized that he wasn't a man but an angel; beautiful white wings protruded from his back, the feathers perfectly aligned and smooth.

The angel walked toward Alisha, his hands clasped behind his back, and stopped a few feet from her. He stood eyeing her intently for several seconds. The silence between them was deafening. Finally the angel in black spoke, his voice emotionless. "Do you know who I am, child?"

Alisha was silent as she studied the figure in front of her. This was the first time she had seen an angel not covered with gleaming armor or wielding a magnificent weapon.

"No," she said after a pause, her eyes never leaving his.

"I am Metatron, the voice of the All-Father. I have been searching for you."

"Am I dead?" Alisha asked. "Have you come to save me from all the demons and take me to Heaven?" Her voice revealed her vain hope that her nightmare would finally be over. Her wide, sea-green eyes silently pled with him to say yes—to say yes and finally put an end to her fear-filled life on Earth.

For the first time in Metatron's long existence, he felt sorrow ... sorrow and compassion for this human child who had suffered so much as a result of the Seraphim's failure, who would have to suffer still more pain and loss.

He knew what her fate was to be, for the All-Father had revealed his plan to him some time ago.

Lowering his body to the floor to rest upon his knees before her, Metatron stared at the child he knew from Israfil's vision. This human child had been chosen by the All-Father to carry out his vengeance and save the remnants of mankind. But at what price would innocence be lost?

"No, child," he said. "I'm sorry, but you are not dead. Rather I have secured your mind for the time being. Your body is still back on Earth, in the care of a human priest." Metatron spoke softly, watching the small spark of hope fade from her eyes.

"So my apartment ..." Her words trailed off.

"We are not in the city of your birth," he said. "Rather, this place represents safety and comfort for you. I pulled the memory from your mind so as not to frighten you further."

Her mind a whirlwind of thoughts and emotions, unsure what was real and what was false, Alisha again brought her eyes to meet his. "What do you want from me, then?"

"Yours is a tale that is, tragically, far from over," he said gently. He took her hands, his touch filling her with renewed energy and strength. Then, swallowing hard and steeling his resolve, Metatron spoke again, staring directly into her eyes. "Child, you have been chosen by the All-Father to restore the Earth and mankind and free them both from the clutches of Lucifer and his minions. Evil will pursue you at every turn, and you will have to be stronger then you ever thought possible. You will draw upon the strength that lies within you and your protectors."

At the word *protector*, Alisha's eyes sparked to life again. "Do you mean the angel with the black wings?" she asked hopefully. "Is it Rai?"

"Yes, child," Metatron said, "although his is a scarred and tragic story. Once Rai and his twin brother, Krillion, served together in the army of Heaven under the All-Father's banner. Then there came a day when Lucifer deceived Rai, who opted to betray the light and join Lucifer in a rebellion against the All-Father and the Seraphim. As the battle drove on into the late hours of the day, brother fell to brother, Rai's knowledge of his prior life was erased, and he was cast out to serve in the legions of Hell for eternity."

Alisha listened intently, never speaking as she learned the story of the angel who had saved her life. Her eyes were locked on Metatron's as he continued.

"Due to the recent treacheries of Hell, the brothers have found each other once again after millennia apart. Though they are now united, Rai can't find his way back into the light. It will be one of your tasks to show him what he has lost and what he must fight for. The bond that will be forged between you will determine the fate of the planet and of its inhabitants forever more."

"How am I supposed to do that? I don't have powers or wings or anything," Alisha said.

A slight smile crept to the corners of Metatron's mouth as he replied. "Child, it will be your innocence, your humanity, your love … and this." Alisha felt something warm as her hands touched Metatron's; she looked down to see her hands glowing. She gasped, fearful and awestruck.

"What is this?" she asked, pulling her hands away and staring at them intently.

"This is a gift from the All-Father, child. With his blessing I give it to you, so that you may complete your task and restore the world to the light."

All traces of fear and doubt now gone, Alisha felt a faint gleam of hope for the first time since her nightmare began.

"Do you now understand the gravity of your situation, child?" Metatron asked.

"Yes," Alisha said. "But even with this gift, how will I be able to defeat the demons?" Her voice was calm and steady.

"Your protectors will show you the way, but be wary: all things come at a cost, child. I tell you now, you will know more suffering than anyone. Your pain will have no limits, and you will have to bear it all for the sake of humanity," Metatron said, standing up and stepping away from Alisha. "I must leave now, child of light, for I have other matters yet to attend to. You must go now—back to Earth. Take your first step into your journey of light. The All-Father is always with you."

With that, Metatron turned and walked away, his figure vanishing from Alisha's sight with every step.

Standing by the apartment window, trying to make sense of what she'd just heard and the task set before her, Alisha heard Metatron's voice one last time echo through the empty room.

"Do not fear the ultimate sacrifice, child …"

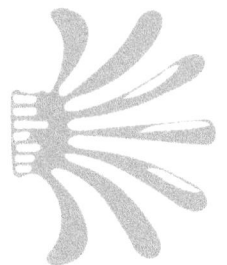 

Chapter 35

THE SKIES ABOVE THE PENS were sparkling with blue energy as the power of Valafor's weapon arm streaked through the air. Meanwhile, Azreal was using his uncanny battle skills to dodge or bat away the angels' daggers, thrown with deadly precision.

For Krillion and Rai, the battle was up-close and personal; the twin brothers who had reunited after millennia apart were once more fighting side by side against a common enemy, the angel of death himself. To those watching from the ground beneath them, it looked like a graceful dance, death in motion: one brother on defense, the other on offense, both trying to find a chink in the impregnable armor of their foe across the sky. This was to be the final battle of the day; it would set the Seraphim back on the path of victory from which they had drifted so long ago.

This righteous victory would show mankind, nearly destroyed by Hell's invasion, that the Seraphim were still here, that they would not stop fighting for humanity as long as a single angel drew breath.

"This is it, Azreal!" Rai yelled, darting in low and slicing the air with his long, slender blade in the hope of distracting Azreal from Krillion, who was flying behind, his war hammer poised for the kill. Easily parrying Rai's efforts, Azreal answered him with a swift boot to the gut, simultaneously dodging Krillion's blow.

As Azreal brought his flaming sword up to slice Krillion's rib cage, Krillion blocked the blow with the metal shaft of his hammer. The two floated above the scene of death and carnage below, their weapons locked together as each combatant tried to overpower the other.

"You've killed your last Seraphim, bitch!" Krillion grunted, trying to exert more raw strength over his opponent.

"Wrong, dog," Azreal shot back. "I still have a few more to kill before this day is out!"

Speeding up from the ground, straight toward both combatants, came a powerful beam of pure blue energy. (Valafor couldn't fly, but he had been taking potshots whenever he could.) Before the blast hit, the combatants broke apart, each pushing off the other to put distance between them.

Krillion finally slowed his flight and turned to see his foe. He let his hammer hang slightly in his right hand, giving his muscles a rest from hours of fighting. Breathing heavily, trying to form a plan that would end Azreal once and for all, he noticed Zara in the distance. She was racing toward Azreal from behind, her twin blades bared and eager for his blood. Her wings pumped furiously as she gained more speed, trying to catch her opponent unawares. Her mind held a single thought: extinguishing the life of this traitor.

Zara was so intent upon her kill that she realized too late the folly of her actions and she missed the slight shift in Azreal's wing posture.

When her blades were within feet of completing their task, Azreal moved ever so slightly to the left and then whirled in a complete circle, using his flaming sword of death to slice clean through the soft, exposed flesh of Zara's lower back, below her armor. She screamed in agony, and as her bloody and battered frame passed Azreal, she began to lose altitude.

Horror filled Zara as she plummeted toward her death. Weak from blood loss and constant fighting, she could do little more than close her eyes and wait for the inevitable.

"Zara!" Krillion cried. Tucking his wings to his side, he dove like a bullet to the ground to try and catch her before she hit.

His move did not go unnoticed by either Azreal or Rai.

Seizing his chance to end the commander of this motley team—along with Israfil's vision for the salvation of the planet—Azreal made his move. "Die, bitch," was all he said, aiming his flaming sword at Krillion and Zara. He was seconds away from letting loose a streak of flame hot enough to incinerate both angels and anything else unfortunate enough to get in its deadly path.

Oblivious to the danger, Krillion had focused his full attention and strength on catching his teammate. Even if Valafor on the ground tried to catch her, the speed of her fall would likely shatter her bones or even kill them both.

Rai was also in motion, flying toward Azreal from the left. His wings strained to propel him faster, to stop the angel of death from releasing his flaming bolt. Eyes glowing red, holding his sword in a reverse grip, he flew with the force of a hurricane. Time was of the essence. He had to get this just right or the consequences would be dire.

Azreal watched the flames lick around the edges of his sword, which was glowing hotter and brighter, the heat building until he would set it loose. A smile of triumph spread across his face as the flame left the sword and began its evil descent toward Krillion.

At that moment Rai flew directly into the path of the fire, his sword slicing cleanly through Azreal's armor and flesh. Azreal felt hot, searing pain in his side as blood began to trickle down in steady streams. Not once in his long, storied history had anyone been able to breach the armor of the angel of death, much less make him bleed. Clutching his side and gritting his teeth, he watched as his last airborne enemy began its fall to the ground below. Tucking his grey wings to his side, Azreal hurled himself toward Rai's falling figure, intent on ensuring his death.

The cooling wind rushed all around Zara, permeating every inch of her limp body.

This is it. Avenge me, Kane, she thought, just as her body was jerked out of its smooth fall. Opening her eyes, she gazed upon the features of her commander, who had caught her seconds before impact.

Carrying Zara in one arm, Krillion landed hard on the ground. He heard a snap in his leg, but at least they were both alive.

"Krillion!"

He heard his name being shouted, and he tried to push his massive body up from the ground to stand. Instead his knee gave under his own weight, and he realized that it had shattered from the impact. Valafor was rushing toward him, yelling and pointing at the sky. Looking up, Krillion saw something else falling and realized that Rai had been hit by a flame blast from Azreal's sword. The gaping hole in Rai's side was obvious as he fell from the skies with Azreal right behind him.

Inhaling sharply, fear written on his face, Krillion knew he wouldn't be able to save his brother. Once again, all he could do was watch Rai fall.

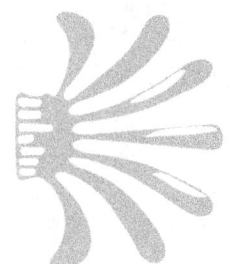 # Chapter 36

PAUL'S HANDS WERE A BLUR of motion as he used a damp rag to wipe the face of the unconscious child laid out before him on the blood-soaked ground. Just when he believed all his efforts were futile, Alisha's eyes flew open and she gasped for air.

As the priest helped her sit up, patting her on the back to get precious oxygen into her lungs, he felt a change about the child—something he could not put his finger on.

"Where are they?" she choked out between coughs. "Where are the angels? I have to find them." She started to her feet, but Paul grabbed her by the arms to steady her.

"Child, you must calm yourself. Everything's all right. You're safe here," he said, perplexed.

"No, Father," Alisha said. Her focused, determined look caught Paul off guard, piercing him to his soul. "We are most definitely not all right."

There, she thought, as her eyes caught the streaks of fire cutting through the dark skies above her. "Father, I have to go. Please care for him," she said, nodding at Kane. Then she grabbed a torch from a human who was walking past her, and she burst into a dead sprint away from them.

"Child, wait!" Paul yelled after her.

Alisha headed toward the last sounds of battle in the distance, running as fast as she could without tripping over weapons and the bodies of the slain. She didn't know what she would do when she got there; she just knew that Rai was in trouble and it was her turn to help him.

† † †

Struggling on her hands and knees in the mud, her back bleeding from where Azreal's sword had sliced her, Zara was working as hard as she could to get her feet under her and rejoin the fight above. "Too fast, didn't see it," she grunted through the pain, still trying to figure out how Azreal had managed to catch her off guard.

Shaking her head to clear her hazy vision, she saw Alisha, the girl she had left with Kane, running toward her at full speed.

As Alisha drew near, Zara's body gave out and she slumped back to the ground.

"Alisha," Zara gasped through pain and blood, "you must ... must leave here. Head back to the others. Tell them we failed. Azreal ... too strong..." Her words cut off as she began coughing, flecks of blood flying from her mouth.

Kneeling down next to the battered, bloody angel, Alisha feverishly patted her back, trying to help clear her airways. "Zara, I have to find Rai. Where is he?" she asked, panting for air and looking around.

"All is lost, child. We have failed you," whispered Zara.

Alisha could hear her breaths becoming shallow and unsteady, and her fading voice indicated she was on the brink of death.

"Krillion!"

Alisha heard the shout from behind her. She turned to see a huge, hairy demon pointing to the skies and yelling. Krillion was on the ground a short ways away, trying to stand and yelling Rai's name between his own screams of pain.

The girl was filled with dread as she turned her gaze upward and saw the lifeless form of Rai falling through the air. As he neared the ground at incredible speeds, she knew the impact would shatter every bone in his body. Without another thought she ran toward his projected point of impact. She ran past Krillion, who was crawling through the bloody mud of the pens, trying in vain to reach the spot before his brother did.

Seeing all the flyers of the team down and out, Valafor used his muscular legs to propel himself across the battlefield. Perhaps he could catch Rai before he followed the fate of so many angelic warriors before him. "Come on, Val, *move!*" he yelled, urging his body to go faster. He had to try, no matter the result. Otherwise Rai would surely die. Waiting until the last feasible second, Valafor knelt and then sprang up with every ounce of strength he had left, at the same time releasing a beam of blue energy that shot past his falling comrade just as the angel of death closed in for the kill.

Rai's body smashed into Valafor's in midair, the impact sending both of them spiraling out of control. The teammates hit the ground simultaneously several yards away from each other. Neither Rai nor Valafor was moving. Their bodies were intact, but they had reached the end of their long fight.

Easily dodging the blast that was meant to distract him, Azreal slowed to alight on the ground. All around him were the broken bodies of Israfil's grand team—the team that had been given the task of retaking the Earth by the All-Father himself. But they had not counted on fighting the most dangerous warrior in the entire Seraphim.

"What a fucking joke," Azreal said, looking at the fallen warriors spread around him, his flaming sword glowing brighter with the anticipation of more blood and death.

Alisha ran past Azreal to Rai's motionless body and fell to her knees beside him, gently rolling him over and cradling his head in her lap. The red traces from the corners of his eyes had dulled from a fiery red to little more than a faint glow, a sign that his life force was quickly fading.

"Rai, you have to get up—you have to keep fighting," Alisha pleaded, brushing the loose black strands of hair from his face. She glanced down and saw the gaping hole where his armor had melted from Azreal's blast, leaving ribs and organs exposed. She knew Rai hadn't long to live. Her mind a blank, unable to think of what to do, her head fell to the chest of the fallen angel as her tears landed on his battered black breastplate. She heard his whispered voice in her ear, "I'm sorry, little one."

Alisha lifted her head and gazed down upon her fallen champion. She watched his eyes slowly close, the red light fading even further, and his head went limp in her hands.

"No!" she screamed, clutching his still body. *"No, no, no!"*

Across the battlefield, Zara lay in a pool of her own blood, her strength completely gone. She had accepted her fate once more.

Opposite her, Krillion was screaming at Azreal, making threats he knew he couldn't back up.

Kane was under the care of the human priest, along with the few humans and angels who had lived through the terrible ordeal of the pens.

Valafor hadn't moved since he and Rai hit the ground.

The team had failed before it had begun. The Seraphim had lost; the demons would remain in control of Earth, with no force left to oppose them.

Azreal, the angel of death, had slain dozens of his brethren in a single battle—the battle that was supposed to have been the Seraphim's first major victory in the bloody war.

Alisha's throat was raw from screaming. And still she screamed.

She screamed for the people across the planet who had suffered vicious deaths at the hands of demons. She screamed for her mother, for the horrors she had endured. Finally, her screams subsided into dull whimpering, and she heard a voice in the darkness, a voice only she could hear: "You will know more suffering than anyone. Your pain will have no limits, and you will have to bear it all for the sake of humanity."

The words were still echoing through her mind as she glanced up to see Azreal walking toward Krillion, who was struggling to rise and face his demon foe. She heard Azreal's taunting voice as he methodically approached the massive angel. "You have failed, oh mighty commander."

"No," Alisha whispered through tears. She glanced at Rai's face one last time before gently placing his head on the ground. Then she turned to face the angel of death, her eyes focused on nothing but him. She stood up and began slowly walking toward him.

Azreal looked from Krillion to the ragged little human walking toward him, and he almost laughed. "This world is mine, human! The end has come," he spat.

Alisha felt her hands beginning to burn. She paused midstride to look down and saw her hands glowing white hot. "Gift from the All-Father," she heard the voice echo.

"No!" she screamed at Azreal, and suddenly the white glow of her hands became flames that spread up her arms, engulfing her torso. "Humans and angels shall stand together, one by one! This world and all life is sacred!"

The pain was searing as the white fire consumed Alisha's body—yet still she walked unhindered toward the angel of death.

"What is this trick, human? Where have you received this power?" Azreal demanded.

"This is the end of your terror, monster! You have betrayed your own kind and so you have been forsaken!" Alisha screamed. Lifting her flaming arms straight above her head, she continued her path to end her nightmare. Every step was agonizing as the white fire began to expand out from her in a solid wide arc, engulfing everything it touched.

Realizing the gravity of this new threat, Azreal was about to lunge at Alisha and extinguish her life when the flames washed over him, and he cringed with pain and a fear he had never known before.

The flames spread over the bodies of her protectors and the bodies of the fallen warriors, purging everything. Demon flesh, too, was devoured by the white, holy flame; it turned to ash and flew away, leaving behind nothing but charred weapons and armor.

The flames grew hotter, continuing to expand and engulf the mutilated angels who lost their lives in the defense of mankind.

Gritting her teeth through the pain, maintaining her steady pace, Alisha noticed her hands had begun to turn black. Her pain was becoming increasingly unbearable with every step she took.

As the flames of the pure and innocent flooded over Azreal, his darkened wings began to break away. Their ashes flew into the maelstrom of light and fire created by the human child, which by now was a small whirlwind circling the radius of the pens.

From the safety of the makeshift defense, angels and humans huddled together as they felt the warmth of the fire wash over them, renewing their faith and replenishing their strength, burning away the fear and horror that had plagued them these past weeks.

As the flames of the innocent reached the embers of the bonfire— the remains of the massive fire that had been built to burn the wings bestowed upon all angels— the ash of those celestial gifts joined the rest of the flying ash. Past horrors moved through the air above the heads of the survivors.

Alisha was mere feet from Azreal when the searing pain became too much for her. She collapsed to her knees on the ground, which now was clear of blood and bodies. She was on her knees in the middle of the whirling tornado of white-hot flame, burning and screaming until her throat began to bleed.

Fear gripped Azreal as he realized that the majority of his wings were burned off and what remained was seared black and cauterized. He turned and ran through the wall of white flame and out of the pens, his glowing red armor burning his skin. As he tore off his breastplate to escape its burning touch, large chunks of bloody flesh came off with it, melted to the inside of his armor.

Alisha remained on her knees, feeling every scream of pain torn from her throat, her hands clutching her head amid a symphony of white flame that danced over the corpses of war, purging the surrounding land of Hell's stench and influence. She did not feel the soft, strong hands that wrapped tightly around her waist.

A soft voice whispered in her ear. "I am here, little one," it said. "You have done it. Let go now. Before it is too late, let go."

Alisha's skin burned. She couldn't turn it off, she couldn't stop screaming, and the holy flame was going to consume her, too. Never before had she felt pain of this magnitude. It was too much to bear, and she passed out. As she faded, the white flames of light died down.

The arms that had grasped her now gently laid her body down. Alisha's eyes fluttered open. It was Rai. He was holding her head in his arms, her body spread across his lap.

"You're alive" she breathed, laying her hand upon his cheek. She noticed the red glow escaping the corners of his eyes once again.

"You brought me back from the brink of death, little one," Rai said. As he stared down at her, he quickly realized that he no longer held the small, red-haired child from before. In her stead was the body of a twenty-year-old. The power of the All-Father had aged her in a matter of minutes. Rai's eyes swept over Alisha, and he saw that her hands were slightly scarred from the white fire. Her face, however, was untouched by its ravaging effects.

Alisha looked up at him, at her champion—her protector. As Rai leaned down and touched his lips to hers, she knew that no matter what the future held, he would always be by her side. He would never waver or fail in her protection, and she would not fail him. She would bring him back into the light of the All-Father's grace, and together with their newfound allies, they would retake the Earth.

"We have to go," Rai said, hoisting Alisha to her feet. As the two looked around, the others were already on their feet. They were looking around in bewilderment, wondering how their wounds had been healed and what had happened to Azreal and the rest of the pens. One by one they walked toward Rai and Alisha; not a word was said as they gathered around the duo. Their silent gazes asked all the questions their lips did not.

Then, as the cinders and ash fell down around them, Rai noticed a lone figure walking through the haze toward them. The figure's arms were folded behind its back, and it was dressed in a hooded, black robe, adorned with a simple beige sash.

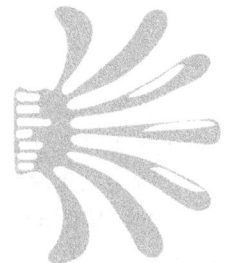 

Chapter 37

Paul lifted his head from Kane's chest to survey the land around them. The air was filled with dirt and ash, and Paul rubbed his eyes vigorously, trying to peer through the dark.

In the distance he saw sparks grow into small flames, and a sense of awe and wonderment came over him as torches slowly illuminated the grounds around the pens. The countless mutilated bodies of the demons were gone completely; all that remained were a few pieces of armor and scattered weapons.

"What happened?" Kane's question brought Paul's gaze back down to the figure on the ground before him.

"I'm not sure," Paul responded in a soft voice.

"Please, Father, help me stand," Kane said, struggling to sit upright. Paul put his arms underneath Kane's and helped him to his feet.

They looked around once more, and Kane saw Raziel and Cassiel running to them, excitement in their voices. "We won! We won!" Raziel cried. "The pens have been destroyed. There are no traces of the demons anywhere!"

"Where are Zara and Krillion?" Kane asked. "And what was that fire that swept over us?"

"Last I saw them they were fighting Azreal," Cassiel said, looking around.

"I'm not sure what that white flame was, but whatever it was, it healed my injuries," Raziel exclaimed. "Look—my wing is no longer broken! There's not even any pain." She stretched out her wings for all to see.

"I have to find them," Kane said. The red aura surrounding him grew brighter, and he began floating in the air before the angels and Paul. "Gather everyone up and be on alert. We don't know what has happened, and we can't afford to be ill-prepared." With that, Kane shot into the sky in search of his teammates, leaving a red energy trail powerful enough to illuminate the pens.

Now that he had a few moments to breathe, Paul looked around at all the survivors, wondering what to do. He glanced at the two female angels standing before him; unlike the angels with whom he had been held captive, these two were whole and pure. As he studied the two celestial beings before him, he realized how hard they had fought to save mankind. Every dent in their armor held part of the story of their struggle for hope and victory. And although their wounds had been healed by the mysterious whirlwind of white fire, they bore scars on the skin where they had worn no protective armor. They may have won the day, but they would bear those marks for as long as angels lived.

"Come, Father," Raziel said, seeing the look of wonder in his eye and holding out her hand. "We have to find out casualty reports and generate a game plan for our next move."

Staring deep into Raziel's eyes, Paul took her soft hand in his. "Never once since our trials started did I doubt that the All-Father would send his warriors for us," he said.

Raziel smiled broadly and gripped his hand tight. "Father, your work is not yet done. Many of the survivors will call upon your faith and skill for the trials ahead. You will have to be a leader to the survivors of the pens. It will be your duty to shepherd them to safety. Come, I will take you to Commander Krillion. He will explain what comes next," she said, and she led him back to the crowd of people.

† † †

The inside of the defense perimeter was a bustle of activity as groups of humans and mutilated angels took stock of their situation, discussing everything from the white flame that had purged everything and healed their wounds to the future and what their next move should be. It was here that Captain Tabbris found Captain Sandalphon amid all the celebration and cheering.

"Sir!" Tabbris said with an air of concern, raising his voice above the surrounding commotion. "Sir, I have an urgent report."

"Easy, Tabbris—slow down and tell me what you have, son," Sandalphon said, grasping the young captain's shoulder in a firm grip.

"During the last few minutes of the battle, sir, my two remaining men and I came upon a weird creature hiding in the shadows. We couldn't get a good look at it before it fired a bolt of orange flame straight into the chest of one of my men, setting him ablaze," Tabbris said.

"Are there any specific details you can give about the creature—anything else you might remember?" Sandalphon asked.

"Yes, sir," Tabbris said immediately. "Before the demon vanished, it said the day was ours, but that he would be back for everyone in the Seraphim, sir. There was hideous laughter and an explosion of fire and brimstone, and then it was gone," he said, shuddering at the memory of the creature's laugh.

"Kobal," Sandalphon said, slowly rubbing his chin. "If he managed to slink away, then this war is far from over. Okay, for now gather up the rest of the captains and then come find me. I'm going to find Krillion and his team. I saw them teleport here during the battle."

"Yes, sir," Tabbris said smartly, and he retreated into the bustling crowd to complete his new assignment.

Turning to look for Krillion, Sandalphon noticed a group of angels off to the side, wingless and mutilated beyond belief. There was a difference in them, he thought. They looked wild, almost feral, as if by losing their wings, they had lost their sanity as well.

Never before in the history of the Seraphim had an angel ever lost his wings. There was no way to know or understand what was going through the minds of the angelic warriors who had paid the ultimate price for the defense of mankind, yet lived to tell of it.

He walked on, searching for Krillion, but he took note of this group, which seemed to be separating themselves from the other survivors, and he decided to come back to it later. Overhead, the sky lit up red from the energy trail left behind Kane as he traveled the length of the pens, looking for Zara and Krillion.

As Sandalphon reached the end of the crowd, he saw them—Krillion, Valafor, Rai, Zara, and a human girl. And then there was another figure with them...

"Oh no," Sandalphon said aloud. He knew who the black-robed figure was. "If he's here ..."

The Fallen | 209

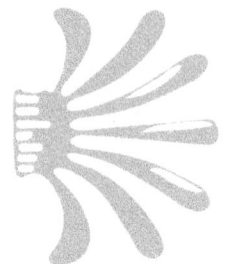 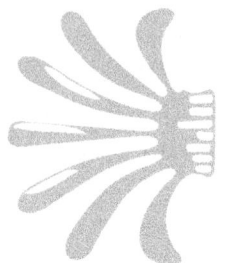

Chapter 38

"WHAT ARE WE GOING TO do? Those fucking demons took our wings!" Chronos declared to the group of angels standing around him.

"I say we stay on Earth and kill every demon we come across until they're all dead or we're dead. There are enough of us that we could use hit-and-run tactics," another angel replied.

"I agree," said a female angel. "There's no point in going back to Heaven. My life there is over. I will kill every demon I come across until I take my dying breath or they are rotting on the ground. That is the only way to serve the All-Father now. Vengeance shall be ours, brothers and sisters."

"Settle down, Serenity—I have a plan," said another. "Chronos, how many do we have here total, not including the humans?"

"Roughly seventy, Magnus," Chronos replied.

"Okay, this is what we're doing," Magnus said. "Serenity, Chronos, spread out with our force to scavenge the area. Any serviceable weapons you find, stockpile them for later. I will go find Commander Krillion and tell him our plans."

"What do you think he'll say when he hears what we plan to do?" Serenity asked Magnus as the group began spread out across the grounds.

"What can he do? Fucking look at us! Our wings have been ripped from our backs. We'll never fly again, never feel the wind in our faces!" Magnus's voice rose in anger, and he looked down at his female companion. "No, Serenity, we will no longer serve in the kingdom of our birth. The best we can do is fight the war from down here, protecting this group of humans from further incursion by the demons. Now go on with the rest. I'll deal with the commander."

"We'll be waiting. Don't be long," Serenity said. Then she headed off with the rest to outfit their makeshift unit with recovered weapons.

Magnus walked away to find Krillion, his eyes scouring the pens. It was here that his brethren and the humans were tortured and suffered horrible nightmares made reality. Now his mind raced with the finality of their new world. Armageddon was over; they had lost. They had failed in their sworn duty to protect the humans from Hell's influence.

"Lost, but not finished," Magnus thought, walking toward the cluster of beings from all realms. Some he recognized; others he did not. Finally he saw Metatron standing among all the tattered armor and bloodied figures. He also noticed a female angel at the opposite side of the group. She was wearing the mark of captain on her armor and escorting a human clad in the robes of the priesthood.

† † †

This meeting would determine the fate of the Earth and the future of both the Seraphim and mankind. Scanning the assembled group of angels, demons, fallen angels, and humans—victors and victims—Metatron organized his thoughts on how to proceed.

"I shall be brief, as time is of the essence," he began. "Some of what I will say you will like; some you will not. Just remember, it is not ours to judge or decipher the will of the All-Father." At this, the members gathered around close, all eyes upon the voice of the All-Father. "Captain Sandalphon and Captain Raziel, gather your remaining soldiers and return to the Crystal Palace immediately. Plans have been set in motion, and your strength and leadership will be needed in the upcoming weeks. Do not ask questions now—all will be revealed upon my return."

"Yes, Metatron," Sandalphon said, a confused look upon his face. He nodded to Raziel, who was standing across from him with a human priest. As the two captains turned to leave, Metatron directed his next instructions to Krillion and his team.

"We have lost the war, Krillion, as you know. We all have our individual parts to play that we may salvage this transgression and perhaps restore light to Earth. You and yours will not be allowed back into Heaven, commander. With Hell's victory complete here on Earth, we will close the gates to the Crystal Palace and prepare for the potential threat of attack."

"Are you serious?" Krillion asked angrily. "We are to stay here on Earth and continue fighting with no hope of returning to Heaven?"

"Control yourself, Commander," Metatron said. "With Hell's successful invasion of Earth and Azreal's betrayal of us all, Israfil has assumed command for the time being until Gabriel is back at full strength. Due to these unforeseen events, the All-Father fears an attack upon Heaven will be Hell's next move. We shall close the gates to the Crystal Palace and prepare, for if you fail here on Earth, then surely you understand that there will be no Heaven to come back to."

"Yes, yes, you are right, Metatron. So what are our exact orders?" Krillion asked, his voice again confident in the face of this new challenge.

"You shall remain here and fulfill Israfil's vision to the best of your abilities or die trying," Metatron said. "As you already know, though, you will not be alone in this endeavor. Amid the evil and nightmares of days past, a candle of hope was lit and has been bestowed upon mankind in a final attempt at salvation." At this, Metatron's eyes rested on the fully matured Alisha, her hands and arms showing scars of the All-Father's gift. "Krillion, you have been reunited with your brother, Rai. Centuries and bitter betrayal have torn the twins of Heaven apart, yet here you stand, side by side on the battlefield, victorious once again. You are the only twins ever to grace the skies of Heaven, two halves coming together as an unstoppable force for all of Hell and the enemies of man to fear."

Metatron's gaze shifted to the red man. "Kane, your history is one of sorrow and undeserved punishment for a crime you never committed," he said. "Because of your immense power, the council decided that you were not to inherit the Earth. I'll admit I played my hand as a deciding factor in your fate. For that I apologize—we were wrong."

Kane gave a slight nod as Metatron's gaze shifted again. "Valafor, you have created the ultimate milestone in the history of all three realms," he said, looking at the massive, hairy demon rubbing the blackened weapon that served as his right arm. "You are the first demon to side with the light. During Rai's time in Hell, you forged an unbreakable bond that rivaled that of brotherhood. Through the weeks and months ahead, you will be the cornerstone of Rai's strength. When all is lost, your strength and battle prowess will be at the forefront of the fight. For the sake of us all, do not fail him or yourself."

Paul entered the circle to stand directly before the voice of the All-Father. Gazing now at his hopes and faith made flesh and blood, feeling the power emanate from this holy servant, Paul felt his knees quiver and he fell to the ground before Metatron. "And what of your faithful servant, sir?" he asked reverently, eyes to the ground as he awaited Metatron's answer.

Staring down at the human prostrated before him, Metatron was filled with hope, although there was no evidence of it on his face. "Rise, priest, faithful servant of the All-Father," Metatron said, placing his hand upon Paul's shoulder. "Be it known that we, the Seraphim, have failed in our duty of protection, thus allowing Hell to administer unimaginable horrors upon you and yours—"

Paul cut him off. "No, no, no—the angels have come to our aid in our time of need. You have shared in the nightmare, as we all have," he said, gesturing to the wingless angel standing on the opposite side of the circle.

Hearing Paul's words, Magnus winced at the thought of never soaring through the skies again with his brethren, and his blood boiled with rage. He thought of the violent revenge he and his kind would inflict upon the demons in the coming weeks.

"It is true, angels and humans both have suffered during this time of evil. But you shall not be alone in your trials ahead—will he Magnus?" Metatron asked, settling his gaze upon the battle-worn angel.

Magnus stepped forward, and he stared around at all the gathered warriors. Then, clearing his parched throat, he responded, "No, Metatron, this priest will not be alone. Our ranks number around seventy, and we have decided that the best way to serve Heaven and the All-Father would be to assist these humans and eliminate as many remaining demons as possible until we win or die in the attempt."

Metatron stood before the group, contemplating the words from Magnus. He knew that Krillion would have to stay with his team, but now another seventy of Heaven's veterans would be remaining as well. Was this for the best, or would their lives be forfeited through insurmountable odds? Every question answered just led to more questions. Then his eyes fell on the young, flame-haired woman standing before him; scars marred her delicate features. She placed her body protectively near Rai's.

"My child..." Suddenly Metatron cocked his head to the side as if listening to something audible to no one but him. "I must depart now," he said. "The pendulum swings, and time sits idle for no one. I wish all of you the best of luck in the coming days. The All-Father is with you." Then, with a whoosh of air, his pure white wings unfurled, starkly contrasting with his black robes, and he leapt into the sky, racing back to the Crystal Palace and whatever had called him there.

"The All-Father with you as well, old friend," Krillion said quietly. He watched Metatron for a few seconds before returning his attention to his team, which was looking to him for guidance on how to proceed.

Emotion flooded the faces surrounding the former commander of Fury Legion. All the hopes and triumphs of mankind now lay upon his massive shoulders, and the odds were stacked against him and his team. Krillion adjusted his grip on his war hammer, taking in the severity of their situation and everything that had transpired in the past thirty minutes.

The battle for the pens was over. Alisha had been granted power by the All-Father, which appeared to have aged her while burning her body permanently. His brother, Rai, was once again fighting by his side. Kane had been brought into the conflict as the Seraphim's wild card. And then there was the most shocking reality of all: they had a demon among their ranks, fighting and bleeding alongside them.

Zara, Kane, Rai, Valafor, Alisha, and Krillion: the fate of everything rested upon these six. Live or die, they were mankind's last line of defense.

"We all know what's at stake, whether we like it or not, and we know what we have to do. Any questions?" Krillion asked, his eyes alight with hope for the future.

Chapter 39
Journal of Alisha Grace

ROUGHLY TEN DAYS HAD PASSED since the first portals opened, extinguishing the light of the sun and unleashing wave upon wave of death upon us.

With mankind forced to the edge of extinction by the savage demon hordes, the Seraphim descended from Heaven to uphold their holy oath to protect us.

They failed.

Then, through the bleak darkness, a small ray of light appeared.

That light was me.

Blessed by the All-Father and given a small sliver of his power, I am to be his hand in the coming days of Earth. But I will not be alone through the trials ahead. Through a perverse twist of fate, I have been given a group of protectors from all the realms, brought together through circumstance and united by a common cause.

Krillion and Zara are angels from Heaven who served their armies before the majority of angels fell under Hell's heel.

Before Adam and Eve, the All-Father had begun creating another race of humans. Kane was due to inherit the Earth with his future brethren, until Gabriel and the Seraphim council deemed him too powerful to remain there. Taking Kane's destiny from him, they put him in Purgatory for all time to make way for humans.

Valafor, a demon in the armies of Hell and the best friend to Rai, has taken up arms with us for our cause, wielding his deadly, blackened weapon arm. He crafted it centuries ago after he lost his original arm in battle, killing one thousand demons and forging them into a new limb. Valafor stays with the group out of his love for his friend Rai.

Rai, an angel who fell from Heaven during Lucifer's revolt against Gabriel and the All-Father, has again embraced the light, although his physical appearance has changed drastically since his shame-filled fall; his wings are black, and his eyes remain red from the anger and rage within him.

He is my champion and my love. No harm shall befall me as long as he draws breath.

Some have called this time "dark genesis," the beginning of Hell's reign on Earth.

With the fallen assembled and accepting of our fate, it is time to end the nightmare and begin a new chapter for mankind. It's time for retribution.

We come from different realms and planes of existence, to which none of us will return if we fail.

We are the fallen, and we are not done.

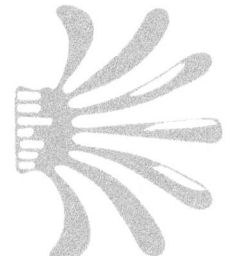 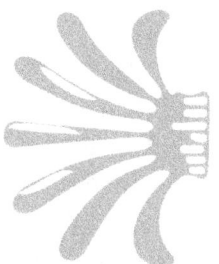

Epilogue

IN THE DEEPEST LAYERS OF Hell, where no average demon dares tread, sits a castle crafted from the souls of evil humans from throughout the ages. It is a place of raw power.

It is here that a demon cringed in fear on a floor made of human skin. The demon was ravaged by morbid fear because he failed to eliminate all the angels and humans on Earth, as ordered by his master. From the moment he retreated from the battle at the pens, he knew this meeting would come to be, and now he shook at the very presence of the figure before him.

It was the dark prince himself: Lucifer.

"You have failed me, Kobal, have you not? Through your failure, the angels have been allowed to live, and what's more, they have amassed a power source capable of defeating all my plans." Lucifer's voice echoed over the screams of tortured souls all around them.

"Master, we might have lost the pens, but the Earth is still ours. It is but a matter of time until we have killed them all," Kobal stammered, his eyes never leaving the floor.

"True, the Earth is ours," Lucifer said, "but Azazel and Leonard are both dead, and the accursed Seraphim are still live, imp! Perhaps I put too much faith in your evilness to spearhead my war. Fret not, little demon, for I have a plan for you to right your failures and eliminate the angelic scum." Lucifer pointed to the far end of the castle room. "Come, my pet, come and devour the flesh and souls of the living," he said.

Kobal dragged his gaze from the floor to look where Lucifer pointed. A massive hole had opened in the floor shooting flames into the air. Coming from the flaming hole was a horrible screeching noise intermingled with an indescribable roar. A smile crept over the face of the demon master of hilarity, his eyes fixed upon the hole as the sounds of chaos and destruction rang through his ears.

Then a creature began emerging from the hole to do his master's bidding.

"What is that, Master?" Kobal asked, his clear voice showing confidence that he would not die this day.

Two huge paws appeared on the edge of the hole, pulling behind it an incredibly large body. Once the beast had fully emerged, Kobal could see it had the torso of a leopard, the mouth of a lion, and the paws of a bear. Seven heads protruded from its neck; each head had a blasphemous name written upon it and sported ten horns, and each head bore a crown.

"This, Kobal, will be your tool in eliminating the rest of the humans and angels," Lucifer said. "Unleash it upon the Earth and finish your task."

"What of the impending attack upon Heaven and the Crystal Palace, Lord?" Kobal asked.

"Because of your failure you will remain on Earth and not concern yourself with that battle. That battle will be forthcoming very soon. For now, you focus upon the extermination and cleansing of Earth. Do you understand?"

"Yes, Master," Kobal said, chastised.

"You will not be alone, as I have summoned other demon lords from their realms to assist you in your task and to ensure that it's done properly: Gaap, master of the water demons and Andras."

As the two names left Lucifer's mouth, two figures materialized in the center of the room next to the dark prince. Gaap's body seemed to flow as he moved to stand before Kobal. Across from Gaap, sitting atop a huge, black wolf, was Andras; he had the body of an angel and the head of a raven, and wielded a sharp, bright rapier.

At the sight of his new allies, another smile crept across Kobal's face in anticipation of his upcoming revenge.

"You will not fail me again, or your suffering shall know no bounds. Are we clear, Kobal?" Lucifer said in a commanding tone.

"Yes, Master. Game on," Kobal answered. And he began laughing, still eyeing the three new demons.

CPSIA information can be obtained
at www.ICGtesting.com
Printed in the USA
LVHW111034150820
663270LV00002B/509